"THIS IS A WONDERFUL APARTMENT," SAID BARBY.

The drink relaxed her, took away the last lingering bit of self-consciousness.

Ilene smiled. "That's why I don't want to sublet it. But it's too big for me alone."

"Can't you find someone to share it?" Barby asked.

"It would have to be someone special—someone who meant a lot to me, personally. I don't believe in grieving for the past. One has to move ahead." She poured coffee into a heavy pottery cup, set it in front of Barby. Her hand trembled a little.

"I'm a very direct person," Ilene said. "I don't finagle around and try to put over a deal—not where my personal life is concerned." She looked at Barby, the long straight look that had melted her heart the first day, as if she could see through her eyes and into her mind. "You're very young."

"Not that young," Barby said low.

"I don't know if you even know what I'm talking about."

"I've known for a long time."

IN A LONELY PLACE
Dorothy B. Hughes

SKYSCRAPER
Faith Baldwin

THE GIRLS IN 3-B
Valerie Taylor

THE GIRLS IN 3-B

VALERIE TAYLOR

AFTERWORD BY LISA WALKER

THE FEMINIST PRESS
at the City University of New York
New York

Published by the Feminist Press at the City University of New York
The Graduate Center, 365 Fifth Avenue, Suite 5406
New York, NY 10016, www.feministpress.org

First Feminist Press edition, 2003

09 08 07 06 05 04 03   5 4 3 2 1

Originally published in 1959 by Fawcett Publications. This edition published by
arrangement with the Literary Estate of Valerie Taylor/Velma Young. The
Feminist Press especially thanks Tee A. Corinne for making this edition possible.

Library of Congress Cataloging-in-Publication Data

Taylor, Valerie, 1913–
        The girls in 3–B / Valerie Taylor; foreword by Livia Tenzer and Jean Casella;
    afterword by Lisa Walker. – 1st Feminist Press ed.
        Originally published: Fawcett Publications, 1959.
            p. cm. – (Femmes fatales: women write pulp)
        ISBN 1-55861-462-1 (library cloth: alk. paper) – ISBN 1-55861-456-7 (pbk:
    alk. paper)
        1. Working class women—Fiction. 2. Man-woman relationships—Fiction. 3.
    Female friendship—Fiction. 4. Women employees—Fiction. 5. Chicago (Ill.)—
    Fiction. 6. Young women—Fiction. 7. Lesbians—Fiction. 8. Iowa—Fiction. I.
    Title. II. Series.
        PS3570.A957G57 2003
        813'.54—dc21

                                                                    2003013432

Text design by Dayna Navaro
Printed on acid-free paper by Transcontinental Printing
Printed in Canada

Women write pulp? It seems like a contradiction in terms, given the tough-guy image of pulp fiction today. This image has been largely shaped by the noir revival of the past decade—by reprints of classics by Jim Thompson and best-sellers by neo-noir writer James Ellroy, the rerelease of classic film noir on video, and the revisioning of the form by Quentin Tarantino. Fans of such works would be hard pressed to name a woman pulp author, or even a character who isn't a menacing femme fatale.

But women did write pulp, in large numbers and in all the classic pulp fiction genres, from hard-boiled noirs to breathless romances to edgy science fiction and taboo lesbian pulps. And while employing the conventions of each genre, women brought a different, gendered perspective to these forms. Women writers of pulp often outpaced their male counterparts in challenging received ideas about gender, race, and class, and in exploring those forbidden territories that were hidden from view off the typed page. They were an important part of a literary phenomenon, grounded in its particular time and place, that had a powerful impact on American popular culture in the middle of the twentieth century, and continues to exert its influence today.

Pulp fiction encompasses a broader array of works, and occupies a more complex place in the literary, social, and commercial culture of its era, than the handful of contemporary revivals and tributes to pulp suggest. Pulp emerged as an alternative format for books in the 1930s, building on the popularity of pulp magazines, which flourished from the

1920s to the 1940s, and drawing on traditions established by the dime novel of the nineteenth and early twentieth centuries. The dime novel had developed the Western, the romance, the sleuth story, and the adventure story as genres, with narratives geared largely to young readers, in particular on the frontier. Pulp magazines, needing to compete with early motion pictures and to connect with an urban audience, offered similar stories with an edge. Grouping fiction or believe-it-or-not fact under themes like crime, horror, and adventure, magazines such as *Black Mask*, *Weird Tales*, and *Dime Adventure* demonstrated the existence of a market for inexpensive and provocative teen and adult reading matter. The move to book-length narratives provided an expanded scope for a voracious literature rooted in American popular culture, reflective of American obsessions, and willing to explore American underworlds.

Printed on wood-grain, or pulp, paper, and cheaply bound, the books were markedly different from hardbound editions. These first modern paperbacks served different purposes, too—entertainment, thrill, or introduction to "serious culture"—and were presumably read differently. Books intended for the pulp lists were undoubtedly produced differently, with less time given to the writing, and less money and status accruing to the authors. As pulp publishers grew in number (Fawcett, Pocketbook, Bantam, Ace, Signet, Dell), economic patterns emerged in the treatment of authors and texts: pulp authors often received one-time payment (no royalties); editors focused on keeping books short, tight, and engrossing; and author identity was often submerged beneath the publisher's pulp brand name and the lurid cover art that sold the books. Some pulp authors used pseudonyms to conceal an everyday identity behind a more saleable one, often of the opposite gender. Georgina Ann Randolph Craig (1908–1957) wrote prolifically as Craig

Rice. Some used several names, each evocative of a genre they wrote in: Velma Young (1913–1997) published lesbian pulp under the name Valerie Taylor, poetry as Nacella Young, and romances as Francine Davenport. Eventually some contemporary authors emerged as brands themselves: a Faith Baldwin romance was a predictable product.

At the same time, classics and contemporary best-sellers were reincarnated as pulp, as the format absorbed and repositioned literature that might otherwise have been inaccessible to working-class readers. Pulp publishers seem to have selected classic fiction with an eye to class politics, favoring, for example, the French Revolution and Dickens. They tended to present science as an arena where good old-fashioned ingenuity and stick-to-itiveness win the day. The life of Marie Curie was a pulp hit. When classics were reprinted in pulp editions—for example, *The Count of Monte Cristo* or *The Origin of the Species*—author identity might move to the fore on covers and in descriptive copy, but in becoming pulp the works acquired a popular aura and gravitated into pulp genres such as adventure and romance. Again, when new titles like William Faulkner's *Sanctuary* or Mary McCarthy's *The Company She Keeps* were issued in pulp editions, the cover art planted the works firmly in pulp categories: ruined woman, Southern variety; the many adventures and many men of a fast city girl. The genre, more than the author's name, was the selling point.

As the stories in pulp magazines were marketed by themes, so book-length tales were distinctively packaged by genre—Dell used a red heart to mark its romance line, for instance. Over time there were Westerns, science fiction, romance, mystery, crime/noir, and various others to choose from. Genres were to a large extent gendered. Crime/noir, for instance, focused on a masculine world of detectives, crooks, femmes fatales (positioned as foils to men), corruption, and violence, all described in hard-boiled prose. Romance focused on women's problems around courtship, virginity, marriage, motherhood, and careers, earnestly or coyly described. Since genres were gendered, the implied assumption was that men wrote and read crime/noir and women wrote and read romances. In fact, this assumption proves largely false.

Because pulp genres tended to rely on formulaic treatments, it was not difficult for writers to learn the ingredients that make up noir or, for that matter, how to write a lesbian love scene. The fact that authorial name and persona were rarely linked to real-life identity further permitted writers to explore transgender, or transgenre, writing. In so doing, they might self-consciously accentuate the gendered elements of a given genre, sometimes approximating parody, or they might attempt to regender a genre—for instance, writing a Western that foregrounds a romance. These freedoms, combined with the willingness of pulp publishers to buy work from anyone with the skill to write, meant that women had the chance to write in modes that were typically considered antithetical to them, and to explore gender across all genres. Leigh Brackett (1915–1978), a premier woman author of pulp, wrote hard-boiled crime books, science fiction, and Westerns, in addition to scripting sharp repartee for Bogart and Bacall in *The Big Sleep* (director Howard Hawks hired her on the basis of her novel *No Good from a Corpse*—assuming she was a man, as did many of her fans). Other women authors wrote whodunnit mysteries with girl heroines, science fiction battles of the sexes, and romances that start with a Reno divorce. Women wrote from male perspectives, narrating from inside the head of a serial killer, a PI, or a small-town pharmacist who happens to know all the town dirt. They also wrote from places where women weren't supposed to go.

Notoriously, pulp explored U.S. subcultures, which then often generated their own pulp subgenres. Where 1930s and 1940s pulp depicted gangster life and small-town chicanery, 1950s and 1960s pulp turned its attention, often with a pseudoanthropological lens, to juvenile delinquents, lesbians (far more than gay men), and beatniks, introducing its readers to such settings as reform schools, women's prisons, and "dangerous" places like Greenwich Village. These books exploited subcultures as suggestive settings for sexuality and nonconformism, often focusing on transgressive women or "bad girls": consider *Farm Hussy* and *Shack Baby* (two of a surprisingly large group in the highly specific rural-white-trash-slut subgenre), *Reefer Girl* (and its competitor, *Marijuana Girl*), *Women's Barracks, Reform School Girl,* and *Hippie Harlot.* Other books posited menaces present in the heart of middle-class life: *Suburbia: Jungle of Sex* and *Shadow on the Hearth.* A growing African American readership generated more new lines, mysteries and romances with black protagonists. Though the numbers of these books were fairly small, their existence is significant. With a few notable exceptions, African Americans were almost never found in pulps written for white readers, except as racially stereotyped stock characters.

While a strengthened Hayes Code sanitized movies in 1934, and "legitimate" publishers fought legal battles in order to get *Ulysses* and *Lady Chatterley's Lover* past the censors, pulp fiction, selling at twenty-five cents a book at newsstands, gas stations, and bus terminals, explored the taboo without provoking public outcry, or even dialogue. (Notably, though, pulp avoided the four-letter words that marked works like *Ulysses*, deploying instead hip street lingo to refer to sex, drink and drugs, and guns.) As famed lesbian pulp author Ann Bannon has noted, this "benign neglect provided a much-needed veil behind which we writers could work in peace." Pulp offered readers interracial romances during the segregation era, and blacklisted leftists encoded class struggle between pulp covers. The neglect by censors and critics had to do with the transience of pulp.

Circulating in a manner that matched the increasing mobility of American culture, pulps rarely adorned libraries, private or public. Small, slim, and ultimately disposable, they were meant for the road, or for easy access at home. They could be read furtively, in between household chores or during a lunch break. When finished, they could be left in a train compartment or casually stashed in a work shed. Publishers increasingly emphasized ease of consumption in the packaging of pulp: Ace produced "Ace Doubles," two titles reverse-bound together, so that the reader had only to flip the book over to enjoy a second colorful cover and enticing story; Bantam produced "L.A.s," specially sized to be sold from vending machines, the product's name evoking the mecca of the automobile and interstate highway culture; Fawcett launched a book club for its Gold Medal line, promising home delivery of four new sensational Gold Medal titles a month. To join, one cut out a coupon at the back of a Gold Medal book—clearly, no reluctance to damage a pulp volume would impede owners from acting on the special offer.

The mass appeal of pulp proved uncontainable by print. Characters and stories that originated in pulp soon found their way onto radio airwaves (e.g., *The Shadow*), onto the screen in the form of pre-Code sizzlers, noirs, and adventure films, and into comic books and newspaper comic strips. Through all these media, pulp penetrated the heart of the American popular imagination (and the popular image of America beyond its borders), shaping as well as reflecting the culture that consumed it.

Far more frequently than has been acknowledged, the source of these American icons, story lines, and genres were women, often working-class women who put bread on the table by creating imaginary worlds, or exploring existing but risky or taboo worlds, to fulfill the appetites of readers of both genders. But these writers, and the rich variety of work they produced, are today nearly invisible, despite the pulp revival of the last decade.

This revival has repopularized a hard-boiled, male world of pulp. Today's best-remembered pulp authors are not only male but also unapologetically misogynistic: pulp icon Jim Thompson's *A Hell of a Woman* and *A Swell-Looking Babe* are not untypical of the titles found among the noir classics recently restored to print.

In fact, it is interesting to note, even in a broader survey of the genres, how many male-authored, and presumably male-read, pulps were focused on women (remember *Shack Baby* and *Reefer Girl*)—a phenomenon not found in the highbrow literature of the period. Men even wrote a fair number of lesbian pulps. But more often than not, the women in these books are dangerous and predatory as well as irresistible, exploiting men's desire for their own purposes. Or they are wayward women who either come to a bad end, or come to their senses with the help of a man who sets them straight (in the various senses of the word). Some critics have noted that such female characters proliferated in the immediate post–World War II period, when servicemen were returning to a world in which women had occupied, briefly, a powerful position in the workplace and other areas of the public sphere—a world in which the balance between the genders had been irrevocably altered.

In contrast with these bad girls and femmes fatales were the heroines of traditional romance pulps, most of them relentlessly pretty and spunky girls-next-door. They occupied the centers of their own stories, and navigated sometimes complicated social and emotional terrain, but in the end always seemed to get—or be gotten by—their man.

Given this background, and given the strict generic dictates to which all successful pulp writers were subject, did women working in undeniably male-dominated pulp genres such as crime/noir write differently from their male counterparts? And did women writers of formulaic romances, both heterosexual and lesbian, reveal the genuine conflicts facing real women in their time, and explore the limits of female agency? They could hardly fail to do so.

Relatively little scholarship has been done on pulp fiction; less still on women writers of pulp. It is not possible to speculate on the intentions of women pulp authors, and few would suggest that they were undercover feminists seeking to subvert patriarchal culture by embedding radical messages in cheap popular novels. Yet from a contemporary vantage point, some of their work certainly does seem subversive, regardless of the intention behind it.

Women writers provided the first pulps with happy endings for lesbians: Valerie Taylor's *The Girls in 3-B* is a prime example of this suprisingly revolutionary phenomenon, and still more intriguing for its contrast of the different options and obstacles faced by heterosexual and homosexual women in the 1950s (with little doubt as to which looked better to the author). The femme fatale of *In a Lonely Place,* the luscious Laurel Gray, has brains and integrity, as well as curves—and in the end, she is not the one who turns out to be deadly. In fact, Dorothy B. Hughes's bold twist on the noir genre can be seen as addressing the crisis in postwar masculinity, with its backlash taken to the furthest extremes. The protagonist of Faith Baldwin's *Skyscraper* is typically pretty and plucky;

she longs for domestic bliss and she loves her man. But she also loves the bustle and buzz of the office where she works, the rows of gleaming desks and file cabinets, the sense of being part of the larger, public world of business—and she epitomizes a new kind of heroine in a new kind of romance plot, a career girl with a wider set of choices to negotiate.

These premier books in the Feminist Press's Femmes Fatales series were selected for their bold and sometimes transgressive uses of genre forms, as well as the richness of their social and historical settings and their lively and skillful writing. We chose books that also seemed to have some impact on public consciousness in their time—in these cases, rather inexactly measured by the fact that they crossed over into different, and even more popular, media: Both *In a Lonely Place* and *Skyscraper* were made into films. And we can only speculate whether *The Girls in 3-B* played any part in inspiring *The Girls in Apartment 3-G,* the syndicated comic strip about three young working women (heterosexual, of course) living together in New York City, which debuted in 1961.

In the past three decades, feminist scholars have laid claim to women's popular fiction as a legitimate focus of attention and scholarship, and a rich source of information on women's lives and thought in various eras. Some scholars have in fact questioned the use—and the uses—of the term *popular fiction,* which seems to have been disproportionately applied to the work of women writers, especially those who wrote "women's books." The Feminist Press views the Femmes Fatales series as an important new initiative in this ongoing work of cultural reclamation. As such, it is also a natural expression of the Press's overall mission to ensure that women's voices are fully represented in the public discourse, in the literary "canon," and on bookstore and library shelves.

We leave it to scholars doing groundbreaking new work on women's pulp—including our own afterword writers—to help us fully appreciate all that these works have to offer, both as literary texts and as social documents. And we leave it to our readers to discover for themselves, as we have, all of the entertaining, disturbing, suggestive, and thoroughly fascinating work that can be found behind the juicy covers of women's pulp fiction.

Livia Tenzer, Editorial Director
Jean Casella, Publisher
New York City
July 2003

THE GIRLS IN 3-B

CHAPTER ONE

"I bought you some pajamas," Annice's mother said. She laid them on the bed among stacks of washed and ironed clothes, still in their cellophane envelopes from Sears Roebuck. *Corny ones,* Annice thought, red-checked gingham and a repulsive flowered print.

"I don't wear pajamas," she said, thinking, *I won't pick a fight, not the last minute like this, I won't let her make me mad.* She bent over her suitcase, rearranging the blouses her mother had already packed.

Mrs. Harvey said, "You might have a little decent gratitude." She was small and thin like Annice; anyone seeing them together would have known they were mother and daughter. But her reddish hair lacked gloss, her skin was dry, and the two creases between her eyes were permanent. She wore a starched gingham dress and low-heeled oxfords. Annice reassured herself with a glance at her own toreador pants. *Even if I haven't got any chest, hardly,* she thought, *I wouldn't wear house dresses. Or cotton stockings. Or those ugly kitcheny aprons.*

"Even if you won't wear nightgowns, you can wear shorty pajamas like the other girls. It isn't decent to lie around with nothing on, a big girl like you."

"Oh, Mother!" Annice yelled. There, she had broken all her good resolutions—no temper, no shouting, keep it sweet and friendly the last day. She picked up the top blouse and fingered it nervously, meanly pleased to see the wrinkles fan out between her fingers. Her mother had laundered it—had worked her fingers to the bone to keep things nice, was the way she put it whenever she thought the family was guilty of ingratitude. And that was most of the time. Annice dropped the garment on the bed, feeling better. She stretched. Four hours till train time, two hundred and forty minutes, how many seconds? "I'll be glad to get out of this crummy place."

Mrs. Harvey refolded the blouse. "Are you taking this?"

"Makes no difference. I don't care what I take, just so I have my notebooks."

"All adolescents think they can write poetry. They get over it."

And that's a lie, her daughter thought. That prim figure had never been shaken by desire or abandoned to passion; had never wept because an April tree was so beautiful and frail; had never walked in mist like the inside of a pearl. No, her concern on a rainy morning was all for muddy footprints on the kitchen linoleum. Annice lifted her chin. "After today I'll be with my own kind of people."

"If you mean that big sloppy Pat, I don't think much of your taste. I'd rather see you in your grave than have you running after boys the way she does."

Shows how much mothers know. *That night of the Senior Prom, when we danced till three and then drove to Uniontown for chicken and fries—well, parents always think you're safe if you square-date.* It was Pat's date—that good-looking Johnny Cutler, who had wanted to stop at the motel—anyhow, the first one to come out and say so. But after the boys had paid and made up fake names, it was Pat who had chickened out. *Not me,* Annice thought proudly. She remembered the urgency and excitement, and then, driving home, the letdown half-ashamed feeling because they hadn't gone through with it. *The very first chance I get,* she promised herself, ashamed to be so inexperienced at eighteen. Aloud she said, "Pat just happens to be my best friend."

"Speak of the devil," Pat said from the bedroom doorway.

She flashed a good-natured smile at both of them, knowing how all the mothers hated this business of walking in without knocking. Until this year, when she was finally allowed to drive the family car, the Harveys' place had been too far out in the country for free and easy visiting; now she took great pleasure in dropping in at odd hours. She leaned against the doorjamb and lit a cigarette.

Mrs. Harvey's lips tightened. The hem of Pat's skirt was torn and a pack of cigarettes, unevenly ripped open, stuck out of her jacket pocket. Her nail polish was bright, and her legs were bare. She was wearing raffia slippers with little straw dolls on the toes, a man on one and a woman on the other, dancing and bobbling with each step she took. Pat grinned, her face alive and very pretty. "You most ready, kid?"

"I don't think I'll ever be ready. All this junk."

"Mom tossed all my stuff in Kevin's old foot locker. I'm all set." Pat crossed to the dressing table. "Hey, don't forget your glamor."

Annice caught the bottle of Tabu neatly and dropped it into the suitcase, on the disarrayed blouses. Her mother glanced at the rejected pajamas, then at the slip straps and unmated nylons dangling over the suitcase edge. She walked out of the room, ramrod-stiff, closing the door precisely. Pat flopped down on the bed. "Fight?"

Annice scowled. "Doesn't do any good to fight with her, she's always right. You can't tell her anything, she knows it already." She picked the cellophane envelopes up distastefully and shook the despised new-smelling garments out on the bed. "Now I have to be modest when I sleep. The house might burn down or something."

"Take them along. You might be sick some time."

There was a moment of silent struggle. Torn between common sense and resentment, Annice finally laughed and laid them with her other clothes. "I can come home if I get sick. I should be glad I've got a good home to come to."

Her tone implied that she'd rather die in a charity ward. "Or I can write home for money if I run over my allowance." Rather starve, too.

Pat stubbed out her cigarette butt. She lit another, snicking the silver lighter open with a practiced thumbnail. "Four more hours, I can't believe it."

"I never thought they'd say yes."

"Seven of us, Mom's glad to get rid of me."

Smoke curled elegantly out of her nose. Annice made another resolution—to start smoking the minute the train pulled out of the station. It was one of the things her mother hated most about Pat, along with Pat's bare legs, her buttonless blouses, her religion, her casual profanity, her naturally curled hair and the hours she came home from dates. Therefore it was one of the things Annice envied and wanted to copy.

"Do people always hate their parents?"

"Always. It's psychology." Pat rolled over on her stomach. "Especially only children. I never thought Barby's folks would let her go, did you?"

"There's something creepy about that setup."

"All middle-aged people make me feel creepy. They don't really have any more reason for being alive." Pat lowered her voice, glancing at the door. "It's not so awful with a big family though, they sort of spread it around. One reason mine gave in, they think it'll break me up with Johnny."

"If he really loves you he'll write. Or something."

"I don't know. I'm not ready to be married yet."

"I'm not talking about being married. That's for the birds." She giggled. "And the bees."

"Well, but it's a sin. I'm going to wait for the man I marry. I made my mind up that night—honest, Annice, I couldn't go through with it. I know you were mad about it, but I can't help it." She looked at her feet, making the dolls jounce. "It's okay to read poetry about free love and all that jazz, but I bet you haven't gone all the way with a boy yet. Not unless you've been holding out on me."

That's because nobody around here's worth bothering with." Annice stared out of the bedroom window, past the barn and machine shed, the RFD mailbox and the road that led to the county seat. She pictured a future filled with handsome intellectual men—or better—fascinating, *ugly* intellectual men. Her eyes shone.

Pat shrugged. "Anyhow we're going. Big deal."

They grinned at each other, the whole bright-colored future unrolling before them. Chicago. Jobs. An apartment. Annice's jaw set like her mother's. She'd go to college if she had to, but not a day longer than it took to make her first big sale to a poetry magazine. They didn't need to think she was going to spend her life in a classroom, learning dull dates and facts out of books, when there was life to be lived.

"Barby's father thinks it would be nice if we stayed in a girls' club."

"He would."

Annice twiddled the windowshade cord. The familiar landscape was uglier than ever, with rescue so near. She pulled the shade down with a snap, shutting out buildings, combine, and the neighbors' feedlot. "I hate this place. I hate everything about it. It smothers me, it's so fat and bourgeois and corn-and-hoggy. If I ever get out of it I'm never coming back, not even for a visit."

"Sure, sure."

"You don't know. You've always lived in town." She overlooked the fact that the town had a population of three thousand, with three grocery stores, two churches and a handful of filling stations. "You don't know what it's like to always be a country kid and have to go to school on the bus, like a—a peasant or something. It isn't money, it's a question of *soul*."

"Can't be any worse than these little hick towns."

"Anyhow, we're getting out."

Mrs. Harvey mounted the front stairs, her steps light and even but somehow emphatic. The girls looked at each other in perfect understanding. She had worked off her righteous indignation—had defrosted the refrigerator or cleaned the pantry shelves probably—and was ready to make a sign of forgiveness, an overture of friendship that would make them feel adolescent and uncouth. They would rather have been left to nurse their resentment.

"If you girls want to come downstairs you can have some cocoa." Peace offering, because she believed it was bad for the digestion to eat between meals, and she had never become reconciled to the tons of cheeseburgers, salted peanuts, candy bars, cokes, and pizza the high school generations wolfed down. She was ready to meet them halfway by suggesting food, and fattening food at that.

In theory, they despised cocoa and never ordered it in the school lunchroom. They would rather have had black coffee or—more adult because it was forbidden—beer. Actually, the rich, sugary smell floating up the stairs made their mouths water. They arranged their faces into the expression of bored tolerance worn by fashion models, and got to their feet.

"Go ahead," Annice said. "I have to go to the john." She had grabbed at the first excuse she could think of, because suddenly she felt an unexpected need to be alone for a minute.

I'm leaving my childhood behind, she thought, standing in the middle of the floor and looking around at the flowered wallpaper, the familiar bleached-wood furniture.

When I come back, if I ever do, I'll be changed. She tried to feel some suitable emotion, but all she could conjure up was the familiar irritation at the flowered curtains her mother had made and the matching dressing table skirt.

Her going wasn't likely to make much difference here. The empty drawers of the dresser yawned, in the closet a tangle of wire hangers swayed slightly. Her childhood books and high school annuals still stood in the white-painted bookcase, and there were gaps where she had taken out the modern novels and slim volumes of poetry. It could have been any teen-age girl's room. She had no feelings about it at all.

She shut the door behind her quietly, as her mother had done.

CHAPTER TWO

"I don't see why you want to do this," Robert Morrison said. He tried to keep his voice even, to sound reasonable and not querulous. Stuffing tobacco into his pipe, he noted irritably that his hands were shaking; his heart was pounding, too. He had hurried home from the store for one last try, knowing of course that it wouldn't do any good, but unable to accept the accomplished fact of his daughter's leaving home—trunk packed, train ticket bought, job as stock girl in a Loop department store arranged through his own business contacts. He tried to smile. "I'm not standing in your way or anything. It's just that it seems so foolish."

Barby said nothing. She had been standing, taking dresses down off the dining-room light fixture one by one and laying them in the trunk as her mother had taught her, with tissue paper between the folds. At the sound of her father's footsteps on the front porch she became absolutely motionless except for the quickened rise and fall of her chest. She stood with her back against the wall, her eyes fixed on his face. In the bright sunshine of early afternoon her profile, outlined against the cheery wallpaper, was a replica of his.

"It's nothing of the sort," Mrs. Morrison said. She turned halfway from the sewing machine, pushing aside the foam of thin material that was one last dress to go. It was her pride that Barby had better clothes, and more of them, than any other girl in her class; had her hair styled at the beauty parlor when her friends were putting theirs up in pin curls; took dancing lessons and went to a high-priced camp in Wisconsin in the summer. *All the advantages I never had,* she said frankly, not bothering to hide or deny her skimpy farm girlhood because, after all, her friends and neighbors, the women she saw at church and Eastern Star and PTA, had known her since she was a barefooted little girl in feedsack petticoats.

She said, "She's old enough to make her own way in the world. That's perfectly natural."

"God damn it, you can't live by magazines and psychology books."

"There's a good deal of truth in psychology books," Helen Morrison said. A flicker of distaste crossed her round cheerful face. "Even if they do put too much emphasis on certain things. A girl's grown-up by eighteen. Plenty of girls are married then."

"You'd like that, wouldn't you?" Damn it, his heart was pounding like a triphammer now. A wonder they couldn't hear it on the other side of the room. He hated feeling flustered. It disturbed his habitual calm to be reminded of the secret he had kept so long. A line of white appeared at each side of his mouth. He took off his rimless glasses and polished them on a clean white handkerchief, narrowing his sharp blue eyes at his wife. "You'd like to get her married and out of the house, wouldn't you? You're jealous of her. All older women are jealous of young girls."

"Don't be ridiculous. Nobody can say I haven't been a good mother."

Barby was going to be sick again. *Oh God,* she prayed, *not now. Not today when it's almost time to go.* She swallowed hard, conscious of the familiar warning symptoms— the hard knot in her stomach, the nausea, giddiness, tension in her arms and legs. Sweat ran down her back, cold under the thin summer dress. Now the rain of black specks and zigzag of dancing lights would come, followed by holes in her vision and the old onesided, bursting pain. Migraine. Ever since she was thirteen and—No. Don't think about that.

I'll have to stay home and go to bed, she thought in anguish, remembering all the days under sedation and the tired, dragged-out crawling back to health. And then, a straw of hope to grasp at—*but it never happens away from home. If I can just hold it off till train time, it's not so long now—*

"Good mother—good God Almighty."

Helen shrugged. She turned back to the machine, obeying the feminine impulse to find comfort in something that could be handled, adjusted, manipulated. "There, it's done. I hope you'll have a chance to wear it, some place exciting to go."

"It's beautiful," Barby said politely. She took the dress in both hands and stood holding it as if she didn't know what to do with it. "I'll have more clothes than I can wear."

"Most likely you'll meet some nice boys," Helen said. "You ought to date more."

"She'll have better things to think about," Robert said. He was shaking inwardly. Why in hell couldn't she understand? Why couldn't she see that Barby was different from most girls, better, prettier, smarter—and more in need of protection? But of course she couldn't know that; for five years he had schemed to keep her from knowing.

He looked with some distaste at his wife, placid and plump as she cleared away the little clutter of sewing. A good woman, as wholesome as bread pudding. Their marriage was as good as most. He thought virtuously, *I'm a good husband, I support my family, I don't drink or chase other women. Does she have to be so goddam stupid?*

Barby bent slowly, focusing her eyes on a figure in the rug to ward off further dizziness, and laid the new dress in her trunk. His eyes followed her movement; he put his glasses back on and watched the nebulous lines of her back and thighs become clear and sharp. A pretty girl, her waist narrow, shoulders and hips softly rounded. That vase-shaped back was wholly womanly. When she turned around, the lines of her bosom would be—ah!

"Mind you use plenty of face cream," Helen said. "City air is awfully hard on the skin. Have your hair done by a good man—don't try to save on it. Don't buy cheap shoes, they'll ruin your feet." She paused, considering what other moral precepts might apply to a daughter about to leave home. "And plenty of sleep. Nothing puts dark circles under your eyes and spoils your looks like late hours."

Barby nodded. She had heard all this before; her mother had been saying the same things since she was in kindergarten. Think about the trip to Chicago. The train—the same one she had taken on so many shopping trips, but different because it was carrying her into the future. The other girls. The job in a big department store, and a chance to earn her own money instead of taking everything from *him.* The apartment, when they could find one and fix it up with cute gadgets from the dime store, fresh paint and drapes. And when she went to bed at night the loneliness and the secret terror wouldn't be there any more—the other girls would be there, her best friends all through high school. *I hate to be alone,* she thought. *It'll be fun to have roommates, almost as much fun as having sisters.*

The churning in her stomach stopped. She felt light and warm with reassurance. "I'll go get my suitcase," she said. Her voice sounded all right.

Robert's eyes followed her to the stairs. A slow graceful walk, with the curves of her legs outlined under the thin skirt. Funny, he thought, she looks like me, but she's all girl—all the curves are in the right places. He tried to picture the days ahead when she would be gone. They stretched out before him in a long drab line, without color or meaning. The store, the basement workshop where he made fine bits of furniture—mostly to get away from Helen evenings—the well-cooked meals, and comfortable bed. All meaningless. This was her doing. His anger kindled against his wife. "You don't have to talk like that," he said harshly. "You trying to make a whore out of her?"

"It's not necessary to use that kind of language," Helen said. Her face was without expression. "I want her to lead a normal life. Any mother wants that."

"You want her running the streets like some cheap tramp."

"If she doesn't know how to behave by this time, she likely never will."

"All this talk about clothes and looks, cheap beauty-parlor trash. It's demoralizing. She has a good mind, she ought to be making something of her life. She could do anything she wanted."

"It's natural for a girl to think about her appearance. Men don't understand about these things."

"You'd like her to marry some ordinary boy and have a flock of snot-nosed brats, I suppose."

"That's not the worst thing that could happen to her."

He raised his head quickly. Her face was turned away from him; she was replacing the little clutter of threads and scissors in a drawer. His mouth went dry.

She didn't know. How could she know? It had happened—oh, God, five years ago. I never told her. I'm almost sure Barby never told her. She'd have thrown it up to me in one of those sweet aggrieved I-told-you-so spells. As far as Stewart's concerned, the sanctimonious bastard would burn in hell before he'd let a thing like that get out about himself.

He shut his eyes, feeling again the unbelieving horror of that evening. He had walked home late from the store, eager to see Barby and hear all the details of her childish day, and at the same time turning over in his mind the possibility of the bank's giving him the loan he had applied for. It was snowing a little; the blue Buick in front of the house was flecked with white. Stewart's car. That meant they were going to let him have the five thousand, because the vice-president of the County Trust and Savings wouldn't have come to him otherwise.

The silence of the house brought him to a stop in the front hall, with his hand on the doorknob. Helen—always a talker, always chattering—should have been entertaining the banker in the living room. He pulled his overcoat off and hung it up, frowning. This was her bridge-club night—but Stewart?

A child's muffled sob brought him to the door of the living room, moving quickly and lightly.

Robert Morrison's face, five years later, was pinched and white at the memory. *Damn Helen,* he thought for the millionth time. *Damn her miserable little soul to hell.* If she hadn't let Stewart in and then gone out to her stupid club— if she hadn't left him alone in the house with a sleeping girl child of thirteen—if Barby hadn't been waked by the door slamming behind her, and come downstairs sleepy in her flimsy little nighty! Morrison clenched his fists.

People don't do such things. Not solid, respectable family men like Stewart. Vice-president of the bank, active in the service clubs. You don't, if you have grown up in a safe middle-class small town, have any qualms about leaving a man like that alone in the lighted living room, knowing your husband will be home any minute to discuss business with him. It was unreasonable to blame Helen. Robert admitted it. But hate filled him every time he relived that evening, like a cold clear poison distilled through his mind and body, drop by drop.

He released his held-in breath and walked into the kitchen, careful not to look at his wife as he passed her. He turned on the cold water. Distracted by the splatter and splash in the immaculate sink, feeling the chill trickle down his constricted throat, listening to the footsteps upstairs, he felt better.

He'd always been a fool about Barby, by Helen's figuring. After all, the only child. But after that night he was conscious of her as a developing woman, and he worried about what life might hold for her. As her leggy angular body took on the curves of adolescence, as she grew into the kind of girl men turn to look after on the street, his pride was tempered by a fearful anxiety. He justified himself by thinking that she was all he had. All that mattered, anyway. And he was the only one who knew what had happened to her.

Stewart had never said anything. Maybe he hoped that Morrison didn't really know, was only guessing—that he had arranged his clothing and wiped his perspiring face before eyes accustomed to the outdoor dark could be sure of what they had seen. He had been genial ever since; but then, he was genial to everybody. And the five thousand, long repaid, had pulled the store through its only real crisis. That it was the best department store in the county was due mostly to Stewart's granting that loan.

She needs me, he thought. *I'm the only one that knows about her. I don't see how she can get along without me.*

He stood with the empty glass in his hand, looking into a future without Barby and without light.

CHAPTER THREE

They had talked about the trip for weeks, planning the details right down to what they would wear on the train. But after they bought the tickets a quietness settled down that even the determined cheerfulness of the mothers and fathers couldn't crack. The three girls mounted the train steps single-file, as solemnly as if they had been climbing to the scaffold; and when they settled down in facing seats, smoothing their skirts and arranging suitcases, they were embarrassed into speechlessness. They looked out of the window at the dull Midwestern landscape, each shut away in a little capsule of her own thoughts.

Annice was troubled. This was the turning point of her whole life, the biggest thing that had ever happened to her, even more important than her first poem—at eight—or her first kiss—at thirteen—and she should have been thrilled to the depths. It was infuriating to feel nothing at a time like this, neither nostalgia for what she was leaving behind nor excitement over what laid ahead. She was tired from packing and from the arguments with her parents. It was their fault she was wordless at a time like this. Annice closed the red leather notebook that held all of her poems, neatly printed in gilt ink. Maybe something would come to her later.

"Well, this is it."

Pat nodded, wide-eyed. "Jeepers, it's big."

"Naturally." Annice kept her voice matter-of-fact, but her lips felt stiff and silly. She watched the shabby streets slide by. "Why do they always have train tracks in the icky part of town?"

"I think the railroads bring down real estate values, or something." Pat pressed her nose against the window, unmindful of dust. Small shabby streets of bungalows with fenced yards had given way to rows of all-alike apartment houses. She saw shabby brick hospitals, schools, and churches; shopping centers with neon-lighted taverns and rundown corner groceries; warehouses. The train came into a widening switchyard with branching tracks and cars waiting on the sidings. Pigeons flew up to settle on the roofs of the freight sheds, warned by the vibration of the oncoming engine. A group of men were standing around a small bonfire—why, in August? Burning trash maybe— two of them leaned on shovels, laughing. One was eating a sandwich out of waxed paper. Between the tracks, grass was growing thin and sparse. Now the train slid in under a roof dotted with small high lights. That was part of the excitement—the yellow lights and the soft gloom beneath, when the sun was shining outdoors. Pat shivered.

"We ought to get our stuff together," Barby said. People were standing up, smoothing their skirts, picking the backs of their skirts away from the seats, lifting their suitcases and bundles down from the overhead rack. Barby sat with her knees crossed; every now and then one dangling foot jumped nervously. She straightened her glasses, noting with relief that her vision was okay again. "We're almost there."

"Let the porter worry," Pat advised. She hadn't changed her clothes for the trip, and she seemed not at all bothered by her shabbiness or the fact that her hair needed cutting and setting. Barby looked at her with wonder. She was always conscious of how she looked and felt uncomfortable if she was untidy. *Maybe,* she thought hopefully, *I'll be a different person from here on out.*

I ought to make a poem about the man with the shovel, Annice told herself, *but then, Sandburg beat me to it. I ought to be* feeling *this more.* She opened her compact and examined her reflection carefully, torn between an artistic indifference to appearances and a feminine urge to look her best for this special occasion. She had a thin sensitive face with a spattering of freckles on the high cheekbones, green-gray eyes, a tangle of reddish hair. People who discovered that she wrote verse—unpublished so far except in the school paper—said she looked like Edna St. Vincent Millay. She snapped the compact shut, satisfied with what she saw.

The train slowed, jolted, gathered speed again, jolted and stopped. A fat matron across the aisle staggered. Pat stood up, gathering her last year's purse and jacket. "Come on, kids, we're in."

Three pairs of high heels clicked in cadence across the vast echoing lobby. *But we're nothing,* Annice thought in sudden panic. *It's too big. All these people living their own lives and going about their own business—there's too many of them. One person doesn't count for anything. I'm nothing; nobody even knows I'm alive.* She hunched her narrow shoulders as though seeking refuge within herself.

Barby took a deep breath. *I'm safe. Nobody's looking at me, nobody even knows I'm alive.* She took off her glasses, which she wore for studying and close work even though her father hated them. A very young sailor turned to look after her with appreciation. She ignored him. She would never see him again.

Pat said crossly, "For Pete's sake come on, I'm hungry."

"How are we fixed for money?"

"I've got a hundred dollars."

"Rich bitch," Pat said. "I've got fifty, and that's all till I earn some."

"I have eighty," Annice said. "But my tuition's paid."

Barby was silent. Her father had found job for her, after all his reasoning and arguing had failed to change her mind. *Oh God,* she thought, *I get so sick of being reasoned with, why can't he just tell me like other fathers do? He only does it to get his own way without acting like a boss or turning me against him, it's a fake, and I never think of any good arguments until too late.* Persuaded against his will, then, that she was really setting off on this wild-goose chase, this crazy scheme her mother had aided and abetted her in, he had strong-armed one of the salesmen who came into the store, and now she had a way to earn her living. Fifty dollars a week. That sounded like a lot of money, but she knew it wasn't—her gray suit had cost more than that. The work would be easy, though; as Mr. Levin described it, it was no more than she had done in the store on Saturdays and through the Christmas rush— tightening buttons, checking zippers, dry-cleaning lipstick spots, making out price tags. Dull, but easy. A job is a job.

Still, she would have like to find something on her own. If only he hadn't had anything to do with it.

"Let's take a taxi. How far is it?"

"Let's walk a while. I want to look in the store windows."

"Where is this Y hotel anyhow? Seems funny for girls to go to a Y."

"It's a regular hotel is all, only cheap. Not like the Y back home."

"Oh."

They came out into the sunshine on Jackson. The bridge vibrated under their feet with the thunder of buses and trucks. Tall buildings rose ahead of them. The people were ordinary-looking. Annice had expected something exotic and citified, not these sunburned men in sport shirts, these barelegged and bareheaded office girls. Two Chinese girls in high-collared, split dresses went by; she was grateful.

The last traces of Barby's unease vanished. The sunshine was so bright. *It's so big,* she thought happily, lifting her gaze from the sidewalk to the row on row of windows. The people hurrying past held no menace for her; they had their own affairs to take care of. The buildings were vast and impersonal. This new glass-brick and cement-block structure, with bits of paper still glued to the windows, with baby trees at either side of the entrance still rooted in balled burlap—how many people would work there, meaning nothing to one another, going home at five o'clock to live their separate lives? She said softly, "I like it."

Pat said, "I'm hungry." This was the time of day when the little kids would be coming in from their play to have a snack. Mom would pour milk and spread peanut-butter for them, and then sit down at the kitchen table and have a cup of coffee before she tackled the ironing. The familiar shabby kitchen wavered before her. *They didn't have to be so damn happy to see me go,* she thought, "Let's stop in a Toffenetti's and eat."

Barby said reluctantly, "There's a girl I bunked with at camp last summer, Jonni Foster—I have her number."

"Well, okay, we'll eat in a drugstore. You can call her."

No, Barby thought, shrinking from touching another life so soon, spoiling the wonderful impersonality of it. *Not somebody we have to know.* But she kept still; she had started this, she had to see it through. *Me and my big mouth,* she thought.

She went into a drugstore booth and dialed with a reluctant finger, while the others took possession of three stools at the fountain and scanned the mimeographed menu.

Barby felt better about it, when Jonni was shown up to their room in the Y. She helped them unpack and politely admired the room, although the impressive bulk of the Conrad Hilton, a block over on Michigan, made it look small and shabby. Barby sat on the edge of the bed, barefoot, checking the want ads in the evening papers. They had bought all of them, pleased because they were so bulky. "We'll find a place right away," she said, running a finger down the To Let columns. "Why do so many places only want men?"

"That figures," Pat said. "Women hang their wet laundry in the bathroom and get cold cream on the pillowcases. I guess they bring men home with them too. Men keep their sex life on the outside."

Annice said, "That sounds like a corny joke."

"Well, I haven't got any sex life, so what difference does it make?"

Jonni Foster giggled. For a year Barby had been thinking of her with shorts and a peeling nose; she hardly recognized the thin, elegant creature in the high-waisted dress and short enameled haircut who sat in the one armchair. Jonni had on the new pointed, thin-heeled shoes; her lipstick was the latest shade; she was fragrant with Chanel Number Five. She had a late date, she said; she couldn't stay. "There's plenty of it around."

"But how do you meet boys—men?"

"The same as anywhere. They work in the same office. Or they sit next to you in a restaurant. Maybe live in the same building. I don't know, how do you meet men in Waterloo, Iowa? That's where I'm from?"

Barby wasn't interested in men. "Says here two and a half rooms. What's a half room?"

"Kitchenette. It would be semi-portioned with a counter and stove, maybe. Where is it?"

"Fifty-six hundred south."

Jonni peered over her shoulder. "That's the University district. It might be okay, or it might not. You run into a lot of fairies down there. Then there's a lot of beautiful old houses, nice people. That's where the artists and intellectuals live, I guess."

"What do you mean, artists?"

"Some are just beard and beret boys. Beat generation fakes. There's some real ones too." Jonni shrugged. "I don't know if they're any good or not. But anyhow the rent won't be too high at that address and the I.C. is handy."

"Is it safe?"

"Safe enough. You don't walk down dark alleys at night even in Waterloo." She had been gone from Waterloo long enough to stop hating it, she explained. A whole year. "It's a nice little town. I only hope I never have to live there, is all. Human nature's the same most anywhere."

"Reminds me of a story I heard," Pat said grinning. "This girl got a scholarship to go to New York and study art, and her mother was all upset about it. So she went to the priest for advice. 'Just think what might happen to my daughter in one of those studios.' And the priest said, 'Just think what might happen to her in an Iowa haymow.' They bale it now, but it's the same idea."

Barby said with distaste, "Don't you kids ever think about anything but men?"

"What else is there to think about?"

Jonni said, "The boys here are exactly like the ones back home. You can tell every move they're going to make while they're still leading up to it real subtle-like, they think."

Annice was silent. She walked across the room and looked at herself in the long mirror of the dressing table. She wore the flowered pajamas her mother had bought for her, the same pair she had rejected so scornfully only this afternoon—it was all right now she no longer had to assert her independence. They were cooler than a dress and more easily laundered than pedal-pushers. The short full top only made her look smaller and thinner. Little, bird-boned, with narrow hands and feet, her chest nearly flat when not helped out with latex and boning, she couldn't help knowing that her looks were right for this year's styles. That pleased her. So did her walk, which was light and graceful. She smiled at her reflection.

"You kids have jobs lined up?"

Annice said, "I'm at the Pier, U. of I. But not for long, I hope."

Pat puckered her eyebrows. "I'm looking."

"Plenty of jobs around. The papers are full of unemployment, but I haven't seen any."

"I don't know how to get started."

"Typing? Shorthand?"

"Some. I can spell."

"There's this girl in my building, she works for a publisher. They might have an opening. I don't know how much they pay," Jonni said, "the more highbrow a job is the less it pays as a rule, but you could ask."

"I could try it, anyhow," Pat said gratefully.

Barby tore off the margin of the Want Ad page for the phone number.

"People are nice," Pat said when Jonni had left. "You hear a lot of stuff about big cities, how cold and impersonal they are and all that jazz. I don't think so."

Barby said, "Maybe it's because everybody comes from someplace else."

After they had gone to bed in the double room Annice sat by the window in the adjoining single, her elbows propped on the grimy sill, looking out. Below were traffic lights, neon signs blinking on and off, the headlamps of cars making a weaving pattern that dazzled her. She shut her eyes, but the glow was still there, behind the lids. A gentle summer breeze blew in from Lake Michigan.

She thought, *this is where I belong. Somewhere in this big city is all the romance and beauty and excitement I've always wanted to find.* She smiled. Let the others fuss about jobs and finding a place to live. Those things would work out; somebody always took care of them. This was her town. This was the place where she would find love and fame. Fame could wait if it had to—she was young, there was plenty of time. But love was the big thing, the thing to look for first of all.

CHAPTER FOUR

There was a mixture of guilt and pleasure in being downtown when everyone else was at work, like playing hooky from school or going to he movies when you were supposed to be home helping Mom with the Saturday cleaning. Pat crossed the intersection of Jackson and Wabash under the clatter and clang of the El and stood uncertainly watching the pedestrians run into the middle of the street after a slowing bus. A couple of men with briefcases bumped into her from behind. She realized that the light had changed and the cop was holding back a block-long line of cars and taxis. She hurried across, feeling in her embarrassment that the tall buildings were going to tip over on her.

The Walgreen's at the corner of State and Jackson looked comfortingly like the Walgreen's back home, and she thought about going in and having a cup of coffee. Then she decided against it, on the ground that she was too nervous to sit still. She turned north and walked down State, irked because she was early for her appointment and anxious to get it over with. Annice and Barby had been out of bed half an hour before the alarm went off, talking loudly enough to wake everyone in the building and trying on all their different clothes and cosmetics. There hadn't been any point in trying to sleep with all that gabble-gabble going on, so she had gotten up too, and now she was out on the sidewalk without anything to do until ten o'clock.

The outlines of the street map she had memorized last night were clear in her mind, but it was hard to relate the complex noisy streets to the line drawings. She paused long enough to verify Adams on a street-corner sign and then walked on with more assurance, reminding herself that she could ask a cop or a newsstand man if she really got lost. Play it cool, she advised herself. It's just a job. If I don't get this one I'll find another. She took a deep breath.

The Fort Dearborn Press was located on the fourteenth floor of an office building on Dearborn, although she found out later that there was no connection. The surroundings were unpretentious; the building was set between a United Cigar store on one side and a Tru-Value dress shop on the other, but the lobby was ornate enough to scare her all over again. It was paneled in marble like pressed veal and had two thick, swirly, obviously genuine oil paintings on the wall—you could see the brush marks. In one, an Indian family was sitting in front of their wigwam, or tepee, with a bunch of pine trees in the background. In the other, a black-robed priest was preaching to a respectful Indian congregation. All of the Indians looked alike, with thin, intellectual faces and long noses.

Feeling snooty about the paintings made her feel better, but then she caught sight of herself in the full-length mirror beside the elevator grille and was depressed again. Her hair was either too long or too short, depending, and much too fuzzy in a town where other people wore theirs lacquered flat. Her navy-blue dress had a couple of buttons missing. *I need about five hundred dollars worth of new clothes and a good diet,* she thought, stepping into the elevator and seeing with a sinking heart that it was self-service. Automatic elevators always made her nervous, not because she was too dumb to run them, of course—she was as smart as any elevator boy—but if the damn thing got stuck between floors she wanted it to be somebody else's fault. She punched the 14 button, put her fingers in her ears to equalize the pressure, and waited for the door to stick when the trip was over.

The door slid open smoothly, and she got out feeling cheated.

The gold paint was shiny on the outer door of The Fort Dearborn Press and the reception room, although small, was lushly carpeted and lined with shelves of books. There was a mahogany and plate-glass desk with three wire baskets labelled Incoming, Outgoing, and Proofs. The girl behind the desk was reading a long strip of printed paper, moving a plastic ruler down slowly, line by line. A sharp pencil was stuck through her sleek chignon. A cup half full of coffee sat on the edge of the desk, and three or four pink-stained butts lay in the pottery ashtray. She said, "Minute," and marked the paper in front of her. When she got to the end of a line she moved the ruler down and, raising her eyes, gave Pat a good searching look. "You're the girl Jonni called about. The regular receptionist isn't here, in fact she's quitting. That's why the job is open. I'll see if I can find somebody."

Pat sat down on a straight chair, looking at all the books in colorful jackets with the log-cabin colophon on the backs, wishing she could open some of them but not wanting to seem too much at home. There were some thin ones that were probably poetry, and she thought about Annice—*she ought to be here and not me, this is her kind of place.* Beyond the open window, office buildings cut sharply into a deep blue late-summer sky dotted with small cottony clouds. *The Loop,* she thought; *this is a Loop office.* And suddenly she wanted to work there more than she had ever wanted anything in her life.

The girl came back. "This way," she said indifferently, and Pat followed her down the corridor, aware that her feet hurt and wishing she had worn her straw sandals. The hall was painted fuchsia and was decorated with book jackets Scotch-taped to the walls. Through partly open doors she could see a man talking quietly into a dictating machine, a boy running dittos, a gray-haired woman typing with machine-gun rapidity. The atmosphere was one of quiet concentration.

"This is Miss Callahan."

"Thanks, Phyllis. Won't you sit down, Miss Callahan?"

Everything about this office said Executive, maybe even Top Executive. Signed photographs of authors covered one wall, there were flowers in a pottery jug on the windowsill, and the rug was what Pat vaguely thought of as Oriental.

This at a glance, before she looked at the man behind the desk. The effect of that look was like sticking a wire hairpin into an electrical outlet. The same jolt, the same zing down the arm and along the backbone.

He was tall and handsome, a college-athlete type getting a little heavier maybe, a little thick around the middle and soft under the chin, but still a man to turn and look after on the street. Maybe thirty-five. He looked like a salesman or a young politician, not bookish. He smiled. "I'm Blake Thomson. Now, this job—"

His voice held her; she lost what he was saying. Resonant, full, with troubling overtones, it stirred her like music. She tried to listen, fixing her eyes on his face. His eyes were not dark, as she had expected, but a deep gray. Blunt nose, charming smile. He picked up a pencil, and she saw that his hands were strong, with curly dark hair at the edge of the starched white cuffs.

This is crazy, she thought. *You can't feel like this about somebody you've just met. Anyhow, he's probably married and has five or six kids.* She shut her eyes, partly to regain her balance and partly, she realized too late, to shut out all other sensations so that deep clear voice could flow over her unimpeded. At once she was conscious of a physical response she had read about and heard described in intimate talk, but had never experienced. Definite, local, unmistakable. She felt her face reddening and resisted a sudden impulse to cross herself. *Keep me from sin,* she prayed silently.

"So if you think you'd like to try it, you can begin tomorrow morning. Our other girl is married, and her husband's being transferred—"

She opened her eyes. She wasn't sure what he had been saying—had, in fact, no clear idea of what she would be expected to do if she took the job. As far as she knew it might be something of which she was totally incapable.

Struggling for clarity, she said in a small voice, "I've never been in this sort of business before."

"It's not too different from regular office work. If you can type and answer the telephone you'll get along all right." He smiled. The smile was more than she could take. Something inside, some deep female instinct, warned her to run. *If you had any sense,* she told herself, *you'd get out of here but quick.* This is more than you can handle. She felt suddenly short of breath, as if her lungs were being squeezed by an iron hand. The floor tilted. She grasped the edge of her chair, and the hard reality of the wood gave her stability. She smiled back at him. "I'd like to try it."

He walked back to the foyer with her. She wondered crazily what would happen if she brushed against him, swayed toward him in that narrow hallway.

"Phyllis, Miss Callahan is coming in tomorrow." He bent over the proofreader, his attitude at once casual and intimate. Envy flared up in Pat.

Going down in the elevator, she realized dizzily that she hadn't settled anything at all. She didn't know what she was going to do, or what her hours would be, or how much she was getting. She crossed the splendid lobby and went out through the revolving door without seeing anything or anyone.

The girls would be full of questions. Barby had made a special trip in to interview her boss and fill out application forms, and she had come back loaded with details: paid vacations, store discount, pension plans, Social Security cards, group insurance, company cafeterias. Annice, bored as she pretended to be by the idea of going back to school, had her schedule all made out for the semester and the pages of her college catalog were dogeared with handling.

Well, she would have to make up some answers. Or stall them off until she found out. She crossed Dearborn and

Madison without noticing the traffic, the lights or the shopping crowds. A deep disturbing voice rang in her ears. *He doesn't even know I'm alive,* she thought, *but I'd go anywhere with him, or do anything in the world he wanted me to do.*

CHAPTER FIVE

New employees, and some old ones, were always complaining because the Store was so big, when they weren't complaining because the customers were snippy or their feet ached. They said you could get lost looking for the restrooms, and it was true. If you had to go to the office and see about deductions or sign up for insurance, it took half a day to find the damn place. You could punch the time clock every day from now until Social Security and never see a familiar face in the waiting line; you could eat in the company cafeteria every day—but nobody did—and the macaroni casserole would be familiar but the face across the table wouldn't. The Store, always upper-cased in memos and bulletins, was a city of strangers.

The girls from Gary and Michigan City and Elgin griped, coming in from the commuters' trains in the morning. So did the college girls working part-time in the Junior Miss department and the tough old birds who had been with the company ninety-nine years, starting as cash girls back in the days when the money-boxes sailed across the ceiling on wires. The pretty Polish girls from South Chicago complained, brought up as they were to the close-knit life of the apartment building, the neighborhood movie, the Sunday family dinner and Mass at St. Ladislaw's Church. All of the complaints were variations on the same theme—sure, the pay was okay, and you got a fifteen per cent discount on everything you bought. But—well, you didn't feel like a person; more like part of a machine. Too big.

Barby liked it. She was the last stock girl in her department to go home after the credit books were filed away and the counters covered with muslin. Between five-twenty and five-forty the washroom was jammed with girls fixing their faces and having a quick smoke; then everyone rushed for the I.C. or subway or the Michigan bus, and quiet settled down. Barby liked to wait until the washroom was empty and take her time. She followed all her mother's teachings about grooming because they had become habitual—washing her face before she applied fresh makeup, rubbing lotion into her hands after she washed off the carbon smudges. That her face as reflected in the long mirror above the basins was prettier than most didn't bother her; it was her face and she was used to it. She put her lipstick on with a little brush, drawing a clear line.

It's big, she thought contentedly, taking her coin purse and tissues from the square plastic box that was like all other plastic boxes except for her name printed on the slip-in card. The Store was staffed by polite strangers who minded their own business and didn't look at her with curiosity or pry into her affairs. The garments she ticketed went out on racks and were sold by salesgirls she knew as dimly familiar but nameless faces; the meals she ate were prepared by anonymous hands. The check she got twice a month was made out by some stranger to whom she was nothing but a clock number. If a man looked at her, eyeing the swing of her hips and the contour of her bosom, it was someone she would never see again and there was nothing to get excited about. She had been accosted on Van Buren two or three times, walking toward a late train, and had walked on calmly without giving the furtive men a second thought.

Everyone sank out of sight at five-forty-five, dismissed by the click of a time clock, and came to life ten minutes before opening time in the morning. It was a neat arrangement.

She walked past the shrouded counters, past the thin stooped Negro who ran a carpet sweeper between the aisles, and took the elevator to first. She went by the cosmetic counters, still delicately fragrant from the perfume that was sprayed into the air several times a day, and out of the employees' entrance, pausing to flash her I. D. card at the watchman. Real life, non-Store life rushed up to meet her with the heat from the sidewalk. She remembered what she had been refusing to think about all day, that she was supposed to check apartment ads.

In her billfold she had a list of names and addresses in the Hyde Park area and two folded five-dollar bills with which to pay a deposit if she found anything at all possible. Apartments were hard to find and rents were high; even the lower-priced places, dirty and infested as they were, had waiting lists, and unscrupulous landlords extorted "fees" and "bonuses" that were nothing but bribes from desperate tenants in search of a place to live. Unemployment in other parts of the country brought Negroes, hillbillies and Latin Americans into the city at the rate of three or four thousand a day, to crowd into overflowing tenements and seek non-existent jobs. White-collar workers, who had a certain living standard to maintain but in many cases earned less than skilled mechanics, were caught between their way of life on one hand and the exorbitant cost of plain necessities on the other.

Annice had said dreamily that she wouldn't mind living in the slums, but Barby thought she was probably thinking about a Greenwich Village–type of quaint little place that had no relation to roaches and rats or noisy neighbors.

She walked up Randolph looking into shop windows. She passed the fifty-cent flower place where the man was putting button dahlias out in tin cans, thinking that when she had a place of her own she would stop and buy flowers every pay-day—they made a place look so nice. She passed the outdoor magazine stand and started down the concrete steps to the I.C. underground station, ignoring the whistle of a punk kid standing on the top step. She studied her list of addresses, walking briskly past the sign that said *Men* and the one that said *Telephones* and the souvenir stand with the silver-and-turquoise jewelry. The flats were all in Jonni Foster's neighborhood; Jonni had briefed her on rentals and utilities. She bought a ticket to 53rd and went out on the echoing wooden platform to catch the South Chicago Special.

It was hot for September, a good dry heat. Across the train aisle a young girl in cotton blouse and skirt snuggled up to a very young boy who put his arm around her shoulders and whispered into her ear. The woman in front of Barby, hatted and gloved, glared at them. Barby didn't like people who glared at smoochers, but she didn't much like all this public affection either—it made her uneasy, reminded her of things she didn't like to think about. She picked up a copy of the *Tribune* that some commuter had left on the seat and read the Carson Pirie Scott ads to see what the competition was doing.

The sunshine was beginning to slant when she got off at 53rd, and the neighborhood had a friendly late-afternoon look. The air was fresher here than downtown in spite of traffic fumes. There was a French film on at the art movie house. Two stout grandmothers were coming out of the supermarket with loaded baskets. At the corner, a vacant lot strewn with bricks gave an unobstructed view of the I.C. platform, and on the next block one of the city-subsidized housing projects stood proudly, all tan brick and shiny glass, among the older buildings. A young Negro mother turned in at the front walk, wheeling a stroller with a healthy-looking baby in one end and a sack of groceries in the other. Barby halfway hoped that this would be the building she was looking for; but it was a half-block farther on, dark-red brick in two wings with a recessed entrance like a glass showcase, displaying an inner door and a row of mailboxes. There was an eighteen-inch strip of tan grass and wilting petunias along the sidewalk. Barby pressed the doorbell and waited, but if there was an answering buzz it didn't reach her ears, so she stood uncertainly poised, unsure what to do.

After a while, heavy steps sounded and a stocky young man in a Marlon Brando undershirt came out of the inside door. "Why doncha come in when you ring? You ring, I push the button and unlock the door and you come in, see?"

"I'm sorry. The apartment—is it still for rent?"

"Sure, a nice apartment. The B apartment on the third floor. You wanna see it?" He shoved the door open. She followed him inside, wishing nervously that one of the other girls had come along. Suppose she took it, and then they didn't like it? Or worse, suppose she *didn't* take it; suppose the rent was too high or it was dirty, or something; how would she tell him? The old miserable uncertainty took hold of her.

She looked unhappily at the bare muscular shoulders of her guide, a common workman in his undershirt and old Army pants. Yes, but sort of good-looking too, the kind of fellow who appeals to women. Male and sensual, with big muscles. Thick curly hair. A good-natured face, with dark eyes and incredibly long and curly eyelashes. She asked, "Are you Italian?" and was afraid she had been rude.

"Sicilian, that's me." He threw out his chest. "Rocco d'Angelo. I live downstairs." She remembered seeing windows just above ground level—half-basement, English basement, whatever they call it. So he would be the janitor or caretaker or superintendent. She smiled politely, trying to convey that a janitor is as good as anybody.

The apartment was all right; living-room with a davenport that opened out, all the standard furniture, rather shabby from a succession of tenants. She parted the heavy flowered curtains that looked clean but felt grimy, and looked out over a beaten backyard with garages and a child's swing. Two could sleep in the double bed, and the kitchenette range was new. Two and a half rooms. "How much?"

"Eighty."

She did quick arithmetic, standing between the bed and dresser. "Can I make a deposit?"

"Sure. Five, ten, how much you want to."

She consulted her little list. "Is there a place where we can do our washing?"

"In the basement. Come on, I show you."

The steps to the basement were cement and not so clean. Boxes of waste paper, tin cans and beer cartons stood on them. Rocco kicked a carton. "Goddam lazy bums, why they don't put their garbage all the way down?"

She realized that he was looking, not at the trash but at her legs. The expression on his face was the strained look she tried not to remember—not liking or admiration, but naked hunger: She felt suddenly cold. She walked ahead, but at the foot of the stairs, confronted with three closed doors, she had to stand back and wait. He brushed against her as he opened the first one. "In here. You put twenty cents here, see? And it does one load. Wash, rinse, everything. This here is the dryer."

"I see." She swallowed hard; her mouth had gone dry. It was quiet in the basement. She could hear the purring of some electrical appliance, and a scrabbling behind the wall that threatened mice. Still, the house must be full of people this time of day. She nodded. "I'll talk it over with my friends and let you know."

"Nice clean house. You can use the phone in the upstairs hall. Close to the bus stop." Rocco gestured. "You want to have parties here, so you don't make too much noise it's okay. Girls they like to have parties sometimes. Pretty girls have lots of company."

She said stupidly, "We don't know anybody yet."

"So what? I wouldn't mind to know some pretty girls myself. I ain't that old, I wouldn't like to look at a pretty girl. No, Rocco he's a good man with women."

Barby backed away a step. "Well, then, I'll give you five dollars and you give me a receipt, is that right?"

"You come in and have a glass of wine, no hurry, just one glass to get acquainted."

She hoped desperately that he had a wife. She could go into some garlic-smelling cluttered kitchen and meet a fat Italian mama and six or seven dark-eyed kids if she had to; it wasn't anything she much wanted to do, but she could do it and drink a glass of vino for politeness. She pulled her skirt seams straight, aware of his gaze fixed below her belt. He smiled deeply. At once she was aware of the first faint nausea, the throbbing at the temples. *Oh,* she thought, *not now, not here nor in the Y hotel, for God's sake, and a new job and everything, I can't stand it.*

She walked mechanically through the door he held open. At once she knew she had made a dreadful mistake. This was no family kitchen redolent of tomato paste and echoing with voices. It was a bedroom, narrow and dark. A pile of detective magazines in one corner and a bottle of red wine on the dresser indicated how Rocco spent his time when he wasn't doing chores. The unmade bed fascinated her and filled her with shuddering revulsion; she couldn't stop looking at it.

He poured wine into two small cheese-spread glasses. "You like Chianti? It's good."

"It's very good." It was sour enough to set her teeth on edge, but the warmth of unaccustomed alcohol spread through her and made her arms and legs feel loose, her apprehension lost. She looked at the empty glass in her hand with some bewilderment.

"More?"

"No thanks. It's very good, but I have to go now." She kept her eyes fixed warily on the open door. As long as the door stayed open it was all right. She realized that she hadn't paid the deposit on the apartment, but it didn't matter. The only thing that mattered was to get out of here, somehow, anyway. She would go away and never come back—she would never go anywhere alone again—she would never—

His hands were warm and insistent. He held her at each side of the waist, carefully, so as not to startle her. "Pretty. I'm a man and you're a woman, huh? Beautiful woman. Why not?"

She wanted to scream. Surely if she screamed someone would hear her. She opened her mouth, but no sound came out; it was like those nightmares, with the snorting animal or the painted Indians chasing her, when her feet were fastened to the ground. She stood frozen while he shut the door, not bothering to lock it. He pushed her down on the unmade bed and sat down beside her. His hands were inside the neck of her dress now, moving slowly but confidently, as though he knew what he was doing and meant to enjoy it fully. She was afraid. And yet—

His mouth was hot, tasting of tobacco and wine. He pushed her back against the bed, fumbling with her girdle.

There was a crack across the ceiling. She opened her eyes wide and tried to focus on the crack, but it wavered and blurred and finally, when she gasped at the surprise and pain of his entrance, it went away. Then it came back again. She thought dimly, "But it's not the first time." On her bedroom ceiling at home there had been a small water stain; her eyes traveled from it down the wall to the doll's house that still stood in the corner of the room.

She stirred, trying to breathe. Such a heavy weight.

When she came out of the building it was dark. The lights of oncoming cars blurred and wavered in front of her, and, looking at the apartment house across the street, she discovered that part of it simply wasn't there—the building had holes in it. The street lights were ringed with halos that shattered when she looked directly at them. Her head throbbed. She staggered, hailing a cruising taxi. The address was gone from her mind; she had to concentrate, frowning, to remember it. "Please hurry, I'm sick." It flashed across her mind that he might reasonably think she was drunk. "I have a migraine headache, will you please hurry."

"Hey, that's tough. My wife has that, she has to go to bed for two, three days at a time. I guess it's no joke."

She was in no state of mind to sympathize with anyone else's troubles.

When she reached the Y she was unable to stand up. The driver half-supported, half-carried her into the lobby and stood there waiting until Annice came down to pay him and help her up to bed.

CHAPTER SIX

"Damn!" Annice said. She stared blankly at the place where she had left her books and handbag, fifty minutes before. There was nothing there except a couple of reference volumes waiting to be returned to the stacks. *Maybe it's the wrong table,* she thought hopefully, looking around. But no—there was the ink stain in one corner, shaped like the map of Australia. She pushed her way through a cluster of last-minute borrowers to the desk. "Has anybody turned in some books and a tan pigskin purse?"

The student librarian shook his head. "Nobody's turned in anything. Where did you leave them?"

"On that table right over there."

"Well, don't holler at me. I didn't take your stuff." He had a pleasant, rather round face and a nice voice with a hint of Southern drawl. Not the kind of boy to steal anything. She snapped, "I never said you did. It's too bad if a person can't set something down and find it there when they get back."

"What did you do, just walk off and leave your stuff?"

"I didn't do it on purpose. I was thinking about something more important," she said with dignity. "I was making up a poem."

"Oh, one of those."

"Why not?"

He smiled. "Honey, this place is just lousy with poets. Every campus is, I guess, but this one's worse than most. Sculptors and painters, too, all fifty-seven varieties, but the poets are the worst." He looked as if the idea pained him. "You don't have to have any special equipment to write poetry, and if the critics don't like it, you can publish an article in the little no-pay magazines and complain how stupid they are. Do you write free verse with no punctuation, or are you one of those romantic sonnet girls?"

"I'm not going to talk about it," Annice said. "You wouldn't understand."

"Okay, okay, what are you going to do about lunch?"

Annice stopped in her dignified retreat. Her own helplessness was suddenly borne in upon her—no carfare, no lunch money, no change for the endless small purchases a student was always making. Not even a dime to telephone home. She could borrow, of course. She had struck up casual friendships with a dozen people who would surely lend her a dime and might even let her have a dollar. It was nothing to get excited about. But for a moment she was filled with pure terror, seeing herself helpless and lost. It was worse than uncomfortable, it was almost physically painful. She said weakly, "I don't know."

He dug into his pocket and came up with a handful of small change which he counted soberly, like a man at a newsstand. "I'll treat you to lunch if you'll order something cheap."

"Oh—all right. When do you get off?" Anything for a free meal, the girls said, meaning not quite anything—but still it was a break to have a man, almost any man, pick up the tab. It lent a girl status. She was happily conscious of curious looks as she tucked her hand though his arm and left the library.

"I meant it when I said cheap. One hamburger. You can have two orders of fries, though, they're only twenty cents."

"And get fat?"

"Little meat on your bones wouldn't hurt you any. I like girls cornfed."

They sat at the counter in Walgreen's, with a magazine rack at one end and a case of electric pads and bathroom scales at the other. "Just one coffee. I'm a poor farm boy."

"You're kidding."

"Am not." His name was Jackson Carter and he came from a wide spot in the road in Missouri, named Jackson Center after his mama's folks. Jackson Center was purely Southern. "Any place where they farm with mules is in the South, I don't give a damn what the Texaco road maps say."

"I'm from the farm too. I hate it."

"Well, I wouldn't go that far. Makes no difference how many electric gadgets they have or how many horsepower the old tractor has, farm folks don't change much, that's true. They've got a good way of living—for them. Of course if it doesn't happen to be your way you're out of luck." He thought this over and nodded. "You have to fit the pattern, you can't diverge."

"Do you diverge?"

"I'm not a fairy if that's what you mean. There's plenty of them around, have you noticed? I'm an old-fashioned guy— I like women." She giggled. "No, I mean—that's a good way to live if that's what you want to do. Me, I want to be a physicist. Turn the atomic stuff to some useful purpose."

"You ought to be at U. of Chicago then."

"That's all I can do to work my way here."

He was twenty, had worked two years in a filling station, been a stock boy in a drugstore, done a short term in a canning factory where the workday was maybe sixteen or eighteen hours. That was tough; when you got a run of peas or beans you stayed on till they were processed, then laid off maybe a couple of days. "You were supposed to sleep, but I had a big deal on with a truck-farmer's daughter and I didn't do a hell of a lot of sleeping." Annice felt a sharp pang of jealousy. *It's nothing to me,* she reminded herself.

Now he worked as a librarian and posed for art classes. "Not in the nude, but I sure would if I had a chance—it pays better." He lived in a cooperative rooming house with seven other boys; they did their own cooking and cleaning. "All

I'm scared is, somebody's mother might come in some day and drop dead."

They went on talking after the tired waitress laid down their check, cleared away the plates and swabbed the counter; they talked through Annice's French class and Jack's gym section. By this time they had known each other since childhood and she felt perfectly at ease with him, partly because she didn't have to impress him.

"Not that I'd ever get excited about anybody like that," she told the girls that evening. "He's too ordinary. But he's nice even if he doesn't have any feeling for important things like poetry."

Pat asked, "Did you get your stuff back?"

"Oh, gosh, no. I put a notice on the bulletin board though. Maybe somebody'll turn it in. I'd like to have my purse back even if they keep the money."

"How much was it?"

"About ten bucks. Most of my money was home under the shelf paper in the closet." The others nodded. They kept their money under the shelf paper too, or in a dresser drawer. "I keep meaning to start a bank account," Annice said. They all meant to start bank accounts as soon as they had enough money saved up. It seemed silly to go into a bank with twenty or thirty dollars and go through all that red tape. "It wasn't just the money," Annice complained, "it was my good pigskin bag I got for Christmas and all the stuff in it. They took my books too. My Civil Government book I paid five dollars for at the bookstore."

"Well," Pat said, "it looks like you got some good out of it. You met a nice boy."

"That's doing it the hard way. There's plenty of nice boys in my classes. Anyhow I couldn't ever really care for Jackson—he's too dumb, he doesn't read anything but physics and history."

"Nobody's asking you to marry the boy. He might be fun to go out with even if he hasn't got any money."

Children, Barby thought in dull silent scorn. *They don't know what they're talking about.* She had nibbled at her supper, trying to eat because it was Pat's week to cook and it hurt Pat's feeling to have anything left on the plates. No matter whose turn it was, they had hamburgers or hot dogs two or three times a week, with frozen peas or canned corn, and there was never any grocery money left at the end of the week. This led all of them to spend too much money on lunch.

Her head ached. She hadn't eaten all day. That morning while she was spooning instant coffee into a cup she had seen from the corner of her eye a small scuttling brown spot that could only be a roach. She had bent to look, but there was nothing under the gas range but some wisps of dust and a forgotten book of matches. Pat had said, so what—be thankful it's not a bedbug, everybody has roaches. But Barby had poured her coffee down the sink, feeling a little sick, and had left for work without breakfast. Then when she had reached the stair landing Rocco had been lounging there, not doing anything, obviously just waiting for her.

He had caught her by the arm. "When you're coming down to see me?" Too frightened to answer, she had twisted away before one of the other tenants could come down and see them together. At lunch time she had sat, sickly, with a bowl of soup in front of her, thinking, *What am I going to do? How can I go back there?* It had occurred to her finally that she could stop by for Pat and help her carry the groceries from the Hi-Lo, a good enough pretext.

But she couldn't dodge him forever. There was tomorrow.

She still wasn't sure how she had fallen, or been pushed, into moving here. During the two days she had spent in bed with migraine her one resolution, the thought she had clutched to her all through the dizziness and skull-splitting pain, was to stay away from this place. But when she was up again and the girls demanded details, she had found nothing to say except, vaguely, that she didn't like the place. The rent was reasonable, the space adequate, the furniture not too bad. "We can't be fussy," Annice had reminded her, a trifle crossly. "Apartments are hard to find right now and rents are terrible. What was the matter with it, anyhow?"

"Oh, I guess it's all right."

She couldn't tell them. There are some things you can't decently tell anybody. She pushed the memory well into the back of her mind, along with that earlier memory, and tried to forget it was there. If she told the truth—but the thought of their startled eyes and questions made that impossible; and she couldn't think of a good convincing lie. She packed her clothes silently, with death in her heart.

Now she sat on the davenport pretending to read *Life* while Annice and Pat talked about some fool boy. *I must have been crazy,* she thought. *I could have said there were rats or bugs or something.* Now it was too late. The other girls were pleased with the apartment. It was big enough, with only a little crowding. There was a supermarket on the next block. *We'll be here forever,* she thought desperately, feeling the walls close in around her like a prison.

I tried to tell him. Just like I tried to tell him, *before. They're stronger than women.* She rubbed her forehead. The colors of the Matisse reproduction Annice had bought at the Art Institute were melting and running together. She struggled to her feet, noting dully that her arms and legs ached. "I'm going to bed. I think maybe I'm coming down with flu or something."

"You better sleep on the davenport," Annice said. "That way the rest of us won't catch it." Her voice was kind, but she wasn't paying attention; she was lost in her own thoughts. *It's true,* she thought, *I could never take a man seriously if he didn't understand how I feel about really important things. There's no reason I can't go out with Jackson, though. If he asks me.* The notion that he might not ask her made her feel unreasonably sad. She took her red leather notebook down from the shelf where they kept their books and turned the pages. The poems, neatly printed with wide margins and curly capitals, didn't read as well as usual. They sounded like echoes of other poems she had read. She put the book back and decided that since she didn't have a date and wasn't sleepy it would be a good time to wash all her underwear.

She gathered slips and panties from the floor, the dresser and closet, and ran warm water into the bathroom basin, picturing a series of long confidential talks with Jackson Carter that would bring him around to deeper understanding of the finer things in life and finally to a lasting romance.

Pat got out of the bathroom so she could get in. Pat had taken a long steamy shower and had washed her hair and set it in bobby pins, tying a green net cap with bows over it; her nails were still damp with polish, she had shaved her legs, and she reeked of Aphrodisia and lotion. She was wearing pink nylon panties.

"Late date?"

"No, but I didn't have anything else to do, so I thought I might as well get cleaned up." This was new for Pat, whose grooming had always been, to say the least, casual. She said, "Shut your mouth before a fly walks in. Didn't you ever see anybody take a bath before?" But she sounded good-natured.

This was the best part of the day, she thought, crawling into the double bed that took up most of the space in the bedroom and stretching voluptuously. Even better than the moment when he came into the office, smiling, and greeted her. The actual daily meeting was always marred by her own shortcomings—she had a run in her stocking, or her hands were smudged by carbon, or something. The sight of him was enough to strike her wordless, even though she had made up a dazzling conversation the night before.

Now she liked to go to bed while her mind was still alert and think up endless dazzling dreams of he-said-to-me and I-said-to-him. So far she had never reached the final intimacy; maybe that was the voice of conscience preserving her from sin. Although goodness knows her thoughts after a date with Johnny Cutler would have disturbed her mother, not to mention the parish priest. So far all of her imaginary encounters with Blake Thomson began with his arrival at the office in the morning and ended with a scene where he leaned over her and said, "Darling Pat, did you think I thought of you only as a typist? I've been watching you for a long, long time."

So far she hadn't been able to picture him anywhere except in the office.

Wonder what kind of shave stuff he uses. Mixed with tobacco—I love to see a man smoke a pipe and that indefinable male smell. He's older than I thought. She had sneaked his dossier out of the file one day when everyone else was at lunch and had devoured all its details. A Dartmouth man. Never been married. Yet. *Darling Pat, you are the first girl I ever really loved.*

She fell happily asleep, her face shining with cold cream.

Annice felt too brisk for bed. Damn the silly college, she thought, double-damn whoever swiped my stuff. But she hummed, rinsing out her nylon pants and her best bra—padded, but not too much. There was something about having a man in your life, almost any kind of a man, even if you weren't going to get serious about him. So far she had never really loved anybody, and it bothered her—because how can you be a great poet until you know the splendor and tragedy of a great love?

She rubbed and wrung as her mother would have done, inspecting each item sharply before she hung it over the shower rod.

Barby was having trouble falling asleep. She turned and twisted, wide-eyed in the dark. Everything was closing in on her. She was trapped. There was no place where you could hide and be safe. At the store this afternoon one of the salesman had asked for a date, and the awful thing was that even though she was in a turmoil about Rocco she halfway wanted to say yes. At the same time the thought of being near a man—any man—filled her with horror. There was this feeling that she was powerless. She wasn't sure what she had said to young Mr. Cohen. For a moment, looking at his pleasant young face, she had seen Rocco's dark features and powerful arms—and behind him, the clear profile and burning eyes of her father.

She wanted to get out of bed and run—but not past those stairs, knowing what peril lurked beyond their turning. She wanted desperately to run to someone who would open comforting arms and take her in and shelter her. But there was no one.

She stared at the oblong of light moving across the wall as a car passed down the street.

Annice was walking around in the bathroom, singing, hanging a week's accumulation of laundry over the tub to drip. Barby could hear drawers being pulled out and slammed shut, and the click of the medicine-chest door. Every sound was magnified in her ears. She sat up. "For Christ's sake, what are you doing in there? Why don't you do your washing in the daytime?"

Annice looked around the door, her face blank with surprise. "I'm sorry. Am I keeping you kids awake?"

Barby glared at her. Then she rolled over and hid her face in the pillow, too miserable to cry.

Poor kid, Annice thought, *she's working too hard. Or maybe it's the old curse.* She pulled the bathroom door shut and ran clear water into the basin, too intent on her own affairs to be in any way concerned.

CHAPTER SEVEN

Professor King's party was really getting under way. All of the chairs were occupied, some by more than one person, and four boys sat wedged together on the davenport, balancing plates and beer glasses on their knees. Half a dozen people were on the floor, the boys sprawled out, all arms and legs, the girls with arms wrapped around knees. When the door opened, the volume of talk rushed out and hit the newcomers in the face. Someone had left a lighted cigarette on the table; there was an acrid smell of scorched varnish. Someone else had upset a stein of beer in a girl's lap. Everyone was having a fine time.

Annice's misgivings vanished. She hadn't wanted to come—a poetry reading sponsored by an English professor didn't sound very exciting. Not what she had pictured in her dreams of studio parties, the great world of people who wrote and did Interesting Things. Now she was glad she had come. She threw back her shoulders and took a deep breath.

The thin bearded boy at her feet said lazily, "Hi. I'm Alan. Who're you?"

"I'm nobody," Annice said smiling. He turned his back on her, then turned around again so she could get the full impact of his sneer. "Emily Dickinson yet. She's reactionary. You ought to read Henry Miller and learn a new idiom."

"I disagree," the dark man beside the fireplace said. "Emily's in the vanguard. You kids are old-fashioned. But then," he said sadly, "your whole damn generation's reactionary."

"You're quite right." The popeyed girl pushed up her pink-rimmed glasses. "We're still hanging on to the standards formed in the Twenties, the Golden Age of revolt. Kerouac says—"

Annice was torn between pleasure and self-doubt. This was what she had longed for back on the farm, listening rebelliously to the supper-table talk about the price of soybeans. Nobody was interested in ideas there, and she had to go around in a fine poetic isolation, scorning her relatives and neighbors. Here, ideas swirled on the air almost visibly, like the smoke that hung above the heads of the talkers or the body heat that made the room uncomfortably warm even though the outside was cool. Two small logs smoldered in the fireplace. She walked across the room and held out her hands to the blaze. Jack stood against the wall watching her progress, unwilling to risk stepping on any outstretched hand.

She said wistfully, "I love this fireplace."

"A pretty act," the bearded boy said. He unfolded his lean length from the floor and moved to join her. He had bold eyes; he looked at her as though he could see through the peasant skirt and the padded bra. She put a hand to her chest to hide her innocent deceits, then dropped it, angry. "You're rude," she said.

"Rude—of course I am. There's too goddam much fake politeness in the world. Intelligent people have a moral obligation to be rude."

She hated him. He was arrogant and unkind. His eyes were clear and bright, and his chin was firm under the arty beat-generation beard. Suddenly, returning his unwinking stare, she wanted him to like her. More than anything in the world she wanted him to put his arms around her and kiss her, instead of looking so superior. Her desire frightened her.

One of the boys said, "Old stuff, Alan. That's reaction against the reaction against conformity."

Annice accepted a plate and glass from a pleasant forty-ish woman who had too much bottom to be wearing tore-ador pants. The hostess, probably, or a faculty wife called in for the evening. She gave Annice a friendly wink and went away again, leaving her to balance the refreshments and clutch her leather notebook at the same time.

It had been Jackson who told her about this party in the first place. "They talk a lot of crap, but maybe it's the sort of stuff you'd like. Lot of arty guys. I don't think any of them had anything published yet. Anyhow, you might as well get it out of your system." She had been offended by the conde-scending tone and at the same time pleased by what was probably a concession to her tastes. At least he was willing to spend an evening being bored in her company.

She had spent a lot of time getting ready, discarding the striped slacks as too casual and the flowered jersey as too suburban, pulling out most of her eyebrows and penciling in new ones. This was her debut into the world of creative people. She felt a little frightened.

Suppose they didn't like her? Suppose she didn't fit in?

It's only an extra-curricular activity she reassured her-self, just a group some professor has to sponsor. They're not even professional authors. She hated to agree with Jack at any point where the arts were concerned, but it comforted her to feel a little scornful in return for the scorn these more assured people might presumably feel for her.

Someone asked, "Are you a Freudian or a Jungian?" and she turned to answer, but the questioner was lost in a babble of other voices. The bearded boy shambled over and sat down at her feet. "What do you do to release your inhibitions? I don't have any inhibitions myself—I just do whatever I feel like doing."

"Hard on the bystanders."

"What in hell do I care about bystanders? I'm completely self-centered. To develop talent it's necessary to be altogether self-oriented."

The girl in pink-rimmed glasses nodded.

The girls, Annice decided while she munched potato chips, were nothing much to look at. Here as in high school the serious-minded femmes were the homely ones. Except for a little Nisei girl who looked like a painting on silk, they were mostly eye-glassed, too fat or too bony, not so much ugly as lacking in some assurance that pretty girls wear from the day of their first lipstick. Annice identified their look of self-depression without any trouble because she herself had worn it until she was almost sixteen. It was the opposite of charm. She had been rescued by an invitation from the captain of the high school basketball team, whose girl fortunately ruptured an appendix on the day of the Junior Prom; grace and poise settled over her with the folds of the formal her mother was persuaded to buy, disclosing—as it were—curves she had never known she had. Except for a woman of thirty-five who in spite of gray-streaked hair and a comfortable dumpiness gave off the unmistakable aura of successful sex, the females at this poetry reading were the type who failed to attract men mainly because they didn't think of themselves as desirable.

Probably here to find a man, she thought unkindly, forgetting that although she had come here with one she was looking around for better pickings.

The boys were more interesting. Used as she was to student fads and eccentricities in dress, she paid no heed to the corduroy trousers, the blue work shirts, the Ivy League stripes and button-down collars or the green velvet-frogged smoking jacket worn by the balding, round-bellied host. Most of them wore moccasins with white sweat socks or no socks. Three or four with bumpy intelligent faces and harsh South Chicago voices she thought were Jewish, but it was hard to tell because this year everybody made a fad of Yiddish slang—he's a schlepp, she's a no-goodnik, you should read a book already. There was a young Arab with a thin startled face, conspicuous here for his tailoring. The Jewish boys kept handing him peanuts and potato chips and refilling his glass, very politely, and after a while he started looking around uneasily like a trapped rabbit. Later, much later, she noticed that he had left.

There were three or four boys with beards, none as well-developed as Alan's, and one weedy boy had an aggressive British moustache. Definitely, in this crowd the men were the ones to notice. She turned an aloof profile to Alan, and after a few glances away he reached up and pulled her down on the floor beside him. "What's your name, woman?"

"Annice."

"Anise like you drink?"

"I don't drink anything."

"Release the inhibitions. I don't drink because I haven't got any inhibitions. I live with complete selfishness."

"You said that before."

"It's still true. I'm completely unable to feel tenderness or compassion for anybody, even the woman I lay."

"How adolescent of you."

In a sudden silence one of the boys said, "I'm writing a novel on homosexual incest." He looked around for admiration.

Jackson said, "Why don't you do a book on cannibalism? That's the most complete form of identification there is."

The popeyed girl in the pink frames grabbed his arm. "Oh, you're right, you're absolutely right, I think that's a simply wonderful idea."

Annice glared at her. After all, Jack was her escort, and nobody else had any business drooling over him until she was good and ready to turn him loose.

It seemed a long time before the volume of the talk lessened and the thin man sat down in an armchair and asked who wanted to read. This produced a long pause during which several people thumbed the pages of their notebooks and looked at once reluctant and hopeful. Finally the boy with the muttonchop moustache spoke up. He had written a novel—not just planned it or talked about it but written it; he said modestly that it hadn't found a publisher yet and he wasn't sure it was any good. Then he read a long chapter. It was about a thin talented young man who came to a big city and endured privations while writing a novel. There was a scene in which, locked out of his cheap room because he couldn't pay the rent, he wandered the streets looking for a rest room. Annice felt herself getting more and more uncomfortable. When he stopped reading, two girls got up and headed for the bathroom.

The host said, "Well, you might call the excerpt scatological," and there was a puzzled silence while they tried to remember what it meant.

Then one of the girls said bravely, "I thought it was quite well written." There was a shout of disagreement.

Annice listened while they tore the story and the author to pieces. Alan sat with his back against a chair leg, listening in silent scorn.

A girl read a poem about standing in the moonlight longing for her dead lover. One of the young Jews read a poem about love in the slums among the smells of broken plumbing and the tiny scrabblings of mice. Alan said, "For Christ's sake, has everybody here got kidney trouble?" He grabbed Annice's notebook and flipped the pages rapidly.

"Hey, give me that."

"Can't weasel out now."

He read silently until he found a sonnet; he read it aloud, accenting rhymes and pausing at the end of each line. "It's crap," he said, dropping the red notebook on the floor. "A lot of bull. Why don't you women learn that your place is in bed? All this futile struggle to create, when all you're really good for is to release some man's inhibitions."

"Fascist."

"I'm not a fascist, I'm neo-communist."

Annice blinked back her tears. *So maybe it isn't a good poem,* she thought angrily. *He didn't have to pick the worst one in the book. He didn't have to read it like that, so—so corny. I hate him.* She turned her back on him, a difficult thing to do in that packed room, because no amount of deep breathing and not-winking could keep a few tears from rolling down her face. She was conscious of his breath on the back of her neck.

After five or six more selections the young people began to leave in groups and couples, tiptoeing out without farewells. Suddenly Alan gripped her shoulder so hard she squeaked. "Come on. I'll take you home."

"I came with somebody else."

"The hell with that. Where do you live? I've got things to talk about."

She looked around for Jack, but he was nowhere in sight. She made her way doubtfully to the bedroom, bumping into people and muttering apologies. The broad-beamed hostess helped her find her pocketbook and jacket. "Alan's a nice youngster," she said, "but he's a wolf. Watch out for him, he'll take everything but your shoes."

"I can take care of myself." She looked with increased interest at Alan, waiting beside the door.

The cool outside air washed her fatigue away as she swung the foyer door open. This was a better or at least a fancier neighborhood than the one she lived in. There were strips of grass along the curb; her thin heels sank into loam as she crossed to Alan's small beat-up sports car. He walked around, leaving her to open her door. "It's not locked. I never lock it. Nothing inside to steal."

They took Lake Shore Drive, magic in the neon-lighted night, with the dark brooding expanse of the lake on one side and the tall cut-out silhouette of the downtown skyline on the other. "Look," she said, "it's like two different worlds."

"Like the essential dichotomy of the human soul."

He drove fast, but well. She hadn't expected him to be a good driver—most of these arty boys were bumblers where anything mechanical was concerned. He laid his hand on her knee. "Where do you live? Do you have an apartment of your own?"

"I'm doubled up with two other girls."

"Tripled up. For God's sake be accurate in your use of language. It's the only thing that deserves respect. Sloppy females." The hand moved up an inch and came to rest.

She waited.

"Do you ever sleep with men?"

"What business is it of yours?"

"I'm no satyr," he said solemnly. "I'd like to go to bed with you, but not unless you want to. You have a kind of immature charm I find attractive." He stopped for a red light and tightened his fingers on her thigh. "Women should have the right to decide these things for themselves."

"I'm not going to decide anything like that," she said angrily. "At least, not the first time we're out together."

He shrugged. "First time or tenth, what difference does it make? You know your own kind of people without any formal introductions." She had said this so many times she couldn't argue with it now. "Besides, sex is pretty much the same any old time. I've tried all the variations. Had my first girl when I was thirteen. It all comes back to the same frustrations and partial satisfaction." He lit a cigarette. "Pretty boring."

"Why bother, then?"

"Why eat when you don't digest everything you eat? It's a gain. Need it to give you health and balance. That's the only rational approach." He guided the little car into a small deserted park and turned off the motor. In the sudden silence she could hear the rustling of dead leaves scudding along the ground and the chirp of a night-sleepy bird.

"It might do you good to kiss me, anyway. I won't do anything you don't want me to."

She spoke thickly, because his beard was already brushing against her mouth. "The trouble is, I don't know what I might want to do."

"Always do what you want. Anything else is death to everything that matters."

She had never been kissed before by a man with a beard. Curiosity overcame her. But she forgot about it when the tip of his tongue found hers; all of her feeling, awareness, desire centered in her mouth. Suddenly she clung to him, unable to keep her hands off him.

She had done enough dating in the two years since her sudden bounce into popularity to keep a half-conscious guard over the progress of a man's hands on her body. After a long time—at least, she supposed it was a long time, in view of all that happened in it—she pushed him away and struggled upright. "No, not that. I won't do that."

"But baby, that's what all this has been leading up to."

"I won't."

"You're not in any danger unless it's the fourteenth or fifteenth day. That's a lot of crap."

"That's not it." And it wasn't; the panic that shot through her went deeper than any fear of getting caught. "I don't want to."

"Okay, I won't ask you again." His hands shook. "I bet you're a virgin."

It sounded shameful. Babyish, sappy, scared. She turned her face away so he couldn't read the disgusting truth. "Whether I am or not hasn't got anything to do with it."

"Well, then, it has to be that you don't like me."

"I do like you!" She did; quite suddenly she felt he was the most attractive boy—no, man—she had ever met. *If you don't like a fellow after you've done all those things,* she asked herself, *then when do you?*

He laughed. "Okay, so don't worry about it. I'll call you up some day when you haven't got so much resistance." He buttoned up the top of her dress for her, his fingers impersonal as those of a window-dresser arranging a mannequin. *He doesn't have to be so damn calm,* she thought angrily. He said, "You don't have much of a milk fund, do you? You wear falsies."

"It's only a slight padding, and besides, it's none of your goddam business."

He laughed.

When she let herself into the apartment, trying to walk softly because the other girls were in bed and the lights were off, she found that her bra was unhooked, the straps of her slip were pushed down off her shoulders, her stocking seams were crooked. *I'm a mess,* she thought with smug pleasure, glowing all over at the memory of Alan's cold hands against her warm tingling skin. She shucked off her clothes and stood looking for a long time at herself in the bathroom mirror, giving her wide-awake reflection a critical going-over. She smiled, pleased, as she turned off the bathroom light and picked her way through the clothes dropped on the bedroom floor.

She was still undecided whether she would go further the next time. If there was a next time.

CHAPTER EIGHT

Phyllis said, "This is a crazy business."

Pat frowned at her notes. She took dictation with speed and every appearance of self-assurance, but she couldn't always make out the pothooks afterwards; and Mr. Thomson—Blake, darling—never forgot so much as a comma once it was dictated. It was different with the assistant editors and production people; with them you could fake a little. She pushed her hair back. "Huh?"

"A crazy business." Phyllis pushed up her horn-rimmed glasses, which were always sliding off her short but pretty nose, and pulled down her skirt. She was a pretty girl and had a remarkably good figure, but Pat had never seen her in anything but a skirt and blouse, with her nose shiny and her long blue-black hair in need of combing. Oddly enough this untidiness gave her a sexy look—she had the aura of a woman who knows herself attractive to men and therefore needs no artifices of dress or grooming.

Ordinarily Phyllis's casual ways would have encouraged Pat to throw on her own clothes and think no more about it, but since her first look into Mr. Thomson's eyes she had taken to spending a great deal of time and money on her appearance. She felt it necessary to be chic and well-groomed and, in a word, worthy of love. Her salary, which was seventy dollars a week before deductions and about fifty-six when it reached her, didn't go as far as she had expected it to, but knowing Barby was a help. Barby did all of Pat's and Annice's shopping on her lunch hour, using her employee discount. The discount was supposed to be for personal use only, but as Annice said, what could be more personal than a roommate?

She said, "It's interesting." It was noon; everyone else was gone, and she was waiting for Miss Miller to relieve her at the switchboard. Some of her best bedtime fantasies were timed at noon, when everyone else was out of the office, although she and Blake usually went on to a honeymoon hotel or a woodland carpeted with spring flowers. So far, in actual fact, nobody but Phyllis had shared her twelve-to-one watch. Phyllis sat quietly smoking and waiting for the telephone to ring; she switched her calls to Mr. Thomson's office, which had a door that shut tight, and talked inaudibly for a long time. The office grapevine had it that she was mixed up with a married man of wealth and social standing.

"Sure, it's interesting. Why do you think I stay here, doing two people's work for the pittance I get? I could go work as private secretary to the manager of a big department store—would, too, if I had the sense I was born with." The telephone jingled. Phyllis grabbed it. "The Fort Dearborn Press." She listened, head tilted. "I am sorry, you have a wrong number. Goddamn."

"Why do you stay?"

"God only knows." She shoved her glasses up. "I guess it's a special form of insanity. It sort of gets you after a while. Looking at the manuscripts when they come in—I started as a reader, what a rat-race that is—and then when you hit a good one it's sort of exciting. Not that it happens very much."

Pat nodded. She had already learned not to be indignant on behalf of the authors whose cherished stories bounced back after a hasty reading. "I could write a better book myself," she said.

"For God's sake don't. The world's full of fools who think they can write books."

"Some of them can, too. Look at Sam Fry."

"Sure. I was here the first time Sam Fry ever walked into this office. He had holes in his shoes. All I'm saying is, not one in a hundred."

"What's really exciting is when the galleys come in."

"Sure, because it starts to feel like a real book. Page is even better. I don't worry much about typos in galley, but I really sweat when the page proofs come in. Then the promotion office gets busy, they start getting in touch with the big mags and the movies and all that jazz. I don't know, it makes every other line of business look dull." Phyllis lit another cigarette.

"And the artists. Like that girl with the long cigarette holder the other day, that you said was going to do the illustrations for the Fairchild."

"Sure, sure, everybody gets into the act then, the ad agency people—you ever go out with an adman? Don't." She sat down, propping her flats on the edge of Pat's desk. "Then all of a sudden—makes no difference how long it's been sched-uled, you might have the date up on your bulletin board for three months, but it always seems sudden anyhow—then the advance copies come in. That's the book."

She paused for breath while Pat answered the phone and took an order. "You know," she said dreamily, "you never think about it as five or ten or twenty thousand separate books rolling off the presses. Maybe the warehouse people do; I don't know, I never worked in a warehouse." She considered, shutting her eyes. "Yeah, I suppose it's different when they start rolling 'em in on skids. In the editorial office though, it's *a* book, a living breathing book. It's something like having a baby."

"I never had a baby," Pat said idly.

"Me neither, but you can imagine how it feels." The phone rang; they both reached, but Phyllis got there first. Pat said quietly, "Watch the board, I'm going to the john," and tiptoed out to give her a little privacy.

She thought it over, sitting in the white-tiled cubicle that was so silent now compared to the nine and five o'clock clatter. Phyllis was right, it was an exciting business. She couldn't tell how much of the excitement was due to her new awareness of herself as a woman and how much was implicit in publishing itself. Even the letters she typed were unlike the letters ordinary businessmen dictated, with a vocabulary and range of subject matter all their own. She had worked summers since she was thirteen, for various uncles and cousins in the dry-goods, coal, and paper-box businesses, and the work had bored her stiff. But this was fascinating. Holding her hands under the hot-air dryer, she counted over the things she had learned in her short eventful weeks with The Fort Dearborn Press.

She had supposed, until this fall, that writers were a special breed of people—more cultured, less interested in money and material things. That wasn't so. She had seen a lady novelist go into hysterics because Blake Thomson wouldn't give her fifteen per cent royalty instead of the usual ten, and she had opened and answered letters from dignified college professors who screamed like wounded tigers because the accounting department had shorted them sixty-two cents on royalties. A famous poet had asked her out to dinner, and, although she had refused to go, she wasn't sure whether it was because she was awed by his international reputation or because he was sixty and practically bald. *Maybe Phyllis is right,* she thought, swinging the washroom door open; *maybe it's a form of insanity that makes us stay. It sure as hell isn't the money.*

Phyllis had retreated to her own cubbyhole and was hunched over an endless stack of page proofs, looking withdrawn and pale. She squinted over her slipped down spectacles. *Wonder how much a copy editor makes?* Pat thought, remembering Phyllis's boast that she had done every phase of putting a book together short of actually setting type. She dropped into her posture chair, which was uncomfortable, and tried to pull her attention back to her correspondence.

In a few minutes Blake Thomson came in, holding the door open for a woman Pat had never seen before. She would have remembered that tall erect form, that finely modelled face if they had ever passed in the street or stood side by side in a department store, because this female looked the way she had always wanted to look. The way she *did* look in her daydreams. The woman was fine-drawn, as though her bones were made of better stuff than other people's. Her taffy-colored hair was pulled back straight from a beautiful thin face and worn in a chignon, no strand out of place. Under arched eyebrows her eyes were not the blue or gray you might expect, but a deep lively brown. She had on a plain black dress that made Pat's own basic black look like what it was—marked down from the moderate-price line for the October sales.

A job applicant? Author? Clubwoman? She ran through the possibilities and discarded them in a flicker of time.

The expression on Blake Thomson's face wasn't that of a businessman looking at a client. It was the look she had dreamed of at night, picturing it accurately before she ever saw it—a look of infinite tenderness, male protectiveness, naked masculine hunger. It was *her* look, directed at somebody with whom she could never hope to compete.

They ignored her as well-bred people ignore a porter or waiter, not rudely, but as though she didn't exist apart from serving them. As they proceeded down the corridor she saw Blake's hand touch the woman's, a caress so slight that it might have been mistaken for an accidental contact if both faces had not registered an intense awareness of it.

Phyllis sauntered in, lighting a new cigarette. "See what just went into the sanctum?"

"Yeah." She turned her betraying face away.

"He makes me furious! That man has laid half the women in this building," Phyllis said, her color high. "They fall for him before he so much as puts a finger on them, and now that he's ready to get married and settle down what does he do but pick something like this. Money, looks *and* social standing. He's no fool; he knows a good thing when he sees it."

"Maybe he loves her."

"He hasn't got it in him to love anyone but himself. He's been in love with himself ever since he was old enough to look in the mirror. Sure, he has technique. Makes you feel like you're going right up through the ceiling and coming down in another world. That's all it is, goddam it, don't mean a thing."

"Well—"

"He keeps a room at the Midwest Hotel all the time, the son of a bitch. I bet he uses it at least once or twice a week, too. I bet he has some other female on the string before they've been married six weeks."

It was true what the love magazines said. The heart really did ache. She could feel it hurting in her chest, a steady, heavy pain that grew and lessened with every beat. She put her hand to the place, feeling as though it should be tangible—heat, maybe, burning through the front of her dress. Phyllis looked at her sharply. "Don't tell me you've fallen for him. He's pure dynamite for a nice girl."

"Oh," Pat said, "don't talk about it."

"Don't say I didn't tell you."

Sap, she accused herself, trying not to cry. *A man like that, you might know he wouldn't be free.* She put her hand to her mouth, trying not to sob out loud, afraid that the others would come in from lunch and hear her making like a hurt baby.

The telephone rang. Phyllis caught it. "It's for you," she said, grinding out her cigarette in Pat's ashtray and sauntering back to her own desk. *Needn't bother,* Pat thought bitterly. *Nobody's going to be calling me about anything private.*

"Pat? Annice. Look, darling, will you do something for me? I told Jack last night I'd go to Penny Williams's party tonight, in fact I had a hell of a time to make him say he'd go. I don't want to get him mad at me, Pat, but there's going to be somebody else there I want to see about something important."

"Sure, sure, and you want me to take old Jack off your hands."

"Not exactly. After all, I told him I'd go with him," Annice said smugly. "I sort of thought maybe we could all come home together, sort of—"

"And drop old Jack off first." She thought, *I'd be crazy to go, all I want to do is just quietly lie down and die. Let Annice work out her own problems.* She said, "I don't think I will."

"Oh, come one. I'll do something for you some time."

"Well—" She considered. Noise, smoke, and talk till hell wouldn't have it. Might as well be smoked and talked to death as sit home alone, feeling bad. "Okay, I'll go. But I don't want to stay out all night—you remember it."

"You're a doll."

"Sure."

When she came back from lunch Blake Thomson's office was empty. She worked half-heartedly all afternoon, jumping every time the door opened, but he didn't come back. She was duly thankful.

CHAPTER NINE

All schools smell alike. Kindergartens, grade schools, high schools, even these temporary college buildings thrown together to take care of the influx of students. Chalk and sandwiches and the girl's perfume, and—of all things— old overshoes. Annice shut her eyes and sniffed, standing in the main hall with the home-coming crowd milling around. Definitely overshoes. She must remember to tell Jack, the next time they were out together.

Not Alan. You didn't share ideas and observations with Alan; he wasn't interested in anyone but himself, and if the conversation turned into someone else's channel he quickly turned it back again or lapsed into glowering silence. Last night, on the way home from the ballet theater, she had tried to tell him how excited she was at seeing Swan Lake the first time, the way the dances and costumes looked exactly as she thought they would from hearing the music

on records. Unfortunately Alan had been reading up on
Mies van der Rohe and was full of theories on modern
architecture. "You're a conceited fool," she told him finally,
giving up. "You don't think other people ever have any
ideas worth listening to."

"They don't."

"I hate you."

"No, you don't. You wouldn't go out with me if you hated
me. I fascinate you."

He did too, damn him. She opened her eyes quickly before
the current of traffic could wash her downstairs and out of
the building. There was something about Alan that made
everybody else seem dull and colorless. She couldn't stop
thinking about him and wanting to see him; when she sat
beside him on the front seat of his ratty little car she could-
n't help wanting to touch him. Being with him made her feel
more alive than she had ever felt before. *If I'm not careful I'll
end up doing whatever he wants me to,* she thought, scared
and thrilled at the same time. *No matter what it does to me.*

She had decided, after the first date, that she would Go All
the Way if he asked her to. After all, she had come to
Chicago in search of love more than fame or independence—
she was dedicated to love. She went to a party with him,
shaking with mingled pleasure and terror, and he didn't
make a single pass. He had been polite to her—for Alan—
and he had escorted her home at one A.M. and deposited her
on the doorstep as if she had been somebody's maiden aunt,
without so much as a good-night kiss. It was maddening.
"What's the matter, don't you like me or something?"

Raised eyebrows. "Sure. Why?"

"Oh, no reason." She flounced inside, slamming the
front door. That goofy janitor, Rocco, was loitering in the
front hall, doing nothing as usual. She didn't know why he
was hanging around at that hour of the night, but she gave

him a dirty look and went on up. A good-looking fellow if you like the bold, fresh type, but she was peeved at all men, since Alan was out of her reach. I'll get even with him, she promised herself. *If he ever calls me for another date I'll turn him down* so fast.

The thought that he might not call chilled her to the bone.

But he called, and they went to the ballet. Dutch. Alan said there was no reason why a man should pay a woman's way any place in this day and age; women earned as much as men. There was no reason why a man should support a woman unless she was gestating, and maybe not then. It was a racket; women had been working for hundreds of years, and he was against it. He would go so far as to pick up the check if he invited a girl to eat with him, and that was a sop to bourgeois morality that he was ashamed of. On the other hand, he said, he hardly ever asked a girl out, and if he did it was to some cheap joint—a drugstore or the Four Arts Grill. If it was her idea in the first place, she could damn well pay her own way.

"If a fellow and a girl go out together, she ought to enjoy the evening as much as he does. Why should he pay for it?"

"Well, but—"

All the way home from the theater—not as far as she would have liked, but far enough for him to develop any ideas he might have—she sat well away from him, wondering miserably if he was angry with her and why; and if he was angry, why had he asked her to go out? She suspected it was a kind of cruelty, or at best curiosity; he was the kind of boy who torments a frog to see it jump, or pulls the wings off a butterfly and watches it flop. At the door, she moved tentatively closer. He ignored the movement. He said, "Good night," leaving her to open the car door, get out and walk to the house by herself. She supposed that was a matter of principle too. Why wait on a healthy able-bodied woman?

She lay awake far into the night, angry at him and hungry for the touch of his hands on her body and the pressure of his mouth against hers, determined to win him back. Back from where? *He's a stranger,* she thought in her mother's cool rational way. And then, hot with longing, *oh, no, you don't go as far as we did that night unless you like each other.*

Or do you?

Are there people who take excitement any way they can get it, whether the other person means anything to them or not?

This morning he had called at seven o'clock, while she was drowsily making coffee. Penny Williams was having a party, and how about it? Bring somebody if she wanted. "I'll bring a boy from school," she said to show that she was independent, didn't need him. "Fine. We can all eat together."

He could at least have been jealous!"

She called Pat at noon, thinking that a foursome would at least look like a date, and Pat hesitantly agreed to go. She was glad. Pat was no competition in this kind of crowd, where exotic ugliness rated higher than cornfed prettiness. It was hard to believe that she had even been envious of Pat's freedom of her romance with Johnny.

Jack put his hand on her shoulder; she turned, startled, and then smiled at him. "Hi. We'll have to eat downtown after all. Pat's going."

"How come?"

"I thought she'd like to. She doesn't have much fun."

"The idea is I make like Pat's boy friend, so you can come home with Lover Boy."

Damn him, he was too bright. That had been in the back of her head from the beginning, although she wasn't admitting it even to herself. She looked away. "We can all go together, can't we? Do we always have to be in twos like Noah's Ark or something?"

"Oh hell, Annie, let's have a nickel's worth of honesty for a change."

"And don't call me Annie."

He grinned, taking her hand kindergarten style. "What's the matter you're so mean? Don't you feel good?"

"None of your damned business."

It was a bad start for an evening, and from there it went on and on in the same key like an amateur composition. Pat was abstracted, and left most of her fettuccini on her plate. Annice knew she was trying to lose weight, but it wasn't like her to order more than she could eat when she was paying for it herself. Jack was polite and remote. Alan didn't show up until they were almost through eating, and there was an air of excited expectancy about him that made her sniff suspiciously. He hadn't been drinking. Some other girl, then? The idea made her feel leaden.

Alan finally put down his fork. "Come on, let's show these kids from the sticks a slice of real life."

Annice scowled at him. "Oh, when you've seen one of these imitation Greenwich Villages you've seen them all."

"You don't have to go, baby," Alan said, grinning. "The rest of us can get along without your company."

Jack said anxiously, "Look, I don't think you ought to talk to Annie—Annice, I mean—like that."

She turned her scowl on him. "You keep out of this. Just because we've gone out together three or four times you don't own me."

Pat sat drinking water, turning her fork over and over in the messy plate. Jack looked around. "What a cheerful bunch."

"Oh, come on."

Whatever was wrong, the meal set the tone for the evening. The party was a replica of others she had gone to, except that this was basically a gathering of musicians. The guest of honor seemed to be a short, very dark brown boy with long sideburns, who played the drums. It wasn't that she had any race prejudice—*of course not,* she assured herself, trying not to stare when a hard-looking blonde threw her arms around the drummer and hugged him possessively. Alan looked at her coldly. "Matter, you-all, you in favor of segregation or something?"

"Of course not. I don't like his type, that's all. He looks like he ought to be wearing a black leather jacket and carrying a switchblade."

"What do you want him to wear, a tuxedo?"

She squinted through a milling drift of people and cigarette fumes and alcoholic fog. Several boys in a corner were smoking brown-paper cigarettes, not talking, simply standing with half-closed eyes and fixed smiles. She nudged Alan. "Reefers. For Christ's sake, didn't you ever get high?" She had supposed people who smoked marijuana did it in private, not out on the middle of a crowded room where everybody could see. "God almighty, everybody does it. Where you been?"

Everybody was talking, with the volume turned way up. Words beat against her eardrums without making sense, like the pounding of surf on rocks or the blowing of wind in a tree. The drummer, Snap Kennedy, had stopped for a drink. He had one arm around the blonde, leaning on her— she was a head taller than he. He was wearing, actually, a canary-yellow tweed jacket and a light blue bow tie, and in addition to the sideburns he sported a neat moustache. His eyes glinted around from face to face, and he smiled widely now and then, in recognition or in answer to a greeting. Annice had the sudden idea that he was making fun of everyone, the whole party; that he was putting on an act— this was how they expected a jazz musician to be, how a hep cat should look, so he was playing the part and getting along okay. She wondered what he was like in real life.

"He's a fake," she said wonderingly.

Alan nodded. "So'm I. So are you."

"Maybe you are, but I'm not."

"Oh, cut out the crap, Miss Millay. How long is it since you've really written a poem?"

"Not so long."

"When?"

She shook her head. It was months, actually. That foggy day last spring, when she had gone walking in a dream world of mist and muted sounds, completely alone, and had come home to throw herself on her bed and weep because life was so sad and beautiful. Later, she had put down five short lines, a cinquain, about the fog and the loneliness.

That was six months ago.

"See, you're outgrowing it. All kids are going to be writers. I was going to be Henry Miller and do another *Tropic of Capricorn,* only in a more modern idiom."

"That's not the same thing."

"Why isn't it? You can't stand it to face the truth, that's all. You can't face yourself without any pretenses. You're like everybody else, a human being who has to eat and sleep and sh—"

"Oh, stop." His accusations didn't bother her as much as his choice of words; he used words she had never heard anybody say out loud before, although everybody knew what they meant and tough kids wrote them on walls and fences. She couldn't help blushing when he brought them into the conversation, and she was never sure whether they were part of his regular everyday vocabulary or whether he was trying to upset her. "You don't need to say those words."

"Which words?"

"You know what you were going to say."

"If you know it, you don't have any business being shocked by it."

She said coldly, "I'm not shocked. I simply think it's vulgar, that's all."

"Sure it's vulgar. So's life." She stood up, stepping over the feet of a sprawling girl in black leotards. He said, "This is a lot of crap. Let's get out of here."

"I ought to go home."

"Come on up to my place. I've got something to show you."

She felt herself redden. "Uhuh," Alan said, "not what you think. My, you've got a dirty mind."

"I wasn't thinking any such thing."

Pat had found an aspiring author to talk to and was giving him professional advice on how to write a book, although so far her closest contact with literature had been to unwrap arriving manuscripts and enter their title, author and date of arrival on index cards. She caught Annice's eye and raised inquiring eyebrows. It was impossible to be heard above all the racket, so Annice pointed to the door and to herself, indicating departure, and Pat nodded good-bye. Jack was nowhere in sight. Annice wrapped her thin coat high around her throat and followed Alan out into the night, feeling alive with curiosity and at the same time terrified.

She was surprised to learn that he lived only a couple of blocks from her own apartment; he had never mentioned it. She wondered if he was ashamed of the shabby rundown building, but it wasn't like him to be ashamed of anything. She followed him up the front steps and into a dimly lighted vestibule, then across a large downstairs living room where a sleeping figure lay on a folding cot. The room was in shadow, but the street light shone in through the dirty panes of a vast bay window and picked out the details of a forest of potted plants. "African violets," Alan said in a loud whisper. "The landlady's nut about African violets. She won some kind of a goddam prize from some garden club for 'em."

"Is that she on the cot?" She leaned against the smudged wallpaper at the foot of the stairs, waiting for him. Alan snickered. "Hell, no. That's Jenni. He's been out of a job as long as I remember, but Madame feels sorry for him because he's a refugee from the Iron Curtain and such a good-looking bastard besides. So she lets him sleep in the front room for nothing. I think she thinks he's going to lay her. She keeps thinking up errands to go down there in the middle of the night and cover him up or some damn thing, but I don't think it's going to get her anyplace. She's about ninety."

"Oh, come on."

"Might as well be." They were at the top of the stairs now; he fumbled for his key. "He doesn't mind sleeping in the parlor. In fact, he's doing a scientific experiment." He swung the bedroom door open. "Every night he gets up in the middle of the nights and pees on those damn flowers."

"You're kidding."

"No, honest. One died the other day," Alan said, very pleased, "a white one. Jenni says the white ones haven't got as much stamina as the blue ones."

So this was where he lived. He turned on the overhead bulb. She sat down in the bed, although she wasn't exactly invited, and looked around. The room was small, and probably looked even smaller because it was so cluttered. There was no inch of floor space that wasn't covered with records, paperbound books, clothes, sheets of paper both blank and written-on. A saucepan and spoon stood in one corner. A plate sat on the bed. At some distant time the bed had been made up, but now sheets and a depressed-looking cotton blanket trailed on the floor. There was a record player in one corner of the room, and a pair of socks hung over a wire hanger from a picture frame. Cigarette butts were everywhere.

"Don't say it," Alan warned her. "Get that little-woman look out of your eyes. Anything I can't stand it's a little housewife who bustles around and picks everything up and makes the joint all clean and sanitary, making life hell for some nice, normal, sloppy guy."

"Hush, don't make so much noise."

"Why not? In this place, who cares?"

"I can't stay long."

"Bull." He jerked open a drawer, rummaged through a stack of underwear and more written-on papers and finally came up with something in his hand. She wondered what he was looking for, cigarettes or a bottle or—shrinking from the idea—one of the things the girls whispered about, that fellows bought in drugstores. For the first time she felt immediately involved, in personal danger. Her nerves tightened. She sat with her feet primly side by side, her hands clenched in her lap.

"Look."

She stared, puzzled. The thing in his hand was a roundish disk, plainly vegetable and green-white. For a moment she thought he was joking. Then a look at his face, intent and excited, convinced her that whatever this was, it was no joke. It had some special meaning to him— he looked both excited and frightened, convinced her that whatever this was, it was no joke. It had some special meaning to him—he looked both excited and frightened, like a man about to make a high jump. "What is it?"

"Mescal. Peyote. Mitch Patterson brought it back from Mexico with him. He used it there."

"Wh—what do you do with it?"

"Baby, you go into another world with it, another life." His hand was tight on her shoulder; he turned her so that the light shone on her face. His look scuttled over her like the feet of running insects. She shivered. "This is our night to dream dreams and see visions, baby. You and me together."

CHAPTER TEN

Running hand in hand, Pat and Jackson caught the last train on the P.M. schedule, the one that left Windsor Park at 11:41. It was almost empty. Sober working people were at home in bed by this time, and carousers hadn't started to think about breaking up. They scrambled on board and selected a seat from a whole row of empty seats, across from a sleeping Negro woman with a bundle in her lap, somebody's maid carrying her uniform home after a dinner party. Jack stood back to let Pat sit by the window. "Hot in here."

"Mmh."

"Wasn't much of a party, did you think?"

"Oh, I don't know. It's all right if you like that kind of thing—I guess."

"Seems like a silly way to spend an evening," Jackson said. "I haven't got anything against artists, or even fake artists. I bet the real ones don't go to these brawls. I bet they're home working, composing music or writing or whatever it is they do."

"Yeah."

"But if Annie thinks it's fun, I guess the least I can do is trail along." He looked down at his hands, arguing the matter out with himself. "What bothers me is, I sort of hoped Annie might feel like going steady with me. We've only been out together about four or five times, but I know I like her enough to want her to really be my girl."

Pat opened her eyes. "You're a nice boy, Jackson. Annice doesn't have any right to treat you the way she does."

"That's all right. She's smarter than I am, I know that."

"You're smart enough."

"I tell you one thing though, I don't like to have her running around with that Alan. A lot of fellows talk the way he does, but they're just showing off. He means it. He plays for keeps."

She wanted to say, *oh, go away and let me die, don't sit here and bore me to death with all this stuff, can't you see my heart is broken?* Instead, she listened politely.

Jack said, "I mean, he really does all the things he talks about, as near as I can tell. I know a lot of kids that have been around with him. He drinks a lot, and smokes tea, and he doesn't have any scruples where woman are concerned."

"Do you, Jackson?"

"What?"

"Have scruples about women."

He blushed. In the dim light from the ceiling fixtures, reflected back from the shiny orange paint of the car, she could see the color rise. "I've been around," he said, not meeting her eyes. "A fellow isn't going to turn it down if it's available, we're not built that way. I've never done anything with a girl I didn't really like though, and I've never pressured a girl. She has to really want to."

"That's nice."

"I mean, I wouldn't take advantage of a girl because she had too much to drink or something like that."

"You'll make a nice husband for some lucky girl."

He grinned. "Don't know how lucky she'll be, but I sure enough figure to do my best."

"Jackson?"

"Huh?"

"Do you think it's possible for a man to be in love with two women at the same time?"

He considered, solemnly. "Not if it's real love. That just comes once in a lifetime. That's why you want to be sure before you get engaged."

"I guess you're right."

"Another thing. If I get involved with a girl, I'd be damn sure nothing happened. You know." He was really embarrassed now. She looked down at her lap, avoiding his gaze in order not to embarrass him. "A fellow's a heel who gets a girl in trouble, that's what I think. But if I did get a girl in a jam I'd marry her. I wouldn't send her to some quack."

This kid is a gentleman, Pat told herself, feeling more like her old flippant self than she had in weeks. She said gravely, "Jackson, if I ever decide to get in trouble with anybody I'll give you first pick."

"What!"

"Relax, boy."

He couldn't drop the subject of Alan. Bright in his mind was the image of Annice, little and light-footed, innocent-eyed and childishly freckled. He wanted to protect her. He was warm with wanting to protect her. Sickly, he remembered a bit of conversation with one of the fellows in his physics class, a guy who had double-dated with Alan. The boy said admiringly, "Jesus, does he make time with women! He started with women when he was thirteen—no kidding, he'll tell you the names and dates. He won't use a safe either. Says it spoils things for him. He says people should make love the natural way."

"But what if the girl gets caught?"

"Then he thinks she should go ahead and have the baby. That's nature." The fellow had shrugged. "Nice for the girl, huh? I can see my old man's face if my sister came walking in with a basket, being natural."

He glanced nervously at Pat. He couldn't tell her that; he didn't know her well enough—besides, she was a nice girl. There were some things you couldn't talk about with nice girls, just as there were things you couldn't discuss with your dad or anybody older. He said weakly, "Anyhow, I wish she wouldn't see so much of the guy. He's poison. You tell her I said so."

"Sure will."

They were the only passengers to get off at 55th; the long wooden platform that ran two full bocks looked longer than ever, the planking more full of cracks, the white stripe along the edge almost invisible. Pat's heart contracted with an old childish dread—suppose she fell off? She grabbed Jack's arm. They went silently down the enclosed wooden stairs, their steps echoing. Jack looked around nervously. "Be a good place for a holdup. Or a murder."

"Don't say such things."

Traffic was at a minimum; there was no one in the corner drugstore except the prescription clerk in his white jacket, sitting bored and sleepy-looking in his little glass cage. She had never seen the drugstore closed before. They walked past the empty lot where the condemned houses had been torn down. Scattered bricks still lay dark against the ground. Buildings were lighted sparsely, with here and there a strip of light under a pulled-down shade or a row of yellowish stripes behind a venetian blind.

"Is this a safe neighborhood?"

"Safe enough. One of the girls in my office was stopped by a hood on the way home from work the other night," Pat said. "She lives a couple blocks west of here. But you're likely to run into that most anywhere."

"Is she all right?"

"Betty? Sure. She gave him the old knee, and he let her loose in a hurry. A girl who gets raped is simply asking for it, that's all," Pat said, bored. "You have to take care of yourself."

They stood at the front door of her house. "Shall I come up?"

"Don't bother, I have my keys right here. Thanks a lot, Jackson."

He gave her a ritual kiss, a polite touching of lips to cheek. "Look, don't say anything to Annice. I don't want her to think I'm worried about her, or butting in or anything."

"All right. You're a nice boy, Jackson. Annice ought to be grateful to have you think about her."

"Yeah. Well, good night."

He walked home slowly, his head bent. *Shouldn't have said anything. If Pat tells her, it'll only make her mad. She's such a spunky little piece. Gee, I hope Pat doesn't say anything to her. I want her to feel friendly to me anyway, even if she doesn't want to be my girl.*

He intended to lie awake and worry, but he had been short on sleep for a few nights. He fell asleep almost before pulling up the covers and switching off the light. It was ten o'clock on Saturday morning when the telephone waked him. He stumbled to the corner table and answered it, too groggy with sleep at first to take in what Pat was saying, then jarred awake by the hysterical tone of her voice. Annice hadn't come home at all, and would he please come over and tell them what to do?

CHAPTER ELEVEN

Barby was sure that the basement room would come back to her in nightmares and in fever as long as she lived, whenever her defenses were down. The tossed bed, scene of so many defeats—she tried vaguely to count back, but failed because reconstructing those scenes nauseated her and blurred her thinking. She looked at the zigzag crack in the plaster ceiling and listened to Rocco's voice cracked with tenderness at her ear. *Why does he always have to get sentimental?* she thought. She wanted to burst into hysterical laughter at the first syllable. He thought he was being gentle and affectionate. He thought—she stuffed the corner of the pillowcase into her mouth to keep from screaming with laughter—that she was enjoying this! Maybe even that she loved him.

Fool, fool, she thought, tightening her arms around his neck because he expected her to and because the ritual had come to be a reflex.

She would surely remember this as long as she remembered anything. The sudden entry, awaited, dreaded, almost welcomed because it would soon be over now. It was no use to object, to say no. You might as well get it over with. She shut her eyes because the dark intense face was too close to her own, the bristles of beard hurt her cheek. His eyes, dark brown, were fixed in hypnotic pleasure. She tried not to remember Frank Stewart's hungry eyes or compare the excited panting at her ear with the quickened breathing of that first time.

There. Roll off. For one exquisite second of relief she felt nothing but the bliss of drawing a free breath. Then the misery settled down on her again and she lay waiting for him to take his hand off her and gather his strength and get out of bed. Only then would she be free to go back to the apartment. She saw herself crawling, slinking to her hole like the other basement animals, the mice that came out at night to feed from the garbage cans, the slick quick roaches and the scuttling thousand-legged worms.

Sunlight poured in through the street-level window, dangerously unshaded. It crossed her mind, not for the first time, that any passerby could look down through that glass and see them twined in this monstrous and horrible act. Children, maybe, taking a shortcut across lots. He didn't care. On other occasions, when it happened at night, he left the light on. She shuddered. Only one thing could be worse than this degradation, and that was the possibility of getting caught, of standing naked and revealed before the whole world. Shamed, lost, doomed. The pleasant face of her mother rose before her, smitten with shocked unbelief, as it surely would look if she ever discovered she had been betrayed.

Rocco walked to the dresser and stood, feet apart, pouring wine into two small glasses. That was part of the total horror, that she couldn't go at once but had to stay here until the whole ritual was played out. She took the wine into her mouth, shrinking from its sharp sourness, as she took Rocco's lovemaking to herself—not because she wanted it, but because it was pressed upon her. Drink quick, don't breathe, and you can adjust your clothes and go.

There were people in the world who like wine, just as there were women who found men and their lovemaking attractive. She looked again at Rocco, his sturdy well-muscled body, his thick curly hair. And shuddered.

Her good tweed skirt was wrinkled. She sat up dizzily, trying to pull it straight. Her stockings were twisted. She fished under the bed with her toes and found one loafer, but had to stoop—fighting off the faintness—for the other. In the mirror her face was reflected dimly, a white disc that belonged to nobody.

"You don't have to go."

"Yes, I do. Somebody might come."

She tried to walk a straight line to the door, knowing that at this hour on Saturday the other tenants would be coming and going, carrying in groceries, taking suits and dresses to the cleaner, leaving on week-end jaunts. She opened the door a crack and looked out to be sure that nobody was going to or coming from the laundry. Ten o'clock on Saturday morning—what a time for it!

She felt, as always after these encounters, bruised and exhausted. Not in body, although at first she had examined herself all over with the help of a hand mirror, surprised because the dark stains didn't show. Her mind, her spirit felt as though the lightest touch would stir up a pain.

Dirty. She shrugged. She had been dirty so long now. Ruined and rotten. What difference could anything make?

In daylight the apartment looked tired and shabby. In the morning when they left for work no one had time to be critical; at night, with the lights picking out book-bindings and colored cushions, it was homey. Barby stood in the living-room doorway, taking in the general effect of shabbiness and clutter. A pair of high-heeled red pumps stood in ballet position at the edge of the davenport. The ashtrays overflowed with lipstick-stained butts, and magazines lay in uneven heaps on the floor and table. Barby shivered. The room looked the way she felt, beat and dirty.

Pat came out of the bathroom, her forehead puckered. "Did Annice phone or anything while I was at the Hi-Lo? She still hasn't showed up."

"She probably spent the night with a girl, or something."

"Sure, but it's not like her not to call. She's the most

dependable one." This was true; it was Annice who wrote down telephone messages, made out grocery lists, remembered to empty ashtrays. Insofar as the housekeeping was done, she did it. She even rinsed the breakfast cups and piled them in the sink, to be washed at night.

Barby poured herself a cup of coffee and drank it standing, hoping to relieve her headache and to kill the sour taste in her mouth. She made a face. "Ick."

"Listen to me, I'm worried. What do we do now?"

"She didn't get drunk or something and spend the night with Jackson, do you suppose? After he walked you home?"

"I called Jackson. He says he hasn't seen her, and I believe him. Anyhow, he isn't that kind of a fellow."

"They're all that kind of fellow."

"Not Jackson."

"Okay, okay, what's the difference? He says he hasn't seen her."

They looked at each other. Pat said slowly, "I keep thinking about all the scare stories in the papers. She might have been slugged and robbed. Or raped. Or run down by some drunk or something."

The city spread for miles, vast and impersonal. A huge honeycomb of buildings intersected with streets, alleys, parks. A human body was nothing, a small fragile thing capable of being hidden in a sewer or a broom closet. Both of them felt their human helplessness, pitted against the uncaring monster that was Chicago.

Pat said bravely, "I think we better call the police."

"No. It'll go on the record, or something." Barby's idea of what went on in police stations was culled from the movies, but the notion of publicity, newspaper reports, made her squirm. Stay out of sight, be anonymous, that's the only safety. She shook her head. "You can't do that."

"Do you have any better ideas?"

"Let's wait a while. You know how those crazy parties are." Pat, who had gone to only one and left early, nodded agreement. "It could have gone on till morning. Then maybe she went out with a bunch of people for breakfast, or something. Or like I said, maybe she stayed over with some girl. There's no reason to think anything's wrong."

"That's true. We don't want to make a fuss about nothing."

"Then what shall we do?"

"Let's wait a while. Then make up our mind. Maybe she'll come home safe and sound. We'd feel silly if we did anything rash."

They stood looking uncertainly at each other, not sure what to do next. Pat began picking up ashtrays and emptying them into the already full wastebasket. Barby said, "I'm going to take a bath."

"Now?"

"Why not?"

"Seems like a funny time for it, is all."

She searched for an answer. "There won't be any hot water later. People doing their washing and all."

"That's true." Pat rolled the electric sweeper out of its closet and plugged it in. A deafening roar arose to drown out the sound of the shower.

Barby thought bitterly, *This would be a fine time to conk out with migraine, complicate everything. No use to myself or anyone else. At the same time it would feel good to black out for a while. Something to make me sleep and stop thinking.* She realized, with a sense of shock, that she hadn't had an attack since the first time with Rocco, almost a month ago.

No need to count the times; this morning made five. Five times of being used, and spoiled. Of lying awake afterward, helpless and wretched. Every time she promised herself, *I won't do it again, I'll kill myself first.* And then, *Oh, hell, what's the use? It's too late anyhow.*

She thought, lathering her arms vigorously as though soap and water could wash off the touch of him. *What difference does it make? I'm ruined anyway. Ruined at thirteen. Like an apple that looks nice and shiny, but is rotten at the core, black and moldy.* She forced her mind back to that nightmare of hurt and shock that had ended her little-girlhood. The dollhouse that still stood in a corner of her bedroom at home, when it happened. Of course a big girl of thirteen doesn't play with dollhouses, but she still liked to rearrange the minute furniture and admire its tiny details. Some day—but not yet—she would let it be packed away in the attic with the blackboard, the expensive dolls with their real hair and sleeping eyes, the educational toys. After Mr. Stewart did the strange frightening thing to her, she went silently up to her own room by the back stairs and huddled over the dollhouse, wanting to cry but not able to. There were voices downstairs, Daddy's sounding low and far-off, and then Mr. Stewart's loud and cheerful, the way it was when you met him on the sidewalk in front of the bank. She picked up the miniature davenport and held it tightly until she saw what it was; then she threw it from her and lay on the floor, feeling the first throbbing and dizziness that were to become so familiar.

She didn't know why she was thinking about this now, when she had pushed it out of her consciousness for so long. As though she had come to a turning point and had to clear the past out of her way before she could go on to the future. But what future could there be? She certainly wasn't ever going to fall in love or get married.

Daddy had stayed out of the sickroom, but he knew. She didn't know how, but she was sure of that. In conscious moments, before the sedative took hold, she jumped with fright every time a footstep sounded outside the door; but it was Mama every time. Wonderful Mama, a wall between her and everything that could hurt her. She shut her lips tightly when Mama asked how she felt, afraid that she would say something to give herself away and then Mama wouldn't love her any more. And later, when that thing happened, she didn't connect it right away with the talk Mama had already had with her about growing up. No, she was sure she was dying—God was punishing her for what had happened, and she couldn't tell even to save her life. What a relief, what a wonderful feeling when she found out what it was! She lay for hours with a hot-water bottle on her tummy, enduring the grinding ache of cramps without complaining.

Only, after she was up, Mama had another talk with her— embarrassed, neither of them able to look at the other— about what men and women do together, and how a girl who lets men do these things to her before she is married ruins her whole life; how sorry she would feel if she had to confess such a sin to the man she loved, when she was older.

Don't think about it.

She rubbed herself dry, pulling the towel across her shoulders. *Feels better now. Think about Annice—but she's all right, she's old enough to take care of herself. You can't look ahead or back, either one.*

Do something. It will be a few days before he catches me again. Maybe we can move. If the other girls don't want to, I can go by myself. But the thought of being alone, without even the protection of this casual companionship, made gooseflesh rise on her damp arms. She put on a terry robe and went out to help with the cleaning.

Pat said, "Habit's a wonderful thing."

"How come?"

"Oh—makes no difference how you feel, you sort of keep busy anyhow."

It wasn't what Pat had really been thinking. She had been thinking that her heart was broken, and yet she could cover up like this. She could even feel worried about Annice and exasperated at Barby's desire to avoid publicity. *See how calm I am,* she thought. The sweeper came unplugged and was suddenly silent, and she jumped. "Damn!"

"No call yet?"

"For God's sake, it's only about ten minutes since you said don't call."

"Well, she ought to be up by this time if she stayed all night with somebody."

"What I think is, she went out and got plotzed," Pat said darkly "She's probably sobering up, that's what I think."

"Well, there always has to be a first time."

"True, true. How do you think I'd look in a chignon?"

"A what?"

"Like this." She made a bun of a tissue and held it at the back of her head.

"Oh, one of those. Why don't you get one and see? We have them at the Store, nine-ninety-eight, real human hair."

"No, I want to grow my own." Pat tilted her head at the mirror. "I'd like a really smart black dress too. Nothing cheap. Gee, I wish I could afford to have my clothes designed for me."

"You're getting awfully fussy."

"You don't have to worry. Your kind of looks go good with everything."

Sure do, Barby though bitterly, *and what have they got me?* She went into the bedroom where their three sets of clothes were kept in confusion when they weren't scattered over the living room and bath. She dropped the white terry robe and stood looking at her reflection in the mirror. A beautiful and sexy body, thin at the waist, urn-shaped in the Greek ideal of womanliness, curving out gently at hips and bosom; the shoulders wide for a girl, the back a long sweet slope of creamy white. The breasts were high and full, pointing out a little—she had read somewhere that this was a sign of passionate nature, and how wrong could you get! A good face, too, smoother and prettier than most, giving no hint of the tumult inside. She moved with grace, and her walk was the rhythmic hip-swinging sort that makes men turn and look.

She took underclothes from her drawer and began putting them on thinking, *I wish I was fat and ugly and had warts.*

Pat, in the living room, was examining her own reflection and not liking what she saw. Chunky peasant, she thought, wanting to be slender and fine-traced and elegant. She hated her solid frame and big capable hands and feet. A tear rolled down her nose and plopped on the dusty rug.

The telephone rang. They both jumped to answer, but it was only Jackson, calling to ask if they had heard from Annice yet. He said "Annice" reverently, as though it would be a sacrilege to call her "Annie," almost like speaking ill of the dead. "I'm coming over. We'll have to think what to do."

It was a relief. Although both of them would have denied it, they were glad to have a man in the house, taking responsibility and making the decisions. They flew downstairs to meet him and escort him upstairs, feeling better even though his pallor and the slight trembling of his lips betrayed that he was worried too. "I think we better call the police," he said soberly. "A lot of people have accidents. It's not anything you can *blame* them for."

"Well, sure, that's what the police are for, to help people."

"It's in the front of the phone book."

He dialed with shaking fingers. The sergeant was kind, "like a good family man," Jack said later. "You sure your girl friend didn't stay all night with one of her school friends, maybe?"

"She would have called up."

"Try not to worry. We'll call the hospitals and let you know. Prob'ly come walking in safe and sound about the time you start to worry. Happens every day."

Pat put on the coffeepot. They felt better, listening to the pleasant gurgle in the glass top of the percolator. After a short wait Barby made some sandwiches, apologetically, feeling that with a man in the house they ought to provide something to eat. They were all a little ashamed of being hungry.

The sun stood high in the sky, and neighbors passed heavy-footed down the hall, laden with bags of groceries for the Saturday night party, the Sunday family dinner. The police station called back.

Annice was not in any of the hospitals, nor in the morgue—a grisly possibility that had occurred to all three of them, although nobody wanted to be the first to mention it. No newspaper had word of an accident involving a young red-haired girl. They were not sure if this was good or bad. They sat drinking coffee and looking silently at one another, terrified by the unknown.

CHAPTER TWELVE

Colors, shifting and swirling. Green, yellow, then a bright bland drift of white like sunlit snow, then bright pink, the color of candy and ice cream. The red, so blinding in its brilliance that Annice screamed. There were two of her, one screaming, the other standing aside and listening with far-away amusement. The red ebbed and wavered away, to be replaced by undulating waves of a sickening dark brown.

Lines, intricately woven and interlaced, undulated across a gigantic screen—a screen as large as the whole world, reaching farther than she could see in every direction. Blades of light chopped through the lines, silvery and sharp, slashing and ripping, growing wider and sharper. Everything was a silvery blade falling and slicing, and in the distance bells were ringing. The ringing became a roar, and the roar closed over her head. She was sinking, her ears and mouth filled with the ringing, her eyes hurting with it, her whole body shaking with it.

She turned with immense effort, and the bells stopped, leaving an echoing ominous silence. At once the colors returned, a confused mass of them, dancing and whirling until she grew dizzy and lost her balance. She was falling—falling—

Somebody's hand lay on her side. She stirred, and the hand melted and ran down like snow water. *Oh God,* she thought, *now I've killed it.* She bent to pick up the hand before it vanished completely. In front of her there loomed a high tower made of thin wires, reaching up and up into the sky. It was so beautiful that her eyes strained to take it in, she cried out in rapture, she was filled with happiness. The tower became a fountain, the water rising up and up, with butterflies flitting through it. The word "cupcakes" suggested itself to her and she said it over and over, recognizing the importance of remembering it. Ruffles, and cupcakes, and doom.

When she said *doom* a small green snake squirmed across her foot, and her knee jerked up in protest. The snake stretched to an enormous length. Behind the door stood a coal scuttle—she hadn't noticed it until now— filled with babies' heads, round and bald, like baseballs. All of the little eyes were open and winking.

Animals in a row, marching into the Ark, flat and two-dimensional. Closer, then receding, then growing to vast size. A prickling in her foot. She was lying on a bed—no, a floor—no, the floor of a forest carpeted with brown oak leaves, and large green caterpillars were hanging from all the branches. The caterpillars were evil. She said, "This is Sherwood Forest," and someone stirred beside her.

Then there was nothing for hundreds and hundreds of years, while time and history slid by.

The animals again. She pried her eyes open, and they stopped still, but now they were painted or pasted on the wall of a room she had never seen before. First they were toy-size, then large, then waiting to spring on her and do her some dreadful harm. Her arms and legs began to shudder, but they were so far away that she couldn't care. The shudder rose into her stomach, and she retched. She fell back into emptiness.

They were shouting at her, a whole crowd of people with green faces and white hair like snow, pushing closer and shouting. She wished they would stop. Her head was sore. Someone had taken a silver axe and chopped her head in two, through the skull and down to the chin, and half of it was gone. She tried to rub her nose, but it wasn't there. Her mouth was enormous, swollen and prickly. They had been sticking needles in it. There was a huge hand in front of her, bright red; as she stared at it, the skin turned green and dissolved. She pushed herself into a sitting position, and the floor waved and heaved for miles in front of her. *Hands and knees,* she thought, very pleased with herself for being so shrewd. She rolled over into a crouching position. Her head was green too. She could stand there looking down at herself, split into two green people, and see how silly she looked inching across the floor. She laughed.

She wasn't sure what she was looking for. A drink of water, maybe. If she could find a drink of water her throat would stop hurting, and she would wake up and everything would be all right.

But she wasn't asleep. Through everything—the colors, the silvery singing, the lines, the fever of intensity brought on by the repetition of a single special word—she had been able to see the tan-colored wall paper and the white net curtain, torn at the bottom. She could move around. Once, she was sure, she had gone to the sink in the corner and run a glassful of water for herself. She opened her eyes and looked, cautiously, because the floor was rolling. The plastic glass lay on the floor in the corner, in a drying puddle.

Her ears started growing. They grew into morning-glory horns like the horn of an old-fashioned gramophone, and long pink vines grew out of them.

She forced her eyes wider. The pink vines disappeared slowly; she could see them against the tan walls, dissolving. A last leaf remained, waving in an invisible breeze. Far in the distance the bells began to ring again, high and sweet and shrill.

Three goats sat on the foot of the bed, grinning at her. They had curved horns and pointed beards, and they were totally evil. The middle one was the tallest—and the most dangerous.

A man sat on the straight chair, his head lolled back against the wall, his bearded face lifted to the vision. He grinned at her lazily. "Beautiful," he said. "Beautiful. All the colors. Did you have colors?"

She nodded. It made her head ache. The goats were gone. Fuzzily, she decided she must be awake. She got to her feet like a camel getting up, trying not to be dizzy.

"I think I'm coming out of it," Alan said dreamily. "Let's do it again some time, it's wonderful."

"I feel terrible."

"Suffering is good," Alan said slowly. He shut his eyes and lapsed into immobile silence.

There was evil in the room. Or was it only stale air? She turned, seeing the floor tilt and slant, and crossed to the window. Outside, rain was falling in a twilight murk. "What time is it?"

Alan said, "Mmm."

She looked around for a glass and, finding none, ran water into her cupped hand and drank. Her mouth felt swollen and sore, as though Novocain had worn off and the prick of needle and drill were just becoming real. "I have to go home."

"What for?"

She considered. The faucet was still running; she shut it off, and in the basin was a perfect seahorse, green, about an inch long. She reached carefully to pick it up. It disappeared. "I'm seeing things," she said, stricken.

"The Indians."

"What?"

"Part of their religion."

"Maybe that's why." This didn't quite make sense, but she was too far gone to analyze it. She began looking around for her belongings. She still had on her dress, very rumpled. But her feet were bare and her face felt stiff. She found her shoes under the bed and got them on, although they were too small, and located her purse. She tried to count the money in her billfold, with some faint idea of calling a cab, but her mind wasn't working and she couldn't remember the numbers.

"Hey, where are you going?"

"Out."

This got him down off his chair. "Don't go away. We did this together, didn't we? Now we have to talk about it. Get it down on paper before it all goes away. Baby, that's what we did it for."

Annice said, "Oh, to hell with it."

He said, "That's what's the matter with all you people.

As soon as you get the real thing, it scares you." He sat down again, folding his arms across his chest. Plainly, he expected her to change her mind and stay. She waited until his eyelids began to droop again, then tiptoed across the room and let herself out.

The stairs were miles long, and the railing curved and undulated as it hadn't done before, but she made it. Out on the street, in the fresh damp air, she felt a little more awake. Some of the sensation of walking in her sleep went away. She saw with dim surprise that it was getting dark. But it had been dark when they left the party; she remembered seeing the sky spattered with small bright pinpoint stars when she got into Alan's car. Then what time was it? What—she blinked—what *day* was it? She looked around, but the few cars cruising past and the people on the sidewalks were no real indication of anything. *Couldn't be Monday,* she reasoned; the neighborhood stores were open on Monday evening until nine, but the corner drugstore and the specialty shop next to it were closed and dark.

She guessed she could walk home. It was only five blocks, half a mile. She looked fixedly ahead, because to turn her head meant losing her balance, and if she fell down she wouldn't be able to get up again. Her knees wobbled, but her mind was clearing. A dim white shape capered on the walk in front of her, and she was stricken with panic at the appearance of another hallucination, but when she reached it she saw that it was a crumpled newspaper blown by the sunset wind.

She didn't feel tired any more, physically. A little cramped from sitting so long—how long?—in the same position, but not tired. With the speedup in circulation and the easing of her muscles she began to feel better. *Maybe that's why it's part of their religion,* she thought, proud of herself for being so logical. *Maybe it makes them feel good.* She was beginning to be curious about the experience. *Have to see what I can find in the library.*

She didn't want to remember her own visions, though. In any case, they were already beginning to fade. The colors couldn't have been as bright as she remembered them or the noises as loud, or the reiterated words as full of meaning. She thought again of the goats and shivered.

Whatever time it was, somebody was home. Lights were on in the apartment. She needn't have fumbled through the bag with huge swollen fingers, trying to find the key. The door into the hall was open a crack, as if they were expecting somebody. She went in, feeling safer and quite calm now that she was at home.

All of the lights were on, and the living room was abnormally neat. Pat and Barby sat on the davenport, close together as though for mutual protection. Their faces were grave and strained. Jackson Carter sat in the armchair, smoking. A loaded ashtray at his elbow indicated that he had been there quite a while. A thin girl in black slacks, whom Annice had passed in the hall once or twice, sat beside the window. The atmosphere was one of silent waiting. She wondered—*what's the matter, what's happened?* She stood in the doorway looking from face to face. "What's the matter?" she said.

CHAPTER THIRTEEN

One thing was sure, Barby decided, she wasn't cut out for excitement and late hours. She woke late on Monday morning headachey and hung-over from all the excitement of the two preceding days, to find that she had slept through the shrilling of the alarm clock and it was now half-past eight, the hour when she was supposed to report for work. The other side of the double bed was empty, so she supposed Pat had got off all right, but through the half-open door she could see Annice still huddled into her blankets like a cocoon. One bare foot stuck out, dirty-soled and defenseless. *Lie there and snore,* Barby thought resentfully, feeling the weight of her two sleepless nights.

She yawned as she pulled on her seersucker housecoat and tiptoed downstairs to call the Store. Sleepy as she was, she was watchful of two things; to leave the heavy front door of the apartment off the latch, and to look around the turn in the stairs before she descended the second flight. She had been locked out once, and had had to sit on the hall floor, with nothing to pass the time, until Pat came home from work. That was annoying enough. But to be caught by Rocco in a flimsy nightgown and thin wrapper, locked out, on a Monday morning when everyone else in the building had gone to work. *I don't think I could stand it,* she thought, closing the door of the phone booth and dropping in her dime.

She was desperate enough to think of praying, and would have except for her long-time conviction that God had forgotten all about her when she was thirteen. Probably a good thing, too. If the Almighty took time out to recall her, He might go into the matter of her guilt and reject her altogether.

She made her excuses mechanically, aware that she sounded vague and that the switchboard girl probably thought she was hung-over, and got back upstairs without meeting anyone.

Her entrance woke Annice. She sat up yawning, her reddish hair tangled, her face pasty and heavy-eyed. "My God, what a night! What is this, Monday?"

"You're late to class."

"Well then, you're late to work too."

"We were half crazy worry all day Saturday and all day yesterday. That's all." Pat's cup stood in the sink, so that was all right—she had gone off on time. Barby made coffee angrily, rattling the can against the sink, lighting the burner with a firmer thumb pressure against the pilot than was called for. "Nobody got any sleep at all Saturday night," she said. "Jackson stayed all night. God only knows what the neighbors thought."

"Probably thought he was laying you both, turn and turn about." Annice stood up, stretching. They had shoved and pulled her into pajamas after the neighbors left, but she hadn't washed, and Barby fancied that a queer acrid odor hung about her. "Drink your coffee. You need a bath."

Annice sat down at the kitchen table and leaned on her elbows, riveting her gaze to the coffeepot as though it held some explanation. "It's the funniest thing," she said slowly. "After a thing like that, everything seems sort of dull and flat. It makes you see how people get to be dope addicts." She raised her head and looked at Barby. "I don't mean I want to be a dope addict. I've never even smoked a reefer. But at that, I'm kind of glad I did it once."

"Just let us know the next time. The cops will appreciate it."

"You didn't call the cops!"

"Sure as hell did."

She let it drop, folding her hands around the warm cup.

"Alan wants us to write it up for some magazine."

"Under your own names?"

"Oh God, how would I know?"

Barby poured herself another cup of coffee. She added canned milk, poking the clogged hole in the top of the can open with a bobby pin. "The farther away you stay from that Alan character, the better off you're going to be," she said. "He's crazy."

"Ordinary people always think that about unusual ones."

"What's so unusual about him, except that he hasn't got any morals?"

Annice was silent. Barby frowned. "God, I ache in places I didn't even know I had."

"We got to his place around one o'clock Friday night," Annice said. "What time was it when I got home?"

"Around ten. Yeah, because Jack had the nine o'clock news on the radio. We listened to all the news broadcasts to see if anybody was found dead in an alley, or anything."

Annice figured. "Then I was out about forty hours. Funny thing, though, I wasn't asleep. I don't know if Alan was or not, but I wasn't. I mean, I could get up and walk around, and everything."

"Will you please shut up?" Barby's hand shook as she lit a cigarette. "I don't want to hear about it."

"But it's interesting."

"Sure, sure. I have to go to work. Somebody has to pay the rent in this dump." Barby rinsed her cup under the cold faucet and turned it upside down on the drainboard. "It's bad enough to come in late on Monday, everybody thinks you had a great big week end. I don't want to get fired."

She pulled her clothes on angrily. *God damn the little brat,* she thought meanly, *she could act a little bit sorry. I'm no angel,* she reminded herself, conscious as always of the hidden corruption no one knew about, *but I don't go around worrying everyone else half to death.* She applied her lipstick carefully, feeling a little proud because she hid her own sufferings so well. "I'm going. I don't suppose you've thought to call the college and tell them you're not coming in."

"They'll find it out," Annice said. A tentative smile wavered around her mouth. "Have a good day."

A fine day, Barby fumed, missing the northbound train by a split second and settling down on one of the platform benches for a twenty-minute wait. *Oh, this looks like being a perfectly wonderful day.*

She clocked in just as Betty Pelecek, the other stock girl in Blouses, was going out for coffee. Betty winked at her. Her expression was a compound of curiosity, resentment and the gloating anticipation of someone waiting to hear a dirty story. Barby hated her. She shifted her coin purse and rattail comb to the plastic box, checked her jacket and handbag and went into the stockroom as quietly as possible.

Miss Gordon, her supervisor, said, "Sick this morning, Miss Morrison?" She shook her head. "My roommate went on a week-end binge. I slept through the alarm."

"Well, that's an honest answer." Miss Gordon's lips quirked. "Most of them come dragging in here hung-over and tell you they're dying with flu, or something."

Barby laughed reluctantly. Miss Gordon patted her on the shoulder. "Get busy now. Betty's not worth a damn this morning."

Ordinarily she would have resented the touch. Today she was so tired and headachey—yes, and so angry with Annice for causing all this bother—that she welcomed a suggestion of sympathy. She looked after Miss Gordon's retreating back with gratitude, and then set to work marking and threading price tags, diverted from her displeasure.

That's the way I'd like to look, she thought, picturing Miss Gordon's calm, intelligent face and her small neat

figure. *Slim and tailored, and not so damn sexy. I look like
a fugitive from a burlesque show even in slacks—especially
in slacks.* Miss Gordon wore suits and simple blouses, with
one good bit of costume jewelry, and she looked all of a
piece. You couldn't imagine her being flustered or doing
anything stupid or awkward. It seemed to Barby a good
way to be, neat and integrated and without problems.

She kept thinking about the supervisor as the morning
passed and, since thinking so often seems to materialize its
object, was hardly surprised to find herself in the same elevator at lunchtime. She smiled and got an answering smile.
Miss Gordon said, "Going to lunch, or do you have an
appointment with your boy friend?"

"I don't have time for boy friends."

"So? My appointment for this noon fell through. Perhaps
we could have a bite together."

So there they were in the Palmer House Grill, where Barby
had never dared to go before because it didn't seem the kind
of place to go alone. They smiled tentatively at each other,
two strangers ready to get acquainted and unsure how to
begin. The prices frightened Barby, but she thought, *Well, I'll
make it up the rest of the week, bring a sandwich from home
or something, anyone has a right to go some place nice once
in a while.* She relaxed in an atmosphere more leisurely and
prosperous than that of the company cafeteria or the corner
drugstore. The people at the other tables looked assured; you
couldn't imagine them having any sordid problems—the
executive-type women, the suburban shoppers in expensive
hats, the well-groomed men. She took a deep breath, forgetting about Annice.

At that moment Annice was standing in the living room of
the apartment, looking vaguely out of the window and
thinking about school. *Why am I bothering with the silly*

place anyway? she wondered, forgetting that Alan had been posing the same question every time she'd seen him lately. Alan's idea was that if she had her days free, she could live on the money her family sent her for tuition and they could collaborate. She wasn't sure what he wanted to collaborate on; he was always talking about writing a book, but she couldn't imagine him staying interested in one thing that long. Also, he claimed that it was impossible to write a good book until you had touched the lowest depths of degradation. This sounded fine and dramatic, and when he said it at a party the women always looked admiring and the men uneasy, but she wasn't sure it would be so much fun in real life. What if you reached the lowest depths of degradation and then couldn't climb back up?

Back to what? Alan would ask. *Stuffy, respectable suburban life?*

She grinned. Here she was putting answers in his mouth, and God knew he was capable of talking for himself. She got up and washed the dishes, her mother's training asserting itself, and picked up her dirty clothes and stuffed them in the hamper. Once more she noticed the stiff order and cleanliness of the apartment, hardly marred by full ashtrays and dented cushions. *They must have really been scared,* she thought guiltily, *to pitch in like that. I should have called them. But how could I?*

Bathed, powdered and combed, she felt more like herself. At loose ends, though. It felt odd to be alone in the apartment—probably alone in the building, since the landlord didn't take families with children or non-working wives. All of the apartments were leased by working couples or single men or spinsters, or two or three girls or fellows sharing expenses. For that matter, apart from her college classmates she hadn't met a single woman who stayed home and kept house, except—at a party—one girl who had a small child and was awaiting the birth of another, and she wrote confession stories to help out with the household bills.

If I ever got married, she thought suddenly, *I'd want a house with a porch and a dining room, and I'd want to stay home and take care of my kids.*

She could call Alan. Except that he didn't have any telephone in the first place, and in the second place he wouldn't like it if she called. A man has to be free. The only way to hold a man is to leave your hand open so he can fly away when he likes, a wild bird. What a man does with his own time is nobody's goddam business.

Or she could call Jack, leaving a message for him in the Registrar's office and asking him to call back. Good old Jack, he had sat with the girls all night, when they must have been scared witless about her. He would scold, or look at her reproachfully, wanting to scold but being patient and forgiving instead. A small flame of anger kindled in her. The girls didn't have any business calling him in. Like a member of the family or something. Sure, she had gone out with him a few times. She liked him. He was a nice kid—like a cousin or something. A date with him was about as thrilling as eating oatmeal.

She looked dimly around the apartment. Might as well take a nap.

She was half asleep when the bell rang, and it took her a moment to come out of her fog and locate the sound. It was Alan at the door. She scrutinized him for any sign of remorse or apology. But he looked just as he always did, with his hair uncombed and a bunch of loose papers sticking out of his pants pocket. "Hi. I brought over the first draft. You can check it for mistakes if you want to."

"I don't want to," Annice said coldly. It was no good to be angry at him; it was like blowing soap-bubbles against a brick wall. The anger broke, leaving him untouched. "How do you feel? Any lingering hallucinations? Any color sequences? I had the God-damnedest experience this morning," he said casually, "I thought there was a dead body in shower stall."

"Wishful thinking."

"Oh no. If I wanted to kill somebody I would." But he didn't sound too sure.

Now that she was no longer alone she didn't feel so depressed. She swung her feet up to the davenport and stretched out lazily on her back. "You look good lying down," Alan said. "You've got good hip and pelvic bones. I'd like to paint you that way."

"Except you can't paint."

"Who says? I can do anything I want to."

He sat down beside her. She felt a sweet mixture of laziness and excitement. *No breakfast,* she recalled. The girls had fixed her a bowl of soup the night before, but she hadn't wanted it. How long since she had eaten? She felt very clear-headed, as if she could float instead of walk.

"You'd be a nice lay," Alan said, smiling.

"Then why don't you do something about it?"

The excitement carried her along. It didn't even seem strange to be undressing here in the middle of the living room, by broad daylight, with a man stepping out of his pants two feet away. Only for a moment, when the first pain stabbed, she was lifted out of her rapturous clarity into a realization of where she was and what she was doing. She saw the afternoon sun lying slantwise across Alan's clothes heaped on the floor, her own panties and padded bra lying on top of them. She felt abashed about the bra. *But of course he's known since the first night,* she reassured herself. She shut her eyes, clutching at him until her fingernails dug into the flesh of his bare back, as the current feeling carried her away.

CHAPTER FOURTEEN

None of Pat's strategy was going to do any good. Not the black dress which had taken her an evening's time to pick out and the better part of a week's pay to get from Will Call, or the suede pumps that made her legs look so thin and elegant, or the chignon which she had bought, after all, when it became evident that wisps and straggles of hair were going to take months to make a decent bun. The girls were lavish with compliments, but she wasn't trying to impress them. Blake Thomson still didn't know she existed.

That is, she corrected herself, *he knows it when I spell a word wrong. I'm part of the office equipment, like the typewriters and adding machines, except that I do get a paycheck twice a month. If I got sick he'd probably call a repairman instead of a doctor.* She laughed, but two tears rolled down her cheeks and made little blisters on the galley proof she was wrestling with.

Once she would have been thrilled at the prospect of learning to read proof, especially as there was the prospect of a promotion—with raise—involved. Phyllis rated an assistant; it was she who pointed out that it meant a chance to do something that was "publishing," not just office work. Pat was trying, but she didn't really care.

You can't forget a man who is within sight and earshot eight hours a day. She saw him at work five days a week, and thought about him the rest of the time. She had never been like this before, not even when her summertime romance with Johnny Cutler was ripening—she had certainly been excited by the touch of his hand and the pressure of his lips on hers, and there were times, parked in some country byroad, when she was sure she would say yes if he asked her to marry him. But her feeling for him hadn't crowded out everything else as this did—she had eaten with a hearty appetite and slept soundly and walloped her little brothers when she thought they needed it.

Thinking about Johnny turned her thoughts homeward. She thought about her mother, who had never seemed like a very interesting person before, although nice to have in the background and useful as a dispenser of band-aids, comfort, and spending-money. Her mother wrote every week, on lined paper torn from one of the kids' school tablets, and although it was good to get the letters they never made her homesick or anything like that. Usually she answered them because it gave her something to do in the evenings. There is a limit to the amount of time any girl can spend washing her hair, doing her nails, rinsing out her nylons or listening to the radio and wishing she was somewhere else.

Today, though, she thought of her mother with deep personal envy. To be middle-aged and overweight, to have your pattern of life all set seemed restful and reassuring. She didn't doubt that her mother worried when the children were sick or did poorly in school, but that sort of unhappiness is part of the large security that outweighs and outlasts it. You know what life has in store for you, and while it may not be so exciting, well, it isn't frightening either. Everything is settled.

She said to Phyllis, "Do you ever wish you were old?"

Phyllis considered, her forehead knitted. "I don't think so. I've wished I was dead—I tried to kill myself once, but I didn't have the guts to go through with it. I think I'd rather be dead than old, but maybe I'll change my mind when the time comes."

"I'd like to be settled."

"Nobody ever is, though. I suppose when you're eighty, life still looks all bright and full of promise." Phyllis shrugged. "The main thing in life is to have a skill. That never goes back on you."

Mr. Thomson passed her desk, on his way in from one of his frequent coffee breaks. She fell silent, looking after him, at his broad back in the well-tailored jacket, the line of his hair, the way he set his feet down. There was no use trying to be sensible about it. You can't reason away magic.

"Handsome is in a good mood today, isn't he? Must be in love."

Pat frowned. Phyllis went on, lighting a new cigarette and flicking ashes on the floor, "It's about time he settled down, if anyone asks you. Only he won't. That kind never does. He'll be stepping out on her before they're married a month—you wait and see."

Pat said grudgingly, "She's pretty."

"If you like that skinny high-bred kind. She has good bones." Phyllis sat down on the edge of the desk, quite relaxed. This was part of her scheme for getting along in the world, she explained—make the management think you're too important to drudge; other people might have to work every minute, but you're entitled to a break when you feel like taking one. "Women all fall for him," she said, looking out of the window. "I knew a girl one time who went crazy over that kind of a man. Couldn't think about anything else. Thought it was the big love of a lifetime when he asked her to spend the night with him."

"What happened?"

Phyllis grinned crookedly. "She didn't have anything to complain of, really. He paid for the abortion. Of course he couldn't stay with her while it was going on, the cramps and all. Somebody might have found out about it." She stubbed out her cigarette and fumbled in her shirt pocket for another. "Cost five hundred dollars. I suppose a girl can't complain if a man is willing to spend five hundred bucks on her without fussing—so very much."

Pat's protest was throttled by a sudden realization that

she knew who the girl was. She looked at Phyllis with mingled awe and curiosity.

"Skip it," Phyllis said. "Maybe this marriage will work
out all right. They do sometimes. She's got all the cards
stacked in her favor."

"Is she so rich?"

"God, yes. She's some relation to the Armours and the
Palmers and half the old packing-house families. Then she
inherited a wad from her first husband, too. She's got that
sweet kind of nature that turns out tough in a pinch—
maybe she'll be okay. Older than he is, though."

"Maybe he loves her," Pat said. She felt that she could
bear to be set aside in the interest of love, but to lose the
thing she wanted most for mere expediency, to be defeated
by money and social position was absolutely unbearable.

Phyllis laughed. "Maybe. Who knows what love is?"

"Supposed to be the most important thing in life."

"If you can put everything but the job out of your mind
from nine to five-thirty you don't worry about what's important. That's what keeps you going, that little old job. After
hours, week ends—get yourself laid if you want, that's fine."
Phyllis shook her head. "Get yourself a good skill you can
depend on, something that doesn't depend on anybody's
whim and won't let you down if times get tough. Men are too
changeable, and banks go bust—you can't count on money,
even. But something you know how to do, that's the answer
to everything."

"Everything?"

"Well—almost everything. It won't keep you warm on a
cold winter night." Phyllis considered, her face brooding. "But
there's plenty of that around too, without getting all involved."

Pat didn't answer, but she shook her head. Maybe if you
had known a lot of men, they all seemed alike. Or if you liked
somebody who was far away and only spent a night with him

once in a while, or something like that, you could be reasonable and keep your mind on your work. But what did you do when every time you got settled down, with nothing on your mind but punctuation and broken letters, *his* voice floated out from the inner office and you felt excited and seasick, as if you were out in a rowboat on a choppy lake?

"How's your proof coming?"

"I keep thinking maybe the author is right and I'm wrong."

"That's the wrong approach. If you start feeling reverent, it's too bad."

"It's these modern ones. They don't bother with sentences."

"Sure. They use words the way the painters use color— to express the way they feel. Some of them must feel like hell." Phyllis decided that the tiny squizzle at the end of the line was meant for a period, and circled it. "Keep your pencil sharp. You can't edit with a dull pencil."

"Double entendre?"

"Could be, if you were a fellow."

That tough practical approach was a good one to have, Pat decided, but how did you go about getting it? Here she was all tied up in hard knots over a man who didn't even know she was alive. Here was Barby going around all moody, refusing to go on dates in spite of the fact that she looked like a movie star and walked like a prima ballerina—a waste of sex appeal. Here was Annice—she had felt responsible for Annice since the first day of freshman year, when the school bus let her off at the corner by the consolidated high school, a small red-headed girl of thirteen with big scared eyes. Annice had an odd, intense look now, and half the time she didn't bother to go to her classes. She hadn't exactly dropped out of school, just didn't go or do her assignments. She wouldn't go out any more with Jackson Carter, who was the kind of fellow other girls drooled over; she spent half her time in Alan's apartment, and Pat tried not to think what she might be doing there. It was evident that most of the problems and woes of the female sex grew out of their preoccupation with men, and no salary check or nameplate on a desk was going to induce that kind of response in anyone under the age of eighty.

Blake Thomson's buzzer sounded. Two shots—dictation. She put a shaking hand to her chignon, which slipped in moments of stress no matter how well she anchored it, straightened her stocking seams, pulled her skirt around before she reached for her notebook and pencil and went in.

CHAPTER FIFTEEN

"I don't want to."

"Sure you do. You always want to, because you have perfect responses. Look who developed them," Alan said, grinning. In the greenish shadow from the window shade his skin looked white and thin; his half-closed eyes and small beard gave him the look of a satyr. He lay back naked against the sheets, relaxed and ready for argument. She marveled, knowing that a touch or a whispered word would trigger him into readiness for love.

"Well, all right then, I do want to. But I'm not going to because it isn't safe."

"That's a poor excuse."

"No, it isn't. I read it in a book," Annice said hotly. "It said this is the worst time, middle of the month this way. That's when anything can happen."

"Where did you find this book?"

"In a drugstore." She forestalled his answer. "But anyway it's so."

Alan rolled over on his side and groped around on the floor for cigarettes. "Come on, get your clothes off."

"Well, all right." But she sat with her arms crossed on her chest, looking at him, begging for understanding. "It isn't because I don't want to. I do want to, practically all the time. Only I'm scared."

"That's unworthy."

"What if I had a baby?"

"Why not? It would get along all right. Do you good to have a baby, fill you out, make a woman out of you. A girl isn't complete until she has some kids." He considered. "One kid, anyhow."

"Without being married? My mother would die."

"That idea's a holdover from chattel slavery. They used to put an iron ring on a woman's ankle to show she belonged to some man. Now they put a gold ring on her finger. As far as your mother is concerned," Alan said, "why should you care what she thinks? She's lived her life—you live yours."

Annice shivered. It was cold in his room; it was always cold, because the rent was so low, and she hated the untidiness. Bourgeois or not, she couldn't shake off her early training. "I have as much right to like things neat as you have to like them messy," she said, and he raised his eyebrows in surprise. "Now how did you get off on that?"

"Oh—I don't know."

"Do you know a better place?"

She didn't. They were safe from interruptions here; the other tenants—raffish young men in their twenties, dressed like Alan and, like him, apparently without human ties or obligations—might leer at her when they came in together, but they accepted her as Alan's girl and didn't ask any questions. She had talked for twenty minutes one evening with that Jenni who was trying to kill Madame's violets, but she still didn't know his last name, and she was sure he didn't care about hers. There was a degree of security in this amoral indifference.

"Anyway, if you won't use a—a thing, I don't see why you won't let me go to a doctor and get fitted with a diaphragm." Her voice wobbled; she knew she was right, but that didn't make any difference. He chuckled. Nothing amused him more than her avoidance of words he used casually. She suspected that he worked them into the conversation just to see her wince. He said, patiently, "It's not right. I don't mean middle-class morality, I mean being natural. Uninhibited. Living life fully. Beating around the bush all the time and saying no to life—that's the only sin."

"It's a sin to bring an unwanted child into the world."

"Well, then, you could have an operation. Mind, I don't approve of that either, but a girl has to make up her own mind about these things."

"Don't you think the father has anything to do with it?"

"Hell no, why should he? Fatherhood is an accident. Maybe when I'm forty or fifty I'll be ready to beget a child," Alan said grandly. "Or maybe not. The children of superior people are likely to be quite mediocre, you know."

She considered. She did want him very badly. They had been going to bed together for three weeks, almost every day. Not quite every day. She never knew whether he would call up or not, and she guessed that he would be angry if she came to his place unasked, since freedom meant so much to him. That didn't matter. What mattered was that since the first time they had been together, on the davenport in her apartment, she had been learning about love. There was this hunger you learned to feel; and then there was the satisfaction that was like nothing else on earth. Thinking about it filled her with desire for his body.

She shut her eyes. "Oh, Alan, it isn't that I don't want to."

"Peel off, then."

She unbuttoned her blouse, conscious of his eyes on her and, as always, half proud because her body was young and slender and lovely, and half abashed because she wasn't as voluptuous as the girls he looked after on the street. Her breasts, free from the narrow strip of nylon and latex padding, were small and proud, and she had the concave front and flat hips of a very young girl. She stepped out of her skirt and knee-length stockings and stood naked beside the bed, hesitating. "I don't suppose you'd marry me if I got caught?"

"God no. Do I look feeble-minded or something?"

"Plenty of people do."

"Marriage is for the birds. Don't let's waste time arguing, baby. We've got better things to do." He took her hand. "Feel that. All for you."

"I'm scared."

"Sissy."

"You never think about anybody but yourself."

"Of course not. You never think about anybody but *your*self, either. Nobody does." He hugged her close. "This is going to be a hell of a lot of fun, with you all tied up in hard knots. Relax."

"You don't love me."

"Sure I do. Don't I take my time and make you feel wonderful? Don't I? How can you say I don't love you?" His hand traveled down her arm and came to rest on her breast. "Stop thinking. Just feel."

She sighed. He had put her in the wrong again. She was mean, selfish and narrow-minded. She never had an answer; she was always wrong, and he was always right. She said, "Well—"

"You don't have to, you know." He rolled over, presenting an impersonal stretch of back. "I can always go out and get something else."

"I'll never speak to you again if you do."

"You won't know anything about it."

"I'd know."

"You wouldn't. And it wouldn't matter. I believe in freedom." He caught her as she moved closer, and lay against her. Desire rose in her, a mounting tide. She cupped her hands over his buttocks. "Turn over," she whispered. "Please."

"I don't care how many guys you lay. You're a free woman."

"I don't want anybody but you."

"Want me?"

"Yes. Oh, yes, I have to."

She turned under him, feeling her whole being rush to meet his passion. She would worry later—oh, brother, would she worry! But she didn't think about that now. She gripped him tightly, feeling the beginning of the slow rise to absolute fulfillment and giving herself to it.

CHAPTER SIXTEEN

"Good looking?" Betty Pelecek said. She looked at Barby over the rim of her coke glass, her lips twisted scornfully. "I guess she's all right—if you like that kind. I like normal people myself."

Through Barby's mind there flashed the names of half a dozen hidden disabilities—TB, cancer, leukemia, all the names that flashed at you from billboards and magazine pages. She said weakly, "Normal?"

"Sure, she's a Lesbian." Barby's expression was all the answer she needed. "Don't you know what a Lesbian is? It's a woman who likes other women."

"Well, I like other women. Don't you?"

"To go to bed with, stupid. Instead of men."

"But I don't see how—" She ran through her considerable knowledge of the relationship between men and women. "I mean, what do they *do?*"

Betty shrugged. Either she didn't know, or, more likely, she considered it an unfit subject to discuss at a drugstore counter. "They find ways," she said darkly. "They're not like other people." She gathered up her handbag, gloves and packages, preparatory to getting down from the high stool. "We better get back. She'll give us both hell if we're late. Unless," she said maliciously, "you're teacher's pet or something."

Barby frowned. Betty sounded so positive; surely you couldn't make up a thing like that, and yet she didn't see how it could be possible. Fragments of talk, ignored at the time; allusions in books; clinical-sounding magazine articles—this might explain a great deal she had ignored or dimly wondered about. "Anyway," she said, "I don't think Miss Gordon could be one. She looks like anybody else."

"You can't always tell. Sometimes they dress in men's clothes. But other times you can't tell them from ordinary people."

"Well, but—what people do is their own business." She fell silent, knowing that Betty didn't agree. When someone in the department got married it was Betty who made a note of the date, to compare it later with the arrival of the first baby; she seemed to know what every girl in Blouses and Sportswear did over the week end and which ones were sleeping around, what married employees were two-timing their husbands and which of the floor managers and department heads got fresh with the girls. Her gimlet gaze frightened Barby, conscious as she was of all she had to hide. She tried to avoid Betty, and when there was no way to avoid a coke break or lunch hour with her, she breathed easier when it was time to get back to work.

She looked at Miss Gordon with new curiosity when they reached the Store, half expecting to discover some disfigurement she hadn't noticed before. But Miss Gordon looked quite ordinary: neat, attractive, with a pleasant smile. In her dealings with the other supervisors and the salespeople she was both relaxed and capable, as if she knew her value to the company and, at the same time, recognized an obligation to do her best. Her girls didn't loaf when she was around, didn't sneak off to the washroom for a smoke or spend their time visiting, but Barby had never heard her reprimand anyone. She didn't have to. *If she's a—if she's one of those,* Barby though confusedly, feeling Miss Gordon's eyes on her and blushing, *they can't be so terrible. Anything she did would have to be all right.*

She thought about it a great deal, and suddenly it seemed to her that Miss Gordon was everywhere she went—in the elevator before and after work, in the third-floor washroom, in the corner drugstore when she stopped for a box of Kleenex. She stopped at the long worktable where the girls were sewing tags in the $3.98 blouses, and stood for a long time looking at Barby. The look went through her like a ray of sunshine and left her feeling warm and shaky, so that she sat for a while doing nothing. Then, catching Betty's eyes on her, she got briskly to work. But she couldn't shake off the memory of that deep, questioning look.

They fell into step at lunchtime the next day, reaching the street together; Barby stood back to let Miss Gordon go through the revolving door first, and was glad but somehow not surprised that she waited. "Alone? Then why don't you have lunch with me? My treat, of course." She looked at Barby, thoughtfully. "You needn't mention it to the other girls, though."

Barby nodded. Nobody is lower in the department-store hierarchy than a stock girl, unless it's the man who sweeps out or the drabbled women who come in at night to scrub. A stock girl is nobody. Even if she is the owner's daughter, learning the business from the ground up, within the walls of the Store she is without status. Barby knew and accepted this. Dimly, though, she realized that something more underlay Miss Gordon's admonition. She walked silently, excited and a little frightened.

They went to a little restaurant tucked away between two taller buildings, a dark little cubbyhole lighted by candles and frequented by couples who looked ardently at each other across the small linen-draped tables. Some of the couples, Barby noticed, were women. Miss Gordon ran a hand through her hair, ruffling it, and smiled. "I love this place," she said softly. "Glass of wine while you're waiting?"

"Well—"

The wine sent a glow through her, making her feel at once relaxed and alert. She looked around curiously. This was a different world from any she had seen—as unlike the expensive hard-surfaced world of the big hotels and department stores as the small-town streets and tree-shaded lawns of her childhood. It was, somehow, more personal. The flicker of candlelight on intent faces, the silence of the deferential waiters, the soft lilting and wailing of violin music that seemed to come out of nowhere—all of these evoked a mood of nostalgia and romantic yearning.

Surrounded by a rosy haze, she realized that she was answering Miss Gordon's questions without self-consciousness. Yes, she lived with two other girls—they had been friends in school, that was how they happened to be together, but they seemed to be making separate friends and doing different things. One was in school and the other had a job with a book publisher. Yes, she liked working in the Store. "Only I don't want to be a stock girl all my life. I don't know just what I want to do, yet."

"Perhaps get married and have a couple of nice children?" Miss Gordon's lips quirked.

"No, I'll never get married."

"Don't you have a sweetheart?"

"I hate men," Barby said fiercely.

Miss Gordon turned her wine glass between her slender fingers. "You don't look like a girl who hates men."

"Oh, I hate the way I look, too. If I were a Catholic I think I'd go into a convent. I really mean that, Miss Gordon."

"Ilene."

"Ilene." She blushed. "All men want to do is get their hands on you all the time. They just go by the way you look, they don't care how you really are."

"And how are you really?"

"I don't know," Barby said slowly. "It's like I'm waiting to find out."

"Yes," Ilene Gordon said, "that's the hardest part of growing up, waiting for someone else to show you your own possibilities. So often the right person doesn't come along."

The waiter refilled Barby's glass, setting a plate down in front of her. The food smelled wonderful, but she wasn't hungry. "I'm doing a lot of talking," she said shyly. "What I'm really interested in is you."

It was a simple story, Ilene Gordon said laughing. She lived in an apartment on the North Side—she named the neighborhood, and Barby recognized it as a very good neighborhood indeed, far better than her own. She had been sharing it with another girl, who was moving out in a few weeks. "She's being married. I'm not sure what I'll do then, but anyway, it will work out."

Barby tried to imagine a marriage that would be better than sharing an apartment with Ilene Gordon, seeing her every evening, talking things over with her. She said, "Your friend will be sorry," and was rewarded by another of those long, searching looks. They left the subject there, as if it were not time to develop it further.

Miss Gordon picked up the check which the waiter presented deferentially, and tucked a bill under the edge of her plate. None of the nickel counting exactitude Barby was used to when she went out with the girls. "We must do this again. It's been fun."

How nice she is, Barby thought, glowing with wine and talk. *How nice and understanding.*

For some reason, she didn't mention the lunch to Annice and Pat.

The book was on her end of the worktable a couple of days later, tucked under a box of tags as though someone has slipped it there, hastily, while she was out. There was no note with it, and nobody mentioned it, but when she opened it she found Ilene Gordon's name on the flyleaf in a clear, small hand, and she knew that it had been left for her with a special purpose. She took it out to lunch, choosing a small cheap restaurant where she was unlikely to meet anyone from the Store. Without paying attention to the young sailor who was ogling her from the next table or to the mediocre food, she plunged into the pages of such a story as she had never read before.

It was the story of a young woman who, growing up, rejected the love of men and was lost in loneliness for the years of her girlhood, only to find a kind of love she had never known existed—the passionate unselfish love of another woman. Barby was fascinated. There was a relationship, then, without force or fear. Tenderness was in it, and compassion. There was a love between two individuals who understood and cherished each other because they shared the same nature. They could even pledge themselves to each other—perhaps not for a lifetime, but then, how many wives could count on their husbands to be faithful after the first weeks of marriage? For the last five years Barby had looked wonderingly at all the serious, respectable married men she knew, wondering what fearful secret lives were hidden by their everyday faces.

She read on, overstaying her lunch hours and not caring, though the time clock was as relentless as death or taxes and her tardiness would mean a deduction. It didn't matter. She was like an explorer who, long drifting on an unfriendly sea, finally sights land and dares to hope he will make it to shore, after all.

She carried the book home with her that afternoon, reading a few pages in the station, a chapter on the train, propping it on the kitchen table while she opened cans and threw together some kind of a supper. Annice was out, doing God knew what—the thought of what Annice was probably doing made her feel a little sick—and Pat was too absorbed in shortening another new dress to have time for food. This concern of Pat's for her looks bothered Barby, who had always been well-dressed with very little effort on her own part; she might have expected it in Annice, but Annice was getting downright careless since she no longer went to school. Pat was all wrapped up in clothes—insane about clothes, in fact. She had thrown away the skirts, sweaters and flats that went so well with her wholesome chubby appearance and was slinking around in a series of glamorous outfits that looked a bit funny on her.

Well, that was another problem to straighten out when she had time to think about it. Tonight there was something more urgent. She filled a plate with canned vegetables, not so very well seasoned, and took it to the davenport, where she sat down with the book. Long after Pat finished her pinning and hemming and went to bed she was still sitting there, the empty plate still on the floor. It was like stepping into a new world, a world where secret hidden emotions ruled people's lives.

Was it possible that she belonged in that world, too?

She was shy about facing Ilene Gordon at work the next morning. She need not have been. Everything went smoothly. She was on time. Her face in the washroom mirror looked the same as always, a pretty girl's face made up in the current style. Only everything in the Store looked brighter and sharper than usual. The stock shimmered with newness and color; the faces of clerks and customers held a depth of feeling she hadn't noticed before. She saw a young mother with two whining children, tired, hungry for some of the pretty clothes the household budget wouldn't cover; she looked at the older saleswomen and saw their ugly comfort shoes at variance with their smart dresses and modish hair styling, and her heart swelled with pity for them. How hard it must be to get older and have nobody to love you, nothing to look forward to except a skimpy existence on Social Security!

But she was young. Her best years were ahead.

She had never felt this identification with other people before. She had always been alone. She wasn't sure whether she liked it or not. When Ilene Gordon showed up, looking as she always did, Barby was conscious of an intense pleasure at the sight of her. That was all. No anxiety. She was sure everything would work out all right.

Nothing in her life had ever worked out right before. But then, nothing like this had ever come her way.

CHAPTER SEVENTEEN

"Why don't we eat here?" Annice rolled over, shivering in the chilly room.

"What for?"

"Just thought it might be fun. I'm a pretty good cook."

"Don't go little woman on me," Alan said. There was a menacing quality in his voice that she didn't like. She propped herself up on one elbow and searched his face, but it was closed, as usual. So far as she could tell he had only two changes of expression—a hard glee when something struck him as funny, and the ravenous look—eyebrows knitted, mouth hungry—he wore when making love. It pleased her sometimes to realize that she could stir him out of impassivity to a display of emotion; it gave her a feeling of power.

Afterwards, though, he lapsed back into his normal blankness. How many times she had looked at his sleeping features as he lay limp and exhausted by love, searching for some trace of tenderness and finding none. Those were the times when she smoothed his hair as he lay against her shoulder or with his mouth buried in sleep against her breast, unwilling to give more than she had received and yet helpless against the upsurge of emotion that followed spent passion.

Now she sat up, feeling for the cigarettes she had dropped on the floor beside the bed—his gesture. She was no longer embarrassed by her own nakedness or excited by his; every line of his body was familiar to her, and she had learned her own body from his hands and the pressure of his weight on her. She thought, maybe being married is like this. She said, reluctantly, "The thing is I'm getting short of money."

"I wondered when that would come up." Alan sat up, wrapping his arms around his bony knees. "Christ, women are all alike. They all resent it if a man doesn't pick up the tab every time."

That was so unjust she couldn't help quavering a little. "That's not true. It's only that I don't make so very much. Forty dollars a week doesn't go very far—and I did pay your rent last week. I've only a dollar to last till payday."

"Hell, if I had any money you'd be welcome to it. That's the middle classes for you, go to bed with anybody but let money come into it and they're all possessive. I won't be like that. What's mine is yours."

"Yes, but—" She stopped, aghast.

"But I never have anything? Aw, Jesus, baby, can't you stop analyzing everything? Can't you ever just live? I know you were raised in a horrible small-town atmosphere, but haven't I made any impression on you at all?"

She wanted to cry. She hadn't felt like this, touchy and weepy, for a long time—not since she started high school and felt the town kids eyeing her clothes and hairdo snootily. She said sulkily, "I do everything you want me to. I skipped work two days last week because you wanted me to stay with you. Any more of that and I'll lose my job."

"So what? You can get another one. It's a lousy job anyhow. Anybody can be a file clerk."

The obvious answer was on the tip of her tongue. It took all the will power she had to keep from saying, "Yes, but it's been supporting both of us." Instead she said softly, putting her hand on his thin corded arm, "Let's not fight. Seems to me we fight all the time lately."

"Well, it's your fault if we do."

"What time is it?"

"How should I know?"

The clock was on the floor too, along with the overflowing ashtray and the empty beer bottles. She leaned out to look. He leaned past her. "Five to eight, if this damn thing's right. What difference does it make?"

"I'm going to be late to work again."

"Aw, come on, stay in bed a while. Let's just snuggle up here and take a nap. Or we could try the ether," he said hopefully, pulling her down against him. "When are you going on an ether jag with me? It beats booze every way, makes you sexy as hell."

"Now I'm not sexy enough for you the way I am."

"No kidding, it's unique."

She struggled to sit up. Not for anything would she have confessed—coward, chicken—the terror that washed over her when she remembered the two days of the mescal experiment. To lose control, to feel your mind slipping out of reach, was the worst thing she could imagine. Even after making love there was a moment of blind panic when the excitement died down and you came back from the far place. She eluded his reaching arm and stood up, naked, beside the bed. It was chilly in the room. She said, "I'm going to stay home tonight and catch up on my sleep."

His eyes flickered. "That's okay. I can always find some way to pass the time."

"It's different with you. You can lie in bed all day and do nothing. I have to save a little energy for work."

"Nag, nag, nag."

She pulled on her bra and wrinkled slip. No pants. Alan said that women who wore pants were just being silly, either advertising their inviolability or, more likely, hoping to have them removed by force. She needed a bath, but the bathroom was at the end of the hall and the lock wasn't very good. One of the young men had come in while she was brushing her teeth, a couple of days before, and hadn't been embarrassed at all. She put on her yesterday's dress and nylons, and her shoes. She picked up her comb, lipstick, and earrings and stuffed them into her bag. Alan didn't like her to leave anything. Sometimes she wondered if he had other girls up there while she was at work. The thought of his making love to another woman stabbed her with painful jealousy.

She hadn't gone out with anybody else since they began sleeping together. Except that Jackson Carter dropped in at the apartment now and then and sat drinking coffee with her and Pat, and she walked down to the drugstore and had a coke with him before he went home. Twice, they had gone to the neighborhood movie. That didn't count. It was just a way of making time pass until she could be with Alan.

She closed the bedroom door quietly behind her.

The bathroom door was open; Jenni was shaving. He motioned her in with a graceful sweep of the hand.

"Thanks," she said, "I'll wait. How are the violets?"

"All dead. Every one," Jenni said delightedly. He grinned at her through the lather, like a cheerful small boy who has played a trick on the grownups. It occurred to her that they were all perverse and dissipated children, Alan's friends— children who wouldn't or perhaps couldn't grow up. For the first time she wondered about Alan. What had his parents been like? What had happened to him when he was little, to set him adrift and make him at once ruthless and casual?

As far as she knew, he might have been created the day they met.

The wind was cold. The end of October, and she had postponed sending home for her winter clothes. She hadn't even written home for longer than she cared to calculate. The thought of her mother's searching look made her wince, as though her guilt and uncertainty would be apparent between the lines of a letter. She had tucked the last two or three letters from home into a drawer, unwilling to read them but unable to throw them away unread.

At the thought of all her winter garments, clean and pressed and stored away in mothproof bags, a wave of homesickness swept over her. She felt hollow and alone. For a moment the sidewalk wavered, and she staggered and then righted herself.

After all, she thought sensibly, I haven't had anything to eat. Alan ate at odd hours, sometimes ravenous, wolfing down huge plates of hamburger and French fries, drinking cup after cup of coffee; at other times he went sixteen or eighteen hours without food. Since it made him impatient to have her mention food when he didn't feel like eating, they went out at his suggestion—but then *she* wasn't hungry.

In addition, she was dangerously low on money. The stop-gap job as a file clerk didn't pay much, and she was ashamed to weasel out of her share of the rent; Pat was squandering every cent she could get her hands on and had a whole closet full of new clothes. Alan's attitude was that her money was his. He had been angry because she had cashed her paycheck at the currency exchange before meeting him and settled with Barby for the rent.

Of course, she thought, if he had anything he'd share it with me. The disloyal thought blossomed before she could uproot it—there's no reason he can't at least earn something.

She had twenty minutes before work time. That was one good thing about a job in the neighborhood; it might not be as glamorous as working in the Loop, but you didn't waste time and money commuting. She hesitated before a little lunchroom and, seeing an empty stool, went in and ordered coffee and a sweet roll. The sudden warmth struck her drowsy, and she yawned.

Someone had left a *Tribune* on the counter; she opened it idly to the society page. A familiar name caught her eye. Mrs. Harrison Aldrich was announcing the forthcoming marriage of her daughter, Mrs. Renée Hahn, to Blake Thomson of Winnetka and Philadelphia. That would be Pat's boss, the one she had talked about so much when she first went to work at Fort Dearborn. It was funny she hadn't mentioned this engagement. A small office was a beehive of gossip; executives would be upset if they knew what the typists and mail boys knew about their private affairs.

Then the dateline caught her eye. November 5. She had been drifting along from day to day, thinking in terms of October. She rubbed her eyes and looked again, unwilling to believe that it could be so late.

Then—

She had figured wrong, of course. She was due this week, not last week. She tried to count back, marking off the days by those personal landmarks women use for computation. *It was the day we went to that French movie, because I had to get up and go to the ladies' room in the middle of the feature and Alan was peeved. That was after we had the party at Lorene's, and Lorene's husband kissed one of the girls in the kitchen and she raised so much hell.*

Or was it before the party?

She struggled backward through a confused tangle of days and nights, trying to get her bearings; but all she could actually remember was going to bed with Alan far more than she had gone to bed in her own apartment.

After a moment's hesitation she opened her billfold and took out a small calendar printed with the advertising of a stationery store. Some of the dates were circled with pencil: one every month, sometimes one at the beginning and one near the end. She traced the lines of figures with a nervous finger. There was no evading it, she had been right the first time. She was nine days overdue.

It's too soon to worry, she reassured herself. *Maybe I'm catching cold, or something.*

Her mouth felt dry. She drank the rest of her coffee, paid her twenty-six cents at the cashier's desk and walked out, leaving the roll untouched.

CHAPTER EIGHTEEN

It was too soon to start worrying. That was easy to decide—
to act on it wasn't so easy. Annice woke in her own bed the
next morning, next to the familiar blanketed lump that was
Barby, and after the first moment of suspended consciousness, she was gripped by pure primitive terror. She was in
trouble. Nothing was going to change that. Nothing was
going to save her. Her arms and legs tensed with animal
fright; for a long time she was unable to move. Then she
was able to get up, weak and shaking, and make her way to
the bathroom. She got there before she vomited.

It was a gray foggy day, and the bathroom was cool, not
bleak like Alan's rented room, but cold enough to make her
shiver. She stood clinging to the rim of the washbowl,
looking around the familiar walls as though she had never
seen them before. All kinds of cosmetics littered the glass
shelf below the mirror, the edges of the bowl, even the
shelf of the toilet: tubes squeezed in the middle, jars of
cream and lotion, a tin of detergent, bobby pins. On the
shower rod hung a pair of nylons and a pair of panties, dry
but forgotten. *Slobs,* Annice thought coldly. *Why don't
they pick up after themselves? Do I have to do everything
around here?*

Her anger steadied her.

Maybe Alan would come in for breakfast. He had done
that once or twice, and although she realized it was because
he lacked money to go out for coffee, she felt that she would
be glad to see him on any terms. She hadn't left him any
money the day before, partly in a half-conscious attempt to
get even with him for being so demanding and unsympa-
thetic and partly because she really was down to her last
dollar. If he couldn't find anyone else to borrow from—and

it wasn't time for Jenni's unemployment compensation check
—he would surely be in for a meal.

She felt a lightening of the heart as she put on water for
coffee and scrabbled through the breadbox in search of a
slice good enough to toast. It was simple, after all. If she
was right—and she felt sure now—Alan might very well
react like any other young man who had got his girl in
trouble. He would be angry and resentful. He would swear
at her, or even hit her. But when it came to a showdown he
would marry her, reluctantly maybe, and they would go to
keeping house somewhere and after a couple of years he
would forget that it wasn't his own idea in the first place.

After all, a lot of families started that way. Two of her
high school classmates dropped out of school in the middle
of the year to get married, and everyone had smoothed it
over and pretended to believe that they were secretly married two months earlier; the girls had showers for them; so
far as Annice could tell, they got along as well as most
young couples. It wasn't the sort of romance a girl dreamed
about, but it happened often enough to be a commonplace.
She would be brave and cheerful and make a good life with
what she had.

It was silly to take his cynicism at its face value. He was
young. She realized that she didn't know exactly how old
he was. He must have the same needs as anyone else—love,
a home, children. *This was his obligation,* she thought,
pressing her lips firmly together. She would have been startled to know how much like her own mother she looked.

She drank the first cup of coffee before calling Barby
and Pat, and when they were out of the house she began
briskly to tidy the apartment, feeling quite calm and cheerful. She would shower and put on a becoming dress before
he got there. She would be affectionate and good-natured,
but firm.

The morning passed.

It crossed her mind that perhaps he had already suspected this. Perhaps he had been trying to provoke a quarrel so she wouldn't make any demands. Of course, it was unlike him to be reticent about any bodily function. He got an impish pleasure out of shocking her, of using short rude words for things she referred to equivocally or not at all. On the other hand—and she didn't like the idea—it would be like him to observe her with cool, impersonal curiosity, waiting to see how long it would be before she realized her plight and what she would do about it. She knew him well enough to believe he would be quite capable of this. He had already written up the mescal experience, which filled her with fright and humiliation every time she thought about it, and had submitted it to a national magazine under his own name. She decided that he was perfectly capable of using her as a laboratory animal if he felt like it.

Objective Study of a Girl from the Sticks, in Trouble. With names, dates and places, and a detailed description of the way she behaved in bed.

Or maybe he meant what he said—that pregnancy was a normal condition, and the feminine insistence on wedding ceremony nothing but a holdover from a primitive rite; that no man was obligated to stand by a woman he had slept with, or support her and her child. *Well,* she thought, *life isn't like that. He'll simply have to grow up.*

She whisked through the kitchen, straightening things on the cupboard shelves, while her early-morning terror changed to resentment and then to hot, clean anger. *God damn him,* she thought, he made me do it. I didn't want to. It really seemed to her, from this vantage point, that she hadn't. *I told him it wasn't safe, and he wouldn't use anything or let me go to a doctor for equipment or anything.* It crossed her mind that she could have gone anyway, or, failing that, have broken off with him and begun looking around for a more amenable male. She brushed the thought aside. It was too reasonable; it interfered with her good self-justifying rage.

By evening she had convinced herself that the whole thing was simple. She went to bed early and fell asleep in the midst of planning her campaign. He would have to listen to her; he would have to marry her. Even if it meant taking him into court, or threatening to. She fell asleep, seeing her plans already materializing and wondering what she would wear to be married in.

He didn't come the next day, either. Maybe, she thought, he hasn't got a quarter for bus fare. He could walk, of course. It was barely five blocks, half a mile. But then, he never exerted himself—except in bed—unless he absolutely had to. This reminded her that he was penniless, and that blood tests, a license, and a ring would cost money.

Never mind, she could work that out. The main thing was to tell him right away, so he could share it with her.

She wondered how long it would be until a doctor could be sure. There was something called a rabbit test—but that would cost money, too. She was engulfed in the same feeling that had overcome her the day her purse was stolen—the sense of being alone, friendless and penniless in a big unfeeling city.

Around ten o'clock a tap at the door broke into her worry, and she hurried to open it, weak with relief. But it was the janitor, Rocco, who stood there. For a moment she was dumb with surprise, she had been so sure of Alan. Rocco grinned uncertainly. "I just think I'll come up and see if everything is okay up here, huh? You warm enough? Everything all right?"

"We're fine, thanks."

"The pretty young lady, I don't see her for a while. She's not move out, no?"

"Thanks," Annice said dryly. "She's all right." She shut the door gently but definitely, and went back to her cupboards, diverted.

Now that she thought about it, Barby was hardly ever home any more. She had been gone most of the time, herself, and she had assumed that their hours just didn't coincide, but it had been—how long—a week or ten days?—since she had seen Barby except in the early morning. She supposed Barby had left a ring or handkerchief in the basement when she went down to do the laundry. Nice of him to think about it, but she didn't like the man. He was good-looking enough, but there was something—

She stood shivering in the fall air, which was a mixture of sunshine and coal smoke and the smell of frying fish from next door. The emptiness and silence of the apartment were getting on her nerves. So far as she could remember, she had never spent two days alone and at home, before. Summer vacations on the farm had been full of housewifely activity in her mother's company—canning, cleaning house, processing fruit and vegetables for the freezer, making drapes and slip covers. She slammed the window down and decided that there was really no reason for not going to Alan's place and having it out with him. I'll get this settled right now, she resolved.

She changed her pedal-pushers for a dress, obscurely wanting to look her best—*see, you're getting a wife you don't have to be ashamed of*—and brushed her hair. She looked all right, and that was reassuring. *Maybe I'm all right,* she thought, tying a ribbon around her head. *Maybe it's a false alarm, after all.*

But she knew it wasn't.

She walked the five blocks quickly, feeling light and free now that her mind was made up. The fog had lifted and the sun was shining; it was one of those clear, crisp late-fall days that make the heart beat faster. She smiled at groups of children playing on the sidewalk. *Poor kids, they shouldn't have to live on concrete walks and vacant lots. I'll raise mine in the country. Or anyway, in a small town with yards and trees.*

Alan's door was open—it was always open, he hardly ever locked it, even when he was making love. She pushed it open and went in. He wasn't there, but that didn't mean anything. He could be at the grocery, or downstairs playing poker with the boys, or at a party, or down at the corner tavern. He could be and probably was out trying to chisel five bucks off one of the characters he knew. He could even be in bed with somebody else, since he hadn't had her for two whole days. She was obscurely comforted by the thought that anyway, he wasn't making love to some other girl in the bed where they had been so happy together.

She threw her coat across the one chair, and sat down on the bed to wait for him.

It was perhaps five minutes, perhaps ten, before she realized that something was wrong. Something had been subtracted from the clutter. Vaguely alarmed, she got up and prowled around the room. Alan's undershirts and jockey shorts, mismated socks and blue shirts were gone from the dresser drawers. His suntans, corduroy pants and the one pair of tweed slacks were no longer hanging in the closet. The duffle bag and beat-up suitcase she had looked at without really seeing them every time she opened the closet door were gone too. One crumpled sock lay under the hanger bar. In the top drawer of the dresser a few shreds of tobacco and a torn handkerchief were the only indication that he had ever lived there.

The saucepan and plate had been tossed into a corner of the room.

She began to shake.

Jenni was at the telephone, talking softly and emphatically with a hand cupped around the mouthpiece, when she let herself out. "Where's Alan?" His eyebrows shot up. "Oh, he went. Last night. He went to Mexico, I think," Jenni said. His eyes were gay, his mouth twitched. He said to the telephone, "Just a moment, darling, I have another woman here," and turned to her. "Some magazine bought an article from him, maybe. Can I do anything for you?"

"No. No, never mind."

She was halfway down the block before she realized that she had left her coat in that place. The cold wind, blowing through her thin dress and forcing itself upon her abstraction, was like a knife. But she walked on, stumbling over cracks in the sidewalk, ignoring traffic when she came to a crossing, half-blind and wholly deaf with shock and anger. "The bastard," she said aloud. "The low bastard." A drunk grinned at her, lurching by.

She heard the telephone ringing before she unlocked the apartment door. Her heart expanded, growing soft with relief. *I'll go with you,* she promised silently, running to answer. *I'll live anywhere you want to, on any terms you like.*

It was Barby, calling to say she would be late getting home. Annice hung up and stood for a long time beside the telephone table, looking at nothing.

CHAPTER NINETEEN

Barby had known this would be the day, even before she was out of bed. She woke with a feeling of bright anticipation, like the expectant tingle a child feels on Christmas morning—a feeling of happy, calm assurance that was not excitement, but pure joy. Pouring coffee, too pleased to be hungry, she thought, *It has to happen today, it simply has to. I'm ready for it.*

It was the first time in her life she had ever been sure of anything good.

They had lunch together in the candle-lighted hideaway that had become their special secret place. It warmed Barby to enter the small, smoky room, dim after the sunshiny street, and cross to the corner table where they had sat the first day. When someone else was there first, her pleasure was flawed. Today the table was empty, as she had known it would be, and she hung her coat and Ilene's on the old-fashioned rack in the corner and sat down, smiling across the checkered cloth. "I love this place."

"The trouble is that we haven't long enough to talk." Ilene moved the silver at her place, then moved it back again. "I've been wondering. Would you like to come up to my apartment this evening? It's rather nice—and I do have a fireplace, and we'd be free from interruptions." She bent her head to examine the spoon. "We could have a real visit."

"I'd like to."

"Do your roommates ask questions if you're late?"

"No. They quite often stay out late themselves. It's funny," Barby said thoughtfully, "but the longer we live together, the less we seem to have in common. I suppose eventually we'll all know different people."

"I suppose it's cheaper, sharing a place?"

"Partly. And then partly, our families all know each other. That's one reason they let us come, because we were going to live together and they thought we'd sort of check up on each other. That shows how much parents know."

"But you don't have to stay together."

"Oh no. We'll split up, sooner or later. Annice is sure to get tired of running around and get married, one of these days. Pat, too. She's the kind to settle down and have one of those big Catholic families."

"You're not thinking of marriage?"

Barby said low, "No. Never. I told you before, I hate men."

"I'm not going to ask you any questions, who hurt you or how," Ilene Gordon said. She reached across the table and laid her slender, well-manicured hand on Barby's. The touch tingled up her arm. "I've learned not to ask questions. The past doesn't matter for people like you—and me."

"No."

Ilene straightened up. She smiled. "Well then, you will come up this evening, won't you? Around seven, maybe? It's better if we don't go home together."

"Of course. I can take the subway."

"Take a taxi. Here, I'll give you money for it."

Barby took the dollar slowly, folded it differently from her other money and put it in the back of her billfold. It was good to feel provided and cared for. When she went back to the Store, too well-nourished on happiness to know or care what she had eaten, she removed the bill to an envelope and sealed it shut. *I'll keep it,* she thought, *and when I'm old it will remind me.* She knew she was being young and silly, and romantic; but it didn't matter. She felt that she had never been really happy before, in her whole life. It was like feeling well and light-bodied after a long illness.

She called to tell the girls that she would be late, not

because they would be concerned even if she stayed out all night—a thought that made her dizzy with anticipation— but because she passionately wanted everything about this to be just right, to be perfect. Annice was at home, as she had expected. She sounded tearful. Damn the girl, Barby thought, she used to be so steady and reliable, and ever since she quit going to school she hasn't cared about anything. Half the time she doesn't even show up for that crummy two-bit job. It's that bearded bohemian character she runs around with, that comic-book character. I wouldn't trust him around the corner. She turned away from the telephone, her good mood shattered.

Forget about it. Forget everything, she told herself, except the work you're doing. She couldn't think about the evening ahead; it was too bright; it dazzled her inner sight.

The twilight street was delicately dusky when she emerged into it, and a light snow was falling. It blurred the outlines of the tall buildings and put halos around the street lights. The first snow of winter. She smiled self-consciously, knowing it would turn to a dirty mush as soon as it reached the sidewalk, knowing she would have more than enough snow before the winter was over. She could see herself standing on a bus corner with the icy prairie wind whipping her skirts and piercing through her heavy coat; slipping on the frozen sidewalks, begging the landlord for more steam in the lukewarm radiators. This was Illinois winter, worse here than at home because of the Lake. But for a few minutes, she lingered in the muffled streets, recapturing the magic of childhood mornings when, after the dull tan monotony of autumn, she looked out at a world of pearl and crystal.

She wasn't hungry. It seemed unnecessary to eat, but she had to do something for an hour. She went into a drugstore and had coffee, drinking it slowly, watching the clock over the door. From the long mirror behind the counter her reflection looked back at her, wide-eyed and pink-cheeked.

I want to remember every detail of this, she thought, hailing a cab. *The feel of the upholstery and the driver's face and the way the store windows look through the falling snow. I want to remember it as long as I live.*

Ilene's neighborhood was expensive-looking. The strips of lawn between sidewalk and apartment buildings were manicured; the cars at the curb were of two kinds—small, smart and foreign, or large, smart and impressive. She walked across the lobby, heels clattering on the marble flooring, and was wafted up by a sallow elevator boy in a skintight uniform and a chestful of ribbons. Then she forgot to be impressed with the aura of money and splendor, because Ilene was at the door, waiting for her.

She wore Bermuda shorts, with knee socks and sandals; her short hair was ruffled, and she held a thin-stemmed glass. Her hands were warm on Barby's. "I'm glad you could come. Come in and see my place."

It was the sort of apartment Barby had learned to appreciate during her noonday prowlings through department stores and specialty shops. A step led up to the living room, which was long and narrow, decorated all in white and warmed by the jackets of books and the soft glow of a blaze in the fireplace. She stood before it, hands spread wide. "A real fireplace, imagine," she said, and Ilene laid a light hand on her shoulder and said, "Yes, it's marvelous for conversation." The sofa was wide enough for five people and the coffee table that stood in front of it held an elegant service in crystal and silver, glittering in the firelight. The shelves held books, Wedgewood and Spode plates, odd bits of silver. Two china dogs sat at the ends of the mantel. "Staffordshire," Ilene said, turning one of them over in thin, nervous fingers. "See the marking?"

"Is it all yours? I mean, did it come this way?"

A shadow crossed Ilene's face. "I furnished it six years ago with the girl who left to get married."

"I'm sorry."

"Never look back," Ilene said. She replaced the china dog. "Six years is a long time; keep looking ahead."

Barby could accept that. *If I could cut off the past right now,* she thought, *and be born fresh!* Ilene smiled. "You learn to remember the good things, but that takes time. Come on, I'll show you the rest."

There was a tiny dining room. "Silly, because it's too small for guests and we hardly ever used it when we were alone. I like it, though. Leila made the chair seats." She touched the petit point caressingly, and Barby felt a pang of jealousy for the unknown Leila. They moved into the bedrooms, one large, decorated in blue and pale green, with a handful of detective stories on the bedside stand and a row of tailored clothes in the closet; one small, bare, with a single bed. The immaculate bathroom, with a blue and green dressing table. And the small kitchen, best of all, with copper pans hanging on the wall and a shelf of spices in decorated jars. "Best room in the house," Ilene said. She measured coffee into the drip pot, set out a coffeecake, and then, hesitantly, took down a small squat bottle. "Kümmel. Ever drink any? It tastes like hell, but it makes you feel all warm and cozy inside."

The drink relaxed Barby, took away the last lingering bit of self-consciousness. They sat at opposite sides of the linen-covered table. "This is a wonderful room."

"It's the main reason I don't want to sublet. But this place is too big for me alone."

"Can't you find someone to share it?"

"It would have to be someone special—who meant a lot to me, personally. I don't believe in grieving for the past. One has to move ahead." She poured coffee into a heavy pottery cup, set it in front of Barby. Her hand trembled a little.

"I'm a very direct person," Ilene said. "I don't finagle around and try to put over a deal—not where my personal life is concerned." She looked at Barby, the long straight look that had melted her heart the first day, as if she could see through her eyes and into her mind. "You're very young."

"Not that young," Barby said low.

"I don't know if you even know what I'm talking about."

"I've known for a long time."

"You don't have to commit yourself to anything. I want you to think it over. But—will you stay here with me tonight?"

Barby's heart missed a beat, then righted itself. She waited a moment, to be sure her voice was steady. "Yes," she said. She reached across the table and laid her hand on Ilene's. "Yes. I've been wanting you to ask me that."

Much later, when they stood together at the bedroom window, watching the soft flakes of snow drive against the glass and shatter, she said, "It's what I've wanted, all my life. How can anybody want a man, when there's this?"

Ilene held her close. "Don't be sorry."

Just before she fell asleep she thought about Rocco and the basement room; and then, dimly of something farther back and more dreadful. But it was all far away, like a dream already dissolving. The experience of this night had washed away all the hurt and terror of it. Nothing could hurt her any more. She fell asleep in the circle of Ilene's arms, safe.

CHAPTER TWENTY

Pat wasn't interested in kids, even good-looking kids. Her heart belonged to Blake Thomson, firmly and steadfastly. This part-time clerk who kept pestering her for a date was nothing but a boy—twenty—still in school—sophomore at Roosevelt—and not so very well-heeled—part-time worker, and probably paid board at home. He looked like the kind of boy who would pay board. Six foot tall and football shoulders; so what? She said, "Good morning," coldly, and waited for him to go away.

He leaned on the edge of her desk, stooping to her from his superior height. I am not interested in children, she reminded herself firmly, recognizing the dating gleam in his eyes. She felt a moment's nostalgia for Johnny Cutler and the days of their courtship, uncomplicated by anything more than the usual passes and negotiations between young adults of different sexes.

"What do you do evenings?"

She doodled on a scratch pad. "I wash my nylons."

"Oh." He smiled. "I bet you don't even know my name."

"Why should I?"

"No reason. I looked you up in the payroll file. Patricia Callahan. You're eighteen. Your birthday is in June. You get seventy bucks a week."

"Oh, really. Nothing about me," Pat said icily, "is any business of yours."

"You're too young to be so narrow-minded."

"I am not narrow-minded. I'll try anything once. Almost anything, I mean."

"Okay. How about a show tomorrow night?"

She looked around for a door to the trap, and found none. "Well. All right." After all, she reasoned, he's not asking me to sign a lifetime contract. It's a long time since I had a date—August, and this is November. She smiled suddenly, not the wistful smile she had been trying to cultivate but the old Pat grin, with teeth. "All right. What time?"

"Oh—seven. Pick you up at your place."

He got down off her desk and went back to unpacking office supplies. She couldn't help noticing how easily he lifted the big cartons and how deftly he pried out the staples and untied string, but when he turned back to look at her, she was concentrating on her work. Nor would she have admitted that after he left for his afternoon classes she looked him up in the payroll file—*turn about's fair play,* she defended herself. Stanley Wyrzykowski, twenty years old, fifty dollars for a thirty-hour week. She figured that he made about the same as she did, hour for hour. She wouldn't have liked going out with a boy who made less—it made him seem unimportant. She put the folder back, guiltily, as Miss Miller came in on rubber heels.

It was good to be dressing for a date. She went home fifteen minutes early to escape the rush, both on the I.C. and in the bathroom. Annice came in while she stood undecided before a row of new dresses, mostly not paid for. "What's the matter, got so many clothes you can't make up your mind?" The overdue rent and unpaid grocery bill were implicit in her tone.

She thought she looked rather nice. She had the right hairdo and the right lipstick, and she had dieted off twelve pounds. Stan whistled when she came to the door. "You look good. Wyrzykowski can pick girls."

He was all dressed up—good gray suit, quiet tie, well-shined shoes. She introduced him to Annice proudly. You could see that his mother had brought him up right. Probably her mother would go for him in a big way, even with a name like that. She asked abruptly, "Are you Catholic?"

"Sure, what else would I be? I don't go to Mass as often as my mother thinks I should, though. You know how Polish Catholic mothers are."

"I know how Irish Catholic mothers are," Pat said grimly.

She thought, *It's a good thing mom hasn't seen this kid, she'd have the bridesmaids all picked out.* She held her full skirt up daintily, following him down the uncarpeted stairs. That crumb, Rocco, was lurking in the lower hall. He turned away without speaking when he saw them.

It was a cold night, with a snowy wind. Chill air crept in around the joints of Stan's Volkswagen. "Little bit cold," he said. "The heater's good, though. By and large it's a pretty good car." His tone was affectionate. He helped her in, slamming the door twice to make it stick shut. "I got tickets for *My Fair Lady,*" he said casually, looking sidewise at her to see if she appreciated his achievement.

"Oh, that's wonderful."

And she was pleased. To be going to a big downtown theater with this polite good-looking boy, to see a highly advertised play—this was fun. She had almost forgotten how much fun it was. After they seated themselves in the big auditorium, and he helped her off with her coat, she slipped her hand into his. His fingers tightened on hers, but his profile, stern and serious, was intent on the stage. She giggled. It was like the old days—fun, and she could handle him if he got fresh, because he was like the boys she had gone with in high school.

Then she forgot him and lost herself in the play, the first live production she had ever seen. *Who'd have thought I'd ever go without a date four whole months?* she marveled. Nobody wants to go with a bunch of girls, like the older women you find in every office who flock together and never have dates, but think they're having a big evening when they dress up for each other and go to the show together, with maybe a soda after. She had seen them, looking wistfully at couples. She was so thankful to be spared this fate that she leaned against Stan, and he put his arm around her shoulders. She settled down into it naturally, not diverting her attention from the stage but aware of the shattering warmth in the background of her thoughts.

They came out into lighted streets and talking crowds. Pat blinked. Stan said, "What would you like to do now? Like something to eat?"

"Not really. I'm too fat now."

"You're too thin. Look good with a little meat on your bones." He looked her over, not unkindly, but appraisingly. "Like to go for a ride? I put in all day Sunday overhauling the heap. It runs pretty good."

Barby's friend Jonni was right—city or country, they were all alike. She had two ones in her billfold, emergency money, just in case—not that she didn't trust Stan, but on general principles. He was a nice boy, but the nicest boy in the world doesn't just want to sit around and talk after he's spent his money on a girl. "Let's not go too far," she said, with a double meaning.

Stan grinned. "I won't go any farther than you want me to. That's a promise."

They drove south and turned into a little park—the same park where Alan and Annice had gone on their first date. Other cars stood beside the curving drive, parking lights glowing dimly. Stan turned off the motor. "Sounds pretty good. If I had the time and the dough I'd give her a complete overhauling." He sounded proud, like a little boy with a new baseball bat. She said, "It's a nice car."

He lit a cigarette. His hand shook a little, which reassured her. She looked at him, smiling a little. He put a tentative arm across her shoulders, and she relaxed into it.

Next the kiss, she thought, and was ready for it when it came, a brush of the lips across hers. She remembered Johnny Cutler and the long, moist kisses that had held them spellbound for hours, parked on back roads, longing to go farther but afraid to.

Stan said huskily, "You know something? I noticed you the first day I came into the office. I thought, there's a girl I'd like to go out with."

That was a lie, of course, because if he had noticed her at the beginning of the school term in September he wouldn't have waited until November before asking for a date. But it was a good polite lie and she accepted it at its face value. He kissed her again, and this time it had more authority in it. She reminded herself that at a certain point she'd have to start objecting—still, that point hadn't been reached yet, and in the meantime she was having a kind of fun she'd almost forgotten. She snuggled closer.

"No kidding, I didn't have the nerve to ask you before. I figured a girl as good-looking as you would have a dozen fellows."

"How do you know I haven't?"

"Hope you haven't anyhow. I'd like to see more of you."

She couldn't decide whether that was a crack or not, and let it pass.

He held her closer, and this time his free hand reached for the buttons at the front of her dress. His fingers, chilly from the night air, slipped inside her neckline. She felt an instant and perilous response and moved away a little. He said, "Aw, don't be like that."

A car turned in behind them. He let her go, and they sat upright without speaking until it passed and drew off to the side of the road. Smoochers, not cops. This time he tried another attack—standard approach number two, starting from the bottom. He slid a hand under her skirt, not high enough for her to object but high enough to feel the soft flesh at the top of her stockings. He moved the hand a little higher, and she pushed it away. He tried it again.

They're so unoriginal, Pat thought, pushing his hand away and wrapping the skirt of her coat around her legs. *If they don't try, then your feelings are hurt and you go home and look in the mirror to see what's the matter with you. If they do, then you have to keep fighting them off.* She said, "Don't get rough, son."

Presumably some time you wouldn't want to keep fending a boy off, and then you crossed the line dividing good girls and bad girls, as ruled off by your mother when you were about twelve. It wasn't so bad to go all the way with a man you loved, or thought you did. In the moral code of her mother and most of the girls she knew, it was taken for granted that young people are subject to temptation and that it isn't really so bad as long as they get married in the church at least six months before the baby comes, and lead sober hard-working lives forever after. You didn't take chances with a married man or anybody who couldn't or wouldn't marry you, if that became necessary. And you certainly didn't go all the way with a man on your first date. She said, "Don't be fresh."

He said, "Aw, don't be that way." If you were a decent fellow you didn't force a girl, especially if you thought she might be a virgin. Never start a girl. You wanted to, of course; when you got hot for a girl you sort of forgot about everything else, and if a girl let you go too far then, well, you couldn't blame a fellow for the way he was made. Girls were supposed to know that.

He said, "I didn't mean to be fresh. I think you're a swell girl, and it's been a wonderful evening."

She said, "It had been nice, hasn't it? Only I ought to go home pretty soon. We both have to work tomorrow."

"Okay." But he kissed her again, instead of starting the car, and this time it was a real kiss. She collapsed against him, hanging on to him with both hands. He put his hand up inside her skirt, feeling her shallow excited breathing against the front of his shirt. Goddam panty girdle in the way. He stretched the lastex edge, making the kiss last to distract her attention from his maneuverings.

"Looking for something?"

"Oh, hell."

She wriggled out of his grasp and sat up, arranging her dress modestly. "I'm sorry. I'm not that kind of a girl."

"None of 'em are." He reflected bitterly that no girl ever admitted that she wanted to make love. Even when they were undressed and in bed with you, moaning with pleasure and biting and scratching—like that little bitch from the Art Institute he'd gone with for a while—they always talked like it was all your idea and they were pushed into it. They only girl he had ever known who frankly wanted it was a kid back in high school—in fact, she suggested it, on the way home from a dance, and he was so startled he was afraid for a while he wouldn't be able to do anything.

He swallowed. "I'm sorry. You can't blame me though, can you?"

"I guess not." She sounded small and timid. "I like you, too. Only I don't want to start something we're not going to finish."

"We could finish it," he suggested.

"No."

She meant it. He kissed her again, lingeringly, and started the car.

She peeked at him to see if he was angry. He didn't seem to be. He seemed to think that was the right way for her to act. If she'd said yes, he wouldn't have liked her nearly so well after he cooled off. This way, he would ask her out again—and try again, too.

Besides, she admitted to herself, she was scared. Suppose you got caught, or suppose it wasn't as wonderful as you thought it was going to be?

"Come on in when we get home; we'll make some coffee."

"Sure, that would be fun."

The lights were on and the radio was giving out rock and roll, so they went in. Annice came out of the bedroom to meet them. She had been crying again, and her face was pasty. Pat made a mental note to ask a few tactful questions after Stan left. She wasn't sure where the line was between being friendly and interfering, but now that she stopped to think about it, Annice had been acting depressed a lot lately. She stayed home a lot, and she hadn't mentioned Alan. Pat hoped that they'd quarreled; she thought, No good can come to her running around with that crumb, and looked at Stan with new regard.

It wasn't until he had gone home and she'd washed the cups and plates that she remembered Blake Thomson. She curled up under the half-cotton blanket and settled down to the fantasy of love that had become a nightly habit, and then it occurred to her that she hadn't given him a thought all evening. She felt shocked, as though she had caught herself in some disloyalty.

But it wasn't Blake Thomson's face that glimmered through the closing fog of sleep. Drowsy in spite of unfulfilled desire and two cups of coffee, she thought about Stan Wyrzykowski's hand on her leg, under her skirt, and in half-sleep she felt the rise of the response and stirred and smiled.

CHAPTER TWENTY-ONE

It was no day for unhappy errands. A thin rainy snow fell
and melted as soon as it reached the sidewalks, and the
crossings were slushy and gray. The wind whined around
corners and reached inside the neck of Annice's thin coat
as she walked, head bent against the blow. She shuddered.
Maybe I'll die of pneumonia, she thought, reaching a drugstore and stepping into its doorway for shelter; *maybe it
would be a good thing if I did. Solve all my problems.
Somebody else could worry about the funeral bills.*

She lifted one high-heeled sandal, then the other to
judge the damage done by melting snow. The thin soles
were soaked, her feet were wet, and a line of muddy spots
up the back of each leg marred her nylons. She tried to
wipe the spots off with her handkerchief, but it was no use;
the dirt was well mixed with city grease, and only spread
and blurred.

There was no reason she couldn't write home for her
winter clothes. No reason, that is, except this idiotic feeling that she was only safe as long as she avoided all com-
munication. The folks would see through any letter she
wrote, no matter how short and noncommittal. She knew
she was being silly. But the idea had taken a firm grip on
her, and she couldn't shake it off; every time she thought
about writing home she was convinced that she would
somehow give herself away. *Maybe it's my condition,* she
thought, *they say pregnant women get silly ideas. Or
maybe I'm going crazy. That would be a solution too—not
as good as dying, though.*

But death is so permanent, she thought with a wry
smile, forcing herself to move out of the doorway. A blast
like ice water struck her in the face, so that her eyes shut

and she staggered a little. *Oh God,* she thought, *if I ever get these clothes off and crawl into a nice warm bed I'll never ask for anything else.*

The hospital was large and dingy-looking. She stopped in front of it, knowing she had to go in but unable for a moment to lift her feet. She pulled her coat collar straight, using the glass front door as a mirror, and took off her sodden gloves. The fake wedding ring she had bought at Woolworth's suddenly looked cheap and brassy. Alan would say it was a sop to bourgeois convention—well, Alan had run out on this problem, it was all hers. *It's my baby,* she thought without humor, shoving the door open and stepping into the blessed, drug-smelling warmth of the foyer.

She had dressed herself carefully for the first time in weeks, partly for morale and partly because, when she got this life-or-death verdict from the lab, she was going to register at the State Employment Office. No matter what the rabbit said, she would have to find a job and work until she was fired. Any job. The papers said there were sixty thousand unemployed in Chicago, more being laid off every day—well, she would take anything she could get, even scrubbing floors. She twitched around the dress that was too loose, smoothed her wet hair, and hoped the shadows under her eyes made her look interesting rather than dissipated. A passing nurse looked at her curiously. She forced herself to cross the lobby, pass the receiving window and ring for the elevator.

The quiet whiteness of the lab was restful. She took her place on a bench beside an old man with crutches, and tried not to think about Alan. *The son of a bitch. All right, so an artist is above convention. What reason does he have to think he's an artist? What has he got to show for all these years of loafing? And why should an artist be different from anybody else?*

She set her chin and tried to look as if she had a right to the services of a hospital and a technician.

A few minutes later she was smiling at the nurse who stood, card in hand, smiling back at her. "I guess there's no question, Mrs. Harvey. You're about as pregnant as a girl can get. Now if you want to sign up for our prenatal clinic—oh yes, and bring your husband in the next time you come. He'll love our expectant fathers' class."

"I'd love to." She twisted her ring, trying to look as if it had initials and a date inside. "I'll talk to him about it."

"You do that. The fee is five dollars. You can pay the office on the way out."

Handing over the five, receiving in its place a small crisp slip of paper, she reflected that one crime leads to another. If she hadn't been pregnant without the blessing of church or state she wouldn't have had to take six dollars from Pat's purse. *Or if Pat didn't leave things lying around,* she thought, trying to shift the blame. Seeing it on the drainboard, with Pat's week's pay stuck in so carelessly, had been such a perfect solution to her problem that she couldn't help taking the five and the change—for bus fare. *Maybe she won't miss it,* Annice thought. *Or maybe she'll think the janitor did it.*

The employment office was crowded in spite of the cold and wet. Always people out of work, always people hoping for a better job, especially here in this neighborhood where dingy children played on the front steps of peeling apartment buildings and the neighborhood stores looked dusty and depressed. She scrutinized the waiting women, familiar types by this time. Fat middle-aged women who looked like scrubwomen and probably were. Yes, and they made more than office help—they had a union. Pretty colored girls in cheap smart clothes, their hair straightened, carrying themselves with the self-conscious independence of those whose mothers and fathers had been pushed off the sidewalks, whose grandparents had known the terror of lynching and the grind of economic slavery. Annice smiled. It made her feel good to hear their pretty soft voices and see them looking so spunky, even in the face of temporary layoffs and job discrimination.

She had less sympathy for the draggled-looking women from Arkansas and Kentucky and southern Missouri, their bad teeth and sallow skins testimony to too much fat pork and white-flour biscuits, their tired print dresses bungled together at home, their cheap run-down oxfords looking as if they would be more at home following a mule down a cotton row than on a city pavement. They came into the city by thousands with their slab-sided overalled men and snot-nosed kids, their rickety furniture piled high on trucks and old cut-down Chevies; they pushed into the garbage-smelling rat-ridden apartment houses of the South Side where their kinfolks already swarmed and went out to look for the jobs that weren't there. They would fall prey to the landlords and the installment salesmen, go hungry and try vainly to get on city relief before they piled their stuff on the old truck and turned home again, beat. With them came pellagra, head lice, illiteracy, rickets. She was sorry for them, but she couldn't feel any kinship.

Then there were young girls from the South Side, seventeen, eighteen, hard-looking, with dime-store earrings and too much rouge, their pastel jackets sewn with sequins and rhinestones, their cheap pumps shabby in the sunshine. They would work for two or three years, marry neighborhood boys and have babies. Polish, Italian, Bohemian. A thin blonde girl smiled at her, and she smiled back. These kids had troubles. They had been born when their folks were on relief; they knew what it was to be hungry, to have holes in their welfare shoes. They lived in a world too big and too complicated for them. But most of them would pull through.

And so would she.

I'm no artist, she thought, *whatever that cheap bum thinks he is. I'm like everybody else.* There was comfort in the admission. She marched up to the desk when her turn came, took card and pencil from a bored staff worker, and filled all the blanks in neatly.

"Don't call us, we'll call you."

"Okay." She stumbled over the patent-leather pumps of a tall girl in the front row of chairs. "I'm sorry."

"That's okay. I hope you find sompin'."

"I hope you do, too."

Her mind was working clearly now. The indecisions of the last few weeks were gone like a nightmare that dissipates at daybreak. This was real, this incredible thing was really happening to her, Annice Harvey. All right, she would live through it. She could work till she was at least five months along—longer, if she could convince her boss she was a widow—and then something would happen.

It's a big, rich country, richest country in the world. Nobody has to starve to death.

If this was a love story, she thought, hovering in the warm doorway, *some nice fellow would come along and marry me and everything would come out all right in the last chapter. But that doesn't happen in real life.*

Or does it?

Her mouth fell open. Actually. She stopped short, and an old woman who had been hobbling along behind her stopped, too, and gave her a sharp curious look before she hitched on past. Annice ignored her. Dime—she was sure she had a dime. Clutching it in nervous-sweaty hands, she riffled through the phone book, then shut herself into the pay booth at the entrance to the agency.

"Yes, I know he's in class. I know it. All I want to do is leave a message. Tell him Miss Harvey has to see him." She stopped, hearing her voice shrill with urgency, and swallowed. The small tinny voice at the other end said something she didn't understand. "Tell him I said it's urgent, of the greatest urgency. Tell him it's Annie."

She lifted her chin, going out into the snowy afternoon. Cold flakes drove down her neck, and her feet were cold. She ignored it.

He would be over tonight, curious, if nothing more. She would have to plan everything before she saw him, or she would never be able to go through with it. Honest or not, fair or not, this was a thing she had to do. She quickened her step, splashing through the puddles.

CHAPTER TWENTY-TWO

"Jackson, it's so good to see you."

"Good to see you too, Annie—Annice. I've been missing you."

She laid her hand on his arm. "Come on in, why don't you? I'm sorry Pat's out right now, she'll be sorry she didn't see you." She reflected grimly that she had had a hell of a time getting Pat out of the apartment; she was all set, in duster and flats, for an evening of mulling over the travel folders that were her newest interest, and she was mad as a hornet because someone had lifted five dollars from her purse. She hadn't, apparently, missed the small change. Annice had covered up pretty well.

"Gee, I'm sorry, I forgot to put the latch on when I went out this morning. Do you suppose they took anything else?"

"The silverware isn't worth bothering about. Why do you suppose they took five and left the rest?"

"Maybe whoever did it thought you wouldn't notice. Anyhow, would you mind getting out and staying out for a while? I have a man coming up."

"Alan?"

"No, Alan and I are all washed up."

"Thank goodness. Is this anybody I know?"

"Jackson Carter. Remember old Jack?"

"Sure, he brought me home from a party once. I didn't know you'd been seeing him."

Annice said, praying for patience and the grace to tell a good long string of lies so they would sound like the truth, "More or less. I have feeling maybe he's getting serious. Anyway, he's a lot nicer than I ever used to give him credit for. Give me a break—I'll do the same for you some time."

"Fat chance I'll ever need it."

"Why don't you start going out with some nice fellow? Like that cute Stan, or somebody?"

"Children bore me," Pat said loftily. But she got up, groaning, and put her office dress back on and went out, still complaining, to the movies. Annice wiped her sweaty palms on the sides of her skirt and took a deep relieved breath. Everything was going to be all right. It had to be.

So here was Jack, looking better than she remembered. Now that he was actually in the house she was light-headed with release from tension. She heard herself burbling. "You knew Barby moved out? Sure, a couple of weeks ago. She went in with some girl she knows at work. She's had a raise, too; they're letting her do some selling, like on Saturdays." She smiled up at him, a little frightened by his size and solidity and the direct gaze of his honest blue eyes. Think about the Salvation Army and the Florence Crittenton Homes, she admonished herself. Think about the hospital bills and the charity wards, and how they treat kids in orphanages. You can spend the rest of your life making it up to him. He'll never know the difference.

She said, "I've missed you." That was a mistake; she'd said it already. The trouble was that she didn't know where to begin. She had it all planned—after a certain point. What held her back was not knowing how to reach that point. Her experience with Alan offered no clue, because he was always ready to jump into bed; and in his sex life, as in all of his dealings, he was dedicated to the principle that the straight line is the shortest distance to anywhere. She said breathlessly, "Sit down, I'll put on the coffee."

She felt easier with her hands occupied. Jack sat on the davenport, smoking thoughtfully, looking at her. When she came back to sit beside him he moved over, politely, to make room. She thought, *Oh, hell.* "Coffee won't take long, it's a good percolator. What's been happening to you?"

"Nothing much. I got two A's in my term exams."

"But that's wonderful."

"I've been planning to call you," Jack said gravely, dropping the term exams into the limbo of social topics. "I've been worried about you."

"How silly. I'm fine."

"You don't look fine. You've lost weight, and your eyes are different."

There was a small silence.

"I bumped into this fellow I used to be in class with, the other day," Jack said doggedly, "and he got off some cracks.

I hit him. I guess I shouldn't have." His face got red. "He's some kind of a refugee, he looks hungry all the time and I guess maybe he is, but he made me mad. He used to live in the same building with that crumb, Alan." There was no way out of it; he looked around, but nobody appeared to help him out. "He said some pretty dirty things."

Jenni, God damn him. Abstractedly, she saw that the percolator had stopped bubbling. She got up, filled two cups, added sugar and canned milk to Jack's, and sat down again—not on the davenport beside him, but in a stiff straight chair. She took a sip of coffee. "What he said was true," she said loudly. "I used to stay up there with Alan all the time."

"I don't believe it."

"You better. It's true." She was afraid to look at him. She stared into her cup. "I can't believe it myself, now—I keep wondering why I was such a sap. But it's true all right. I'm going to have a baby. That's why he went to Mexico."

"Why, the low son of a bitch."

"It was my fault. I knew he wouldn't marry me, he didn't believe in marriage. We used to fight about it all the time," Annice said with a faint smile. She set her cup down, rattling in the saucer, and stood up. "You know why I asked you to come over tonight? I was going to get you to marry me. I had it all planned out, I was going to get you to make love to me, and then later on I was going to tell you I was in trouble and ask you to marry me."

"And leave me with some other guy's baby," Jack said harshly. All the color drained out of his face. "You sneaking little bitch."

She trembled. "I guess I thought you wouldn't let me down, later. I was going to worry about that when I got to it."

He looked strangely at her. "What made you change your mind?"

"I don't know. Well, I didn't know how to get you started."

"Annie, for Christ's sake, how many men have you slept with?"

"Just him. Getting him started was no problem, though."

"You didn't really think you could go through with it, did you?"

"I thought I had to." The dreadful pallor was vanishing; he looked more like himself, and she began to relax. This was Jackson. Now there was no plot between them, she could talk to him—and how she needed somebody to talk to! She sat down again and looked at him, square and honest. "I'm pregnant with this baby and I'm going to have it. It belongs to me. I won't put it in any stinking old orphanage, either. And I won't have an operation, so you don't need to bring *that* up. I haven't got any money, anyhow."

Jack asked mildly, "How are you going to raise this kid?"

"I've got my name in at the employment office. I'll find something any day now."

"And I suppose you're going to strap it on your back, like a papoose, and carry it to work with you."

"Oh God," Annice said, "I'm too tired to think that far ahead. Just let me take one thing at a time, will you? Other people get along, young widows and all, their husbands get killed in accidents. How do you suppose they manage?"

"So now you're a young widow."

"Well, if you think I'd get along any better single, in my condition—"

Jack took a deep breath. He brought his cup over to the table and set it down beside hers. His hands were shaking. "You've got it all figured out, haven't you?"

"I've been doing a lot of thinking."

"I bet you have," Jack said dryly. "Annie, was there anything the matter with him? I mean, any reason a kid of his wouldn't be okay?"

"Like was he diseased, or something?"

"Oh, God, no. I meant, anything a child would inherit?"

"Well," she said, "he was smart enough. He didn't always act like he had much sense, but then, neither did I. I think it's mostly the way you bring up a child that matters, not what he inherits. And believe me, I'm going to bring this one up to be a good man—even if it kills me."

"How?"

"I told you I don't know yet. But I'm smart and healthy."

"I like kids," Jack said. "Makes no difference what kind of kids they are." He pulled out a crumpled pack of cigarettes, took one out, looked at it carefully, then put it back again. "I'm quitting school in June," he said. "Going home to help my brother run the place. The old man's got to have a hernia operation—he'll have to take it easy for a while. He's not so young."

"I'll miss you."

"God damn it, you don't make it easier for a man, do you?" He took the cigarette out again, looked at it, and decided to try it this time. "I don't know why I'm doing this. I'll probably be sorry afterwards. The point is, if you still want to marry me I'll take you along when I go. Nobody needs to know when it was." He narrowed his eyes. "And get this straight, if I ever catch you looking at another guy after we're married I'll beat the living daylights out of you."

"I'd hate you if you didn't."

"How about it?"

"It's a lousy idea. One of the worst ideas I ever heard in my whole life. Every time you got mad at me you'd bring it up. Besides, how do I know you wouldn't hold it against the baby?"

He shook his head. "I wouldn't do that. I'm not saying we wouldn't ever fight. Sure, I guess most couples have some grudge they save up for when they're mad at each other. If it isn't religion it's families or something. I wouldn't take it out on an innocent kid, though. Besides," he said reasonably, "if you hated it too much you could always divorce me, after."

"Oh no. If I go into this it'll be for keeps."

"Okay, then. Give me a kiss and we'll be engaged."

They kissed. He said, "See how easy it is to get a man riled up?" and kissed her again, harder. At that moment the door buzzer sounded. Jackson said, "Saved by the bell," and went to answer it, with Annice a step behind him. A small red-haired woman with familiar features stood in the lower hall, looking around dubiously; behind her, a burly weatherbeaten man, in a pretty good topcoat. Annice shrieked, "Hey!" and flew to them.

"Your mother got a little worried because you didn't write," her father explained, "so we thought we'd come in and see what kind of a place you girls have got here. Brought your winter clothes along. It gets kind of quiet around the place with just us old folks." He followed them into the living room, dropped the suitcase, and looked around. *Plainly,* Jack thought, *looking around for the other girls and wondering what the hell was going on.*

"It's my fault, Mr. Harvey. Annice was scared to tell you—afraid you might be mad at her. We've been married—how long is it now, honey?"

"Seven weeks," Annice said calmly. She reached past him and fished the dime-store ring out of the fruit dish, slipping it on her finger to the astonishment of the other three. "We were just waiting to find a place of our own and go to keeping house. This is Jackson Carter, mom, dad. His folks have a place in Missouri."

I'll be damned, Jackson thought, motioning his amazed in-laws to chairs while Annice darted to take down cups and pour coffee. Wifeliness sat on her like an apron, cut and stitched to measure. *Women are sure enough devious. I'll never be able to put anything over on her.* His grin broadened. "Here," he said bossily, "I'll take another cup myself while you're at it."

Annice said meekly, "Of course, dear." She filled his cup first, skimping on her mother's and father's. Over Mrs. Harvey's head their eyes met, and he had to tuck in the corners of his mouth to keep from laughing out loud.

CHAPTER TWENTY-THREE

Dreams are crazy things. Robert Morrison sat on the side of his bed, one hand still holding the just-throttled alarm clock, trying to piece together the splintering fragments of his night-time fantasy. Not that it meant anything, of course. He didn't have any faith in all that psychological stuff; nothing could convince him that people, normal decent people like himself, were as dirty-minded as Freud and those fellows insisted. He was just curious about his dreams, like anybody else.

He had been at a funeral. He could see the coffin, silver-colored and blanketed with pick carnations, standing beside the chancel railing at the First Methodist Church. Could hear the choir soprano shrilling off-key—had that been the alarm clock? His neighbors were all around him, looking at him, and there was no place to hide from their eyes.

He hadn't wanted to look at the still figure in the coffin, but he knew without seeing that Helen lay there, and that he ought to be frightened at the sight of her. Why? He couldn't tell, but a remembered horror echoed in the farthest chambers of his waking mind.

Then he was at home, in one of those sudden transitions that seem so reasonable in dreams, searching from room to room and finding nothing but silence. Outside on the street were people waiting to harm him—who? He had to keep the shades down. That was important.

A girl came out of the bedroom door. Naked. She was slender and young, with a mass of dark hair hanging to her white shoulders. She came into his arms without a word, and laid her head against his chest, and his arms tightened around her. Then—

He smiled sheepishly, remembering what had waked him. *Dreams,* he thought scornfully. *I shouldn't have eaten that last piece of pie before I went to bed; makes you dream all kinds of wild things, a bedtime snack does.* But he sat there a moment longer, hearing the reassuring housewifely thump of Helen's low-heeled shoes on the kitchen floor below.

Of course, it was easy to see how Barby got mixed up in that kind of a dream. He had been missing her, the way a father does miss a child who's away from home. The house seemed empty without her, although Helen was the sort of wife who chatters and clatters. In the vacuum left by her going he felt himself becoming the dried-up shell of a man, moving through days that had no value or meaning. Was it to go on indefinitely? How much longer could he endure it?

She hadn't even come home for Christmas, although Helen had expected her and had fixed all the traditional trappings—a special dinner, foil-wrapped gifts, baubles on an electric-lighted tree. She'd wired to say that she couldn't make it; no explanation. Helen had spent the evening of the twenty-fifth writing to her, a long prosy letter no doubt. He didn't write.

There was nothing he could say to his bright and shining girl except that he missed her, and there were no words that could convey the depth and intensity of his missing.

Four months of emptiness, a hundred and twenty-six days counting today. He had them marked off on the store calendar, on the wall of the shoe department. The days to come stretched ahead, page after barren page of them.

Barby would never have been separated from him so long of her own accord. Something was keeping her away, either this woman she was sharing an apartment with—all they knew was her name, which didn't tell a thing—or more likely her recognition of her mother's attitude. It was all wrong, whatever the reason might be. She needed him. He was the only one who could give her the guidance and affection she needed. She had never made any decisions for herself, because he had cherished and protected her.

Especially since—

It came to him, as he went about the dull business of dressing and shaving, that the things to do was go and see her. He hardly ever went to Chicago. Times as good as these, if you had a 1-A credit rating the jobbers came to you. But there was no reason why he couldn't take a day off and go, telling Helen he had to make a business trip. If she suspected that he was planning to see Barby she might want to go with him.

Just walk in, that was the way to do it, and see how she looked and where she was living, what this girl friend of hers was like. He had been opposed to the whole crazy idea of leaving home from the start—three young girls on their own, eating God-knows-what and staying out until all hours, probably. But Pat and Annice were harmless enough youngsters even if they weren't in Barby's class. Now he was afraid she might have fallen in with some immoral, promiscuous type who would encourage her to run around with men, might even introduce her to the kind of men who prey on young girls.

At the thought of a man's hands on that young body he burned with anger.

He stood with his finger on the bathroom light button, weighing the pros and cons of the rip. *Play it slow and easy,* he admonished himself. *Go and look, see which way the land lies, and then decide what to do.* By this time Barby might have had enough of independence, and be ready to come home. If not, he'd have to be careful not to antagonize her.

All he wanted—good God, all he'd ever wanted—was her happiness. He'd meet this roommate, see what kind of girl she was, and so on. A father ought to do that much.

Over bacons and eggs he said to Helen, making his voice casual, "By the way, I'm going to run in to Chicago today. There are a couple of new wholesale houses I want to check up on."

She extracted his toast from the pop-up toaster, reached for the butter. He couldn't see her face. "Will you see Barby?"

"I hadn't thought about it. She will be at work, won't she?"

A flicker of something—amusement or contempt— crossed her cheerful features and disappeared. "You might take her to lunch. I suppose she does get off for lunch. Or you could stay in and take her to dinner. I'd like to see her myself."

The skin along his neck and arms crawled with chill. This was what he had been afraid of. If she insisted on going with him, he had no defense. He said quickly, "I don't even know if I'll have time. I've got a dozen things to do. I'll phone her, though."

"Oh."

He bent over his plate. That was a close one! Now he would have to make a few business calls, maybe order some merchandise he didn't particularly need. The miles and hours that had to be traveled before he could see her stretched endlessly ahead.

All the way to the station he was terrified that she might not be willing to come home yet. He would have to find out tactfully, without sounding like a parent. Make her see that he wanted her here for her own sake.

She'd had her fling, proved that she could earn her living. That was the only reason a girl of eighteen ever wanted a job, unless she actually had to earn her own living. The little salesgirls and office clerks at the store quit as soon as they got tired of getting up early, or as soon as they could catch a man to support them.

She needed him. So pretty, so soft that men turned to look after her on the street, she was in danger all the time. And then she had those disabling headaches.

He had worked hard to build up the business; she could have anything she wanted. Clothes, parties, maybe a cruise —Helen's idea of what a young girl should have. Or if she wanted more education, there was a good junior college right here on the outskirts of Huntsville, an all-girl school—no silly adolescent boys dangling around to distract her from her studies. That was what he wanted for her, to develop her mind.

He greeted the ticket agent with more warmth than usual, even though he was a Methodist, a Lion, and a former schoolmate. "Got to see some people about business. It's a bother, but there's no help for it." He moved toward the pay telephone booth, seeing the day suddenly bright with promise and unwilling to put off any longer the delight of hearing her voice.

CHAPTER TWENTY-FOUR

Breakfast was the best part of the day. They never had it in the bijou dining room, but in the kitchen, with electric light winking off the hanging copper saucepans and the coffeepot within easy reach of the pilot light. Barby had never wanted a home of her own, thinking of it as a by-product of marriage—husband, home, and children. But now she had one, and it was wonderful.

I have everything, she thought. *A home, and love, and the chance of a raise at the Store.* More would be too much.

"I'm so happy."

Ilene said softly, "Are you, baby?"

"Yes." She turned from the stove. Ilene had on her favorite lounging pajamas, blue and gold; her eyes were sleepy and her hair tousled. Love rose in Barby. She crossed the kitchen floor and laid her head against Ilene's shoulder, too full of contentment to need words.

"Really happy?" Ilene persisted.

"I think it's the first time in my life I was ever really happy."

Ilene's arms closed around her.

Barby shut her eyes. "I love you so much," she whispered. She had never said that to anyone before. The words, hanging on the still morning air, had a perfect rightness that nothing else in her life had ever possessed.

"I love you too. All the time, not just at night. But the toast is burning." She reached to shut it off, keeping one arm around Barby. "You might rumple your bed a little. This is the cleaning woman's day."

Barby blushed. Technically, the small bedroom was hers. Her clothes hung in the closet and her cosmetics stood in tidy rows on the mirrored dressing table. But she had yet to spend a night in the single bed. She said, to cover her confusion, "We're going to be late for work."

Ilene buttered her slice of toast and sat down, pushing her cup and plate into easier reach. "We can take cabs. You can't afford to be late when you're bucking for a raise."

"Do you think anybody suspects?"

"They always do. As long as nobody can actually prove anything it's all right." Ilene tasted her coffee, added cream. "You need spring clothes. The best will come in around the middle of this month—by February everything's picked over. I'll have a couple of outfits laid away for you."

"But I want to start paying board."

"Don't worry about that."

The telephone rang. Barby jumped. "Who on earth—"

"Answer it and find out."

"I'm afraid to."

"Don't be silly. It's probably for me anyway. You didn't change your address on the payroll records, did you?"

"Then you answer."

Ilene raised her eyebrows and stepped into the living room, toast in hand. The shrilling stopped. Her voice, low-pitched and calm, reached Barby. "Hello. Oh, hello. Yes, she's right here. Just a minute, please." She put the handset down quietly. "It's your father."

The color drained from Barby's face. Her eyes widened. She put her hands behind her back, a childish gesture of refusal. "Do I have to?"

"Afraid so." Ilene made a gesture indicating, *We'll talk about it later.* She picked up the phone and handed it to Barby, who took it unwillingly.

"Don't go away."

Ilene came to stand behind her, both hands on her shoulders.

"Hello." At a standstill, she listened, looking at Ilene's

fingertips for courage. "Why, I don't know. I'll ask her." She put a hand over the mouthpiece. "He wants to take us to lunch. Do we have to?"

Ilene nodded.

"Sure, but— Well, all right, what time? No, it's against the rules. We'll meet you somewhere." She listened again, her head bent, her hair touching Ilene's right hand. "All right, we'll be there at one. I have to go to work now."

Ilene said, "You could have been politer."

"He wants us to meet him at the Brevoort, one o'clock. Some salesman took him there once and he thinks it's the absolute end."

Ilene said reasonably, "Well, it is nice. Expensive, too."

"Do we have to go?"

"You can leave five minutes early. I'll follow." Automatic caution, necessary to keep private affairs from the public. "It could be worse, you know. He could have wanted to come up here."

Barby looked around, horrified. Their home, the place where they were together with the rest of the world shut out. "You wouldn't let him, would you?"

"No." It was a complete promise. Ilene asked curiously, "Do you hate him so much?"

Barby's eyes widened. "I don't know. I've never thought about it like that." She considered. "I've been afraid of him. Because he's the only one that knows—"

"What?"

"Nothing."

Ilene patted her cheek, moved away. "Okay. Now hurry up, or you will be late."

Barby's glance at the clock was perfunctory. It struck her, however, that ten short minutes ago she had been looking at Ilene across the breakfast table, happier than she had ever been in her life—happy for the first time in her life. She thought, *I wish I could die. No, I wish he'd die. I do hate him. Why didn't I ever think about it before?*

Because you were never a real person before, a small inner voice suggested.

"You know something? I haven't had migraine since I left home. Except once."

Ilene's voice drifted back from the bedroom. "Then you better stay away."

She dressed carefully, to look older and more sophisticated than she was. The good black dress Ilene had given her, hand-hammered earrings from a little shop on Michigan Avenue, dark lipstick. Betty Pelecek took it in with one jealous look. "Man?" "A special date," Barby lied, not caring. Ilene was always mentioning that she ought to date, or pretend to date men, in order to avoid suspicion of being queer or different. Barby saw Betty's eyes widen with respect, and a feeling of cool self-assurance filled her.

Ilene passed, murmuring, "Remember, leave early. Take a cab. I'll meet you there."

Her father, waiting in the lounge at the Brevoort, looked familiar and yet strange in this setting. He stood up when he saw her, and she saw that he looked nervous. She had never seen him less than self-contained, and it gave her a feeling of mastery. She smiled at him, seeing the two of them as the onlookers must—charming young girl, attractive older man.

"I thought you girls might like a steak."

"That sounds good."

"Bet you don't get one very often."

"No, we go in more for hamburgers."

She didn't know how to tell him that Ilene wasn't a girl. A moment later the door swung open again and Ilene was there, trim and composed as always. Barby analyzed her father's expression—surprise, approval, and the fatuous wish to please of the middle-aged married man. "Well, this is mighty nice."

Ilene's glance at Barby evidently reassured her. "It's a pleasure to meet Barby's father. We think she has a real future at the Store, you know. I'm quite proud of her."

His gun knocked out of his hands, as it were, Robert Morrison was silent for a moment. Barby looked from one to the other, aware that something she couldn't follow was happening. Ilene wore her Store face—determined, thoughtful—with a social smile on top. Whatever it was, she was in there fighting.

Robert Morrison said, "Her mother and I were kind of surprised when she left the other girls. They were chums all through school, pretty much."

Ilene shrugged. "Barby's outgrown them. She has a real talent for merchandising. Inherited, maybe. She's told me what a fine business you've built up."

"Well—" Robert said. The arrival of the headwaiter saved him from having to sound modest. Barby followed him to the table, relaxing almost visibly. *It won't last much longer,* she promised herself. *One hour. You can stand anything for an hour.*

Morrison said, when he had seated them, "We've never taken Barby's job very seriously. I thought maybe she was getting enough of it, by this time."

Ilene leaned forward, smiling. "Oh, it would be a pity if she quit now. She's lucky to have such understanding parents. Such an up-to-date father." Barby ventured a look over her menu; could Ilene possibly get away with this? But his expression was pleased. "She has a real future. You're going to be proud of her."

"Her mother can't see that."

"Some women can't."

His thoughts were as plain as if they had been printed on his face in large type. This was a damned attractive woman, and she seemed to like him. Older than he'd expected, with enough experience of life and men to know a winner when she saw one. Barby turned away to hide a small smile, remembering some of Ilene's comments on the male sex. She had a good job in a Loop store, so she was smart as well as good-looking. He shifted his gaze from her face to his daughter's, and Barby gave him back a facsimile of Ilene's bright courteous smile.

You take a bunch of young kids in an apartment, away from grownups, Robert Morrison was thinking, *and the first thing you know they're running around with boys, staying out late at night and eating all kinds of crazy stuff in drugstores. But a woman like this—even if she was young enough to speed up a man's reactions—had more sense.* He smiled at her. "I feel better about Barby with you looking after her."

"Believe me, I'll take care of her as well as I can."

Barby, surveying a small bruise at the edge of her sleeve, said nothing.

He said cagily, "I suppose you two go out in the evenings, now and then? Both too good-looking to stay at home."

Ilene's eyes met his candidly. "Not very often, I'm afraid. Both of us keep pretty busy. Then too, most of the men you meet in merchandising are married—all of the nice ones are." She made it sound like a compliment to him. "I'm afraid Barby hasn't done much dating since she began work."

"Well, that's all right too. She shouldn't run around nights, wear herself out."

"How right you are."

The waiter set down their drinks. Barby seized hers and took a deep swallow, thinking, *If I can get just a little fuzzy it won't be so bad. Ilene will fix everything.*

She had never trusted anyone before.

She wasn't sure, listening to the give and take between the other two and watching her father melt into acquiescence, what she ate. The empty plate was whisked away and a dessert, sugary and elaborate, set down before her. She dabbed at it with a spoon. Through the gentle warm haze that liquor always induced in her she heard her father—like any other man, being flattered by a woman—telling Ilene in boring detail how he had built up his store, while she listened with parted lips and shining eyes. The question of her going home dropped out of sight somewhere along the way; and while she knew it would come up again, sooner or later, she felt sure that it was settled for this time.

He shook hands with them at the door. "I wish you girls would let me give you a lift back, if you really have to work this afternoon."

Ilene smiled at him. Her face must be tired, Barby thought. "Thank you so much, but I have an errand in the neighborhood."

"What errand?" Barby asked curiously when they were free again, walking arm-in-arm down the street.

"I want to buy you a flower. Not an orchid this time. Something different." A look like a caress passed between them.

Robert Morrison, looking out at the rushing streets as his car sped back to Union Station, was wondering how he had been made to change his mind so deftly. *That damn woman,* he thought, smiling pleasantly at the recollection of her admiring look. There was no question about it, he'd made a hit with her. He would have to come back soon, see how Barby was getting along. Although she'd be all right with a woman like that keeping an eye on her.

I don't suppose she sees many men, he thought. *Too*

busy making a career. Well, that's all right. I don't want Barby running around with fellows.

He hummed a little, the nameless tune that indicated he was contented.

CHAPTER TWENTY-FIVE

Weather in Chicago has its mean aspects. In summer the tar in the pavement cracks, melts and sticks to the heels of shoes, and the wind off the Lake is sticky and humid, and little typists in sleeveless dresses and flat sandals collapse quietly when they emerge from their air-conditioned offices. The heat rises in visible waves from the pavement and hits pedestrians in the face. Then in the winter it gets down to Eskimo-and-igloo temperature, and an arctic wind blows sixty miles an hour. The pavements are slick with dirty ice, and taxis turn corners on one wheel. Oil heaters set fire to slum apartments on the South Side, killing families of eleven in their sleep, and even the Loop cops with their beefy red faces look cold.

In spring and fall the wind blows, and girls walking down Michigan Avenue find their skirts whisked over their heads; debris whirls up out of the gutters and into the eyes of passers-by. And then it rains, out of a gray and chilly sky, and the El drips rusty water on everybody's shoulders, and the foyers of office buildings are crisscrossed gloomily with muddy footprints.

But in February, sometime between Groundhog Day and Washington's Birthday, the sky turns blue and the sun comes out, and the air takes on a sweet wild tang that induces romantic thoughts in middle-aged secretaries walking back from Toffenetti's after their soup-and-pie lunch. The benches on the grounds of the Art Institute fill up with unshaven thin boys and skinny girls with straight hair and those lumpy cotton knee socks. They sit with their arms around each other, looking ecstatic. This lasts two or three days, and then it snows again, but while it goes on almost anything can happen.

Pat sat at her desk in the reception room of The Fort Dearborn Press, with a pencil in her hand and a stack of copy paper so that anyone who came by would think she was working. It was the kind of day when nobody feels energetic. Pat's chignon was askew, and there was a carbon smudge on her chin. And she was tired—not tensely so, but pleasantly tired and drowsy from hard work, a relaxed mind, and the consciousness that she was on top of her job.

"My God," she said happily, "what a week! I was up till midnight every night getting Annice's stuff packed and ready to ship, you never saw so goddam much junk in your life, and she wasn't any help either. Jackson's working nights now so you might have thought she'd pitch in and help, but no, all she does is sit around and look dreamy. It wouldn't surprise me any if she's pregnant." She glanced at Phyllis and changed her mind about the next sentence. "Anybody'd think she was crazy about the country, and all I've heard out of Annice Harvey all the time we were in high school was how she hated living out in the sticks. It burns me."

Phyllis said equably, "Well, love does funny things to people." She tucked up a wisp of hair. "As long as she's happy."

"Oh, she's happy all right. It's enough to make you throw up. She hangs on every word he says."

Phyllis lit a cigarette. "How's your other friend, what's her name?"

"I don't see her any more," Pat said. "She's living up on the North Side with some girl she works with—I told you, remember? She's all wrapped up in her job. It's funny, because she always used to be a real tense, melancholy kid. I can't see her turning into one of those tailored types."

Phyllis added her smoked-out cigarette to the loaded ashtray. "Nobody ever knows what's in somebody else's mind. Everyone was surprised when I had my nervous breakdown, and I used to be a terribly moody person really."

Well, I'll be damned, Pat thought, watching her amble back to her own office with a fresh cup of coffee in one hand and a cigarette in the other, to spend the next three hours dreaming up a blurb for a new book by a Swedish existentialist. *You never know.*

Look at me, she thought suddenly. *Good old pal Pat with the balloon hips. No worries, no problems. Maybe she's right.*

She pulled open the desk drawer that held her collection of newspaper clippings. The approaching Hahn-Thomson nuptials, as the society editor of the *Sun-Times* elegantly called them, were scheduled in about ten days. The happy pair would go to Bermuda for a month, after which Mr. Thomson would resign his post as an editor with The Fort Dearborn Press and go to Philadelphia, where he would work for a major advertising agency owned and operated by a cousin of the bride. Pat had a complete collection of the articles that had appeared in the four daily papers, and had pored over them until she memorized every detail of the bride's costume at every luncheon in her honor. It was rather like biting down on a sore tooth, over and over again, but she didn't care. If she couldn't be happy she was going to be good and miserable.

Somehow, though, the last three or four weeks had taken the edge off her unhappiness. So much was happening in the actual three-dimensional world where she washed dishes and did castoffs that she had little time or energy left for emotional turmoil. Wearied by scrubbing woodwork and cleaning shelves—now that she was alone she would move into a single room—exhausted from packing and excited past relaxation by the things that were happening in the lives of her roommates, she had no chance to dwell on her own life. She fell asleep night after night almost before she could pull up the top sheet. In fact, she was finding out, as millions of other people have since the beginning of time, that it is almost impossible to earn a living and have your heart broken at the same time.

She stretched, watching the twelve-o'clock exodus; the men drifting out first, then the girls, who had to comb their hair and fix their faces before they felt ready for lunch. Sunshine poured in at the windows and lay across her desk. She put her head down and sat in a blissful half-asleep, half-awake state for a while, not really thinking of anything, but aware of the clock's ticking and muted sounds from the floor below.

After a while the door opened quietly and someone crossed the floor and stood in front of her desk. She looked up, blinking. Blake Thomson smiled at her. "Asleep on the job, huh?"

"Gee, I'm sorry."

"Don't apologize. Can't work all the time." Since his resignation had been announced he had been in the office only two or three days a week; now he looked around casually. "What a rat race this business is. Can't say I'm sorry to be getting out of it."

"We'll miss you." She felt that her whole heart showed in her eyes.

Blake Thomson sat down on the edge of her desk. "Take my advice and stay single. By the time this shindig's over I'll be a basket case."

"Worse for the bride, though."

"She seems to be enjoying it." He looked sulky. "She's in New York for a couple of days, buying frills for her trousseau. Marshall Field's isn't good enough. Leaves me at kind of a loose end." He swung one foot. "Would you care to go out to dinner tonight? Show? Or anything you want to do. Come on, be a nice kid and keep me from being bored to death."

"Why—I don't know." In all her imaginings it had never happened like this. She felt the color rise in her face.

"If you don't feel like going to a show, well, we could find something interesting to do." He laid a hand on her arm. "I'll bet you're a lot of fun when you get going."

There was no mistaking his meaning. She sat shaking and tongue-tied, unable to find an answer. This was the man she had dreamed about night after night, hoping for a miracle that would bring him to her, ready to live in heartbroken loneliness the rest of her life if he didn't love her. She had been so pleased because she hadn't gone all the way with Johnny, because it meant that she could come into his arms with all her virgin pride and purity untouched. Sure, it was corny, it was old-fashioned, it embarrassed her to think about it. The great love of a lifetime, complete with nuptial Mass and a lifetime of bliss. But that was how it was.

She said awkwardly, "You're going to be married in a week."

"Hell, what's that got to do with it? A guy's entitled to a fling before he settles down." He moved his hand to her shoulder. "I bet you'd be a nice playmate. How about it?"

She looked at him.

"Think it over," he said, "and let me know." He sauntered into his own office and shut the door, casual, not concerned about the unfinished work he was leaving behind or the unasked and unrequited devotion she had been offering him, silently, all these weeks. Or—her heart swelled with sudden pity—for the woman who was making herself beautiful to marry him.

She shook her head.

Phyllis came in and found her still looking dazed. "Good God, it's beautiful out. Makes me wish I was seventeen and in love. Hey, baby, what's the matter? You got bad news or something?"

She motioned at Thomson's closed door. "Oh, Handsome in?" Pat nodded, unable to trust her voice. She was afraid that if she opened her mouth she would burst into loud, childish, idiotic crying. Phyllis took a quarter out of her left-hand jacket pocket and dropped it into her right-hand pocket. "I win. I've been making book on you for weeks. He finally got around to it, huh?"

"How did you know?"

"Look," Phyllis said patiently, "that two-bit wolf propositions everybody. If they take him up on it, sooner or later the novelty wears off and they find themselves out on their can." Her lips thinned; her cheekbones stood out in sudden sharp relief. "Only one girl I know of who didn't get fired, and she had something on him. I feel sorry for that society babe he's hooked; she looks like a nice gal, and it's going to be an awful shock when she finds him in bed with the chambermaid or somebody on the honeymoon."

Pat said weakly, "Maybe he'll change when he gets married."

"He asked you, didn't he? Practically on the way to church." Pat nodded. "You didn't tell him you would, did you?"

Pat's look was answer enough.

"That's okay, then," Phyllis said huskily. She took a Kleenex from the box on the desk and blew her nose hard. "You'll get over it."

Pat sat staring after her retreating back. She didn't have to ask whether Phyllis had slept with him or not. You don't go on resenting a man you've turned down. All the pieces of the jigsaw puzzle fell into place—the girl who had the five-hundred-dollar abortion, the insistence on learning a skill, the contempt that was always in her voice when she spoke of Thomson, and his conciliatory and flattering air towards her. She thought, *She's gone through it too, and she knew about me all the time.* The realization was humbling, but oddly comforting.

She looked out of the window, past the serried rows of windows of the Acme Building across the street. All this man and woman stuff, people wanting each other and being disappointed, or else getting what they wanted and finding out they didn't want it after all. It's too deep for me. I better start with somebody my own size.

She felt as though she had lost something cherished, long held precious and irreplaceable—and now that it was gone, it didn't matter as much as she thought. Losing it, in fact, was rather a relief. She didn't have to polish it up and worry about it any more. She saw now that she had been hanging on to a dream that had lost its glitter.

A crush, she thought in sudden wonder, amazed at the revelation. Like the crush she'd had on Mr. Walters in high school, mooning at him all through chem lab and almost flunking his course because she couldn't keep her mind on the experiments. Then it was over, like snapping your fingers, and suddenly Mr. Walters was a small mild man with a reedy voice and a large bossy wife, who favored the prettier girls in class.

She felt good. *I ought to feel terrible,* she thought vaguely, watching the gyrations of two white pigeons against the blue, blue sky. She yawned.

I'm me, she thought, *and not no skinny society blonde with her bones showing.* She looked down with distaste at the black crepe dress. *What in God's name ever got into me? How come I've been trying to be somebody else all the time?*

Anybody that likes me from here on will have to like me the way I am.

Her feet hurt. She pulled off the black pumps with their newly smart pointed toes and thin, spindly heels. Her toes ached with pure relief. From the bottom desk drawer, where she had thrown them last fall, she took the old raffia sandals with the dancing dolls, and slipped them on.

Stan came in from lunch. She turned her biggest, brightest smile on him. "You doing anything next Sunday?" she demanded.

"Why—no. I don't guess so."

"I thought maybe we could go to Mass together, and then maybe you could help me move my stuff in your car. If you'd like to."

"Hey, that would be swell. Tell you what, I'll pick you up and you can go to church with my folks. Mom would love to meet you." He hesitated. "She's always hollering at me, I don't bring some nice girl home to meet the family."

Pat said warmly, "I'd love to."

He grinned at her. "See you later."

She was still smiling as she took the stack of galleys out of her workbasket and ranged the sharp pencils beside them. *By next week,* she thought, *he'll think it was his own idea.*

She looked down the years that stretched ahead, full of promises—love, job, marriage, children. It looked good.

Stan, she thought. Very neatly, she drew a comma and put a roof over it. It looked, she thought, like a little house.

The Girls in 3-B is part of the unofficial history of women in the 1950s. The official history is dominated by the postwar, conservative formulation of the ideal woman as the suburban housewife who found complete fulfillment in domesticity, and the teenage girl who dated frequently, guarded her chastity, and happily anticipated her future as a wife and mother in a house filled with new, labor-saving appliances. Feminist analyses of the era have also tended to perpetuate the myth of domesticity. For example, Betty Friedan's *The Feminine Mystique*, a famous and influential indictment of the suburban housewife's captivity to the domestic ideal, "reinforced the stereotype that portrayed all postwar women as middle-class, domestic, and suburban" (Meyerowitz 3). But there were many women in the 1950s who did not fit the domestic stereotype—women who were not white, middle-class, married, suburban, and happy—and their stories are being recovered by literary and social historians.

Lesbian pulp, a subgenre of pulp fiction, is one of the places where the "other" 1950s is depicted. Lillian Faderman is accurate in her assessment of the majority of pulp novels as "cautionary tales: 'moral' literature that warned females that lesbianism was sick or evil and that if a woman dared to love another woman she would end up lonely and suicidal" (146–47). But a handful of lesbian writers, including Valerie Taylor, tried to treat lesbianism sympathetically, and their work is distinct from the bulk of lesbian-themed paperbacks. Taylor's work, including *The Girls in 3-B,* her second lesbian novel, portrays the supposedly typical women and girls of the 1950s caught between the unquestioned normalcy of marriage, on the one hand, and desires that did not conform to the dominant sexual order, on the other. Her novels are populated by working women, unwed mothers, women seeking abortions, women having affairs, bohemian women, "career girls," and, of course, women who love women.

In *The Girls in 3-B,* Taylor uses the formula of three country girls coming to the big city to explore how the stereotype of domesticity impacts each girl's experience of sexuality as she moves away from a small farm town in Illinois. While each girl's story can be analyzed in detail for what it tells us about women in the workplace, class and sexual morality, and women's relationships with each other, there is also a prominent theme in each narrative. Pat's story renders a critique of sexism in the workplace and the social pressure on girls to marry young or face spinsterhood; Annice's story poses a scathing critique of the machismo of the Beat subculture, and Barby's story provides a remarkably positive representation of lesbianism for the time period, especially in contrast to the novel's relatively negative representations of heterosexual experience.

What the girls in 3-B share with one another and with many of Taylor's characters in other novels is their status as working women that share apartments or rent cheaply furnished rooms in shabby buildings where they make their coffee on hotplates. Eating out is a luxury and wardrobes are basic. They live from paycheck to paycheck, working in traditional female jobs as store clerks, office secretaries, and teachers, with little or no prospects of upward mobility. While their parents understand the girls in 3-B to be working temporarily until they get married and assume the roles of wife and mother, the girls' working and living conditions provide a realistic sense of what the job market was like for women in the 1950s.

Barby's friend Jonni, who greets the girls as they arrive in Chicago, remarks that there are "plenty of jobs around. The papers are full of unemployment, but I haven't seen any" (21). But even Pat's position at a successful publishing house pays poorly, and it is clear that jobs paying living wages are not available to the girls or to the "Negroes, hillbillies and Latin Americans" migrating to the city seeking work and that even "white-collar workers, who had a certain standard of living to maintain" are having difficulty making ends meet (30). Taylor's depiction of the labor force belies the myth of domesticity, which suggested that women in the 1950s were exiting the workforce en masse, and supports the statistics revealing that in the postwar era more women than ever were working to support themselves or to supplement the middle-class lifestyle to which so many families aspired (Eisenmann 133–141).

Of the three girls, Pat has the greatest economic need to work. She comes from a large family, and her journey to Chicago has more to do with the number of children to care for on the farm than with her own desire to explore big-city life. It is in her story that Taylor most explicitly addresses the imbalance of social and economic power between male employers and female employees, and the resulting sexual vulnerability of women in the workplace. Pat has most fully internalized the stereotype of female chastity and domesticity. Unlike Annice, who is on a mission to lose her virginity and so begin her experience of "real life," Pat is saving herself for marriage. At her job interview, though, she falls hard for her boss, Blake Thompson, a rich, socially prominent rake whose engagement to a wealthy socialite does not stop him from womanizing—and office girls are an easy target.

Pat's all-consuming crush on her boss has both economic and social ramifications. She becomes self-conscious about her corn-fed figure, wholesome prettiness, and wardrobe of slightly tattered dresses, comfortable shoes, and undressed hair. Obsessed with her appearance, she begins to remake herself from farm girl to glamour girl. Dieting and going into debt buying clothes, she falls behind on her rent payments because "she felt it necessary to be chic and well-groomed and, in a word, worthy of love" (57). Her unrequited love for her boss takes up the better part of her story, but when Thompson finally makes a pass at her, she learns from Phyllis, her coworker, the dangers of such affairs for career girls. Phyllis has already been in Pat's position, and succumbed to the temptation of an affair. She has gotten pregnant, had an abortion, and tried to commit suicide. The only reason she has not been fired, as have the other office girls who have been involved with Blake, is that she can blackmail her boss with evidence that he paid for her abortion.

Phyllis looms large as the spinster career woman. "Ruined" by her affair, jaded by her experience with Blake, she is disillusioned with love and marriage, and advises Pat that the best thing a girl can have is a skill that makes her economically independent of men. While Pat recognizes the wisdom of Phyllis's practical approach to life, she cannot imagine herself finding fulfillment in a career. Reflecting on her own obsession with Blake, Barby's moodiness about dating at all, and Annice's infatuation with Alan, Pat decides that a career could not substitute for or quell women's sexual response to men: "it was evident that most of the problems and woes of the female sex grew out of their preoccupation with men, and no salary check or nameplate on a desk was going to induce that kind of response in anyone under the age of eighty" (107).

Anxious that her future might take her down Phyllis's path, and finally aware that Blake Thompson will choose a wife according to money and social position, neither of which Pat has, she turns down the long-awaited proposition from her boss. Instead, she accepts an invitation to a date from Stanley Wyrzykowski, a nice Catholic boy whom she had previously considered a "kid" not worthy of her attention. Recalling that it's been four months since she's been on a date, she thinks with pity and dread of the older women in every office who have only each other's company for evenings out, and who can be observed looking longingly at heterosexual couples. Here, Taylor represents the enormous pressure Pat feels at the advanced age of eighteen to avoid the fate of being unmarried. Stan suddenly gains in value because he can rescue her from that fate—she is on a date, proving that she won't become one of those women (141). While Pat admits that her mother has "never seemed like a very interesting person before, although [she was] nice to have in the background and useful as a dispenser of band-aids, comfort, and spending-money" (103), she warms to the idea of what she imagines to be the security of a middle-aged housewife; if not exciting like the work at the publishing house and the attention of powerful men, it is at least not frightening.

As if she could set aside her own perception of her mother as a blank, almost invisible figure, she looks at her own future as a housewife and sees a life "full of promises—love, job, marriage, children. It looked good . . . . Very neatly, she drew a comma and put a roof over it. It looked, she thought, like a little house" (177). Here, Pat literally edits her desires so that they fit into the tidy package of domestic life.

Although Annice will also ultimately choose a life of domesticity, her story is one of disaffection from small-town values. Her exploration of the bohemian counterculture of the Beat generation can be read as evidence of "young white middle-class feminine dissidence in the 1950s" (Breines 384). Of the three girls, Annice most overtly rebels against the life of social conformity and middle-class femininity that her mother represents. She sets off for Chicago with two goals: to lose her virginity and experience real love, and to attend college only until she begins to publish her poetry. Waiting for the train, she imagines a future filled with "fascinating, *ugly* intellectual men" (5). Her focus on men, particularly ugly intellectual men, speaks to the male dominance within the bohemian subculture that Annice hopes to join. As Wini Breines explains in her article on women and Beat culture, "because Beat and delinquent subcultures were predominantly male, and often working class, and were masculine in conventional and chauvinist ways, girls' processes of identification were complex. . . . Males who were inappropriate as boy friends and potential mates and who represented an alternative to their bland teenage world played a significant role in girls' psychic lives" (385).

It would seem that Taylor writes Annice's story to expose the chauvinism of Beat culture through Alan, whom Annice's family would definitely find an inappropriate boyfriend, and whom many readers will find to be the most detestable character in the novel. He incarnates misogyny the night that Annice meets him at a college party for writers, where he picks up Annice's poetry journal and reads aloud a sonnet, deliberately emphasizing its lack of sophistication, and then turns to her and says, "A lot of bull. Why don't you women learn that your place is in bed? All this futile struggle to create, when all you're really good for is to release some man's inhibitions" (52). But his reputation as a "wolf" makes him more interesting to Annice than the well-mannered Jackson Carter, whom she promptly ditches to go home with Alan.

Annice's dismissiveness of other women at the party also reveals the centrality of the rebellious male for women in the Beat scene. Although she recognizes a slightly younger version of herself in them, she was rescued from "their look of self-depression" that is "the opposite of charm" by a fortuitous date with a football player during high school (49). She promptly learned and internalized the lessons of feminine popularity, and now she rejects the possibility of female companionship, intellectual or otherwise, that she might find among the women in the Beat scene, because she perceives them to be social rejects, "the type who failed to attract men mainly because they didn't think of themselves as desirable" (49). Annice's disidentification with Beat women means that it is not too long before Annice's involvement in the Beat subculture amounts to her involvement with Alan.

In addition to satirizing the sexism and machismo of the Beat philosophy, in which each boy tries to define the most "modern idiom," and to shock everyone else by writing about defecation, Taylor also exposes the racism of Beat culture in a brief party scene where Annice is startled to see an interracial couple—a "short, very dark brown boy with long sideburns, who played the drums" with a "hard-looking blonde" (68). At heart, Annice is still attached to bourgeois culture, as is evidenced by her penchant for doing dishes and hand washing her underwear, her sensitivity to foul language, and her shock at the sight of the couple. She tries not to stare, but suddenly experiences an uncharacteristic moment of insight in which she suspects that the drummer, Snap Kennedy, was "making fun of everyone, the whole party; that he was putting on an act—this was how they expected a jazz musician to be, how a hep cat should look, so he was playing the part and getting along okay. She wondered what he was like in real life"

(68–69). Annice pronounces him a fake, but the scene suggests less that he is a fake than it exposes the way that black music, black culture, and black people signify authenticity for whites seeking experiences outside the mainstream.

Annice's insights are short-lived, however, and she continues her exploration of bohemian life, experimenting with sex and drugs in spite of her bourgeois reflexes, until it becomes painfully obvious that women literally cannot afford the amoral stance that Alan assumes. Annice works at meaningless jobs that Alan eschews and spends her college tuition on their expenses, allowing him to disdain making money as a bourgeois goal. When he does get paid for a magazine article about their peyote trip, he does not share the money with Annice but uses it to go to Mexico. This leaves Annice to face the consequences of being a "natural" woman who doesn't use birth control and to accept the fact that for Alan "fatherhood is an accident" (109).

Taylor renders the negative consequences of downward mobility for women in the Beat scene most explicit when Annice, pregnant and without a job, visits the unemployment office. In place of her romantic ideas about slumming, Annice faces the prospect of becoming one of the working or out-of-work poor, raising her child in substandard housing with no prospects of a well-paying job. Scanning the women at the unemployment office, Annice decides for the first time that she is not destined for fame: "*I'm no artist,* she thought, *whatever that cheap bum thinks he is. I'm like everybody else*" (150). At the same time, her identifications shift as she regards different types of women. She admires the "pretty colored girls in cheap smart clothes," and smiles at the "young girls from the South Side," representing immigrant ethnic groups who "lived in a world too big and too complicated for them" but who would pull through as she would. She has no kinship for the newly arrived poor white Southerners, "the draggled-looking women from Arkansas and Kentucky and Southern Missouri." These are the women who will not pull through, but who will "go hungry and try vainly to get on city's relief before they piled their stuff on the old truck and turned home again, beat" (148–150). This is a version of being "beat" that Annice refuses, for it refers not to the fatigue of a generation of artists but to the absolute defeat of the impoverished underclass.

Having given up her aspirations to become an artist, Annice returns quickly to the bourgeois values that she had been unable to shed in her brief career as a Beat girl. Jackson, the boy she had previously deemed boring, comes to the rescue with an offer of marriage, and Annice seems happy at the prospect of moving back to the country to raise her children. Watching Annice wait on him after they have informed her parents that they have been married for seven weeks, Jack observes that "wifeliness sat on her like an apron, cut and stitched to measure" (157–158). Annice, like Pat, does seem to have found her right place in a return to the domestic, but the critique of Beat culture and its misogyny revealed through her story call into question what alternatives there are for women who truly could not be happy with their mothers' lives.

Barby is the only one of the girls whose refusal of bourgeois sexual morality is successful. Barby, obviously, moves farthest from conventional female sexuality when she discovers lesbianism. Lesbianism here is represented as sheltering and nurturing, and it allows Barby the economic and emotional security of a heterosexual marriage, without the danger of rape, pregnancy, and abortion that Taylor associates with heterosexuality. Barby's discovery of lesbianism is self-affirming, and leads to the escape from small-town life that Annice, in particular, desires. Taylor emphasizes Barby's happiness by structurally juxtaposing pivotal scenes in each girl's story. Barby is anticipating her first evening with Ilene, remarking that it "was the first time in her life she had ever been sure of anything good" (132) at the moment Annice realizes that Alan has abandoned her (130), and Pat is shortening a new dress in her ongoing efforts to get Blake's attention (117).

For Barby, the myth of safe, middle-class, small-town life has been the most damaging. Its veneer of respectability hides secrets of pedophilia, rape, and incestuous desire, and the necessity of keeping the fiction in place has left Barby with crippling migraines and low self-esteem. She was raped at the age of thirteen by the respectable vice president of the local bank, a scandal judiciously repressed by her father, who pulled his business through hard times with bank loans. The secrecy around the rape, to which only her father is a witness, results in Barby's estranged relationship with her mother, from whom she hides the shameful event. Even more damaging, it leads to her father's incestuous desire for his daughter; what begins as protectiveness about his daughter's vulnerability turns into sexual possessiveness that grows in the repressed environment of the small town and the nuclear family. Barby's interest in moving to Chicago has everything to do with escaping this atmosphere of secrecy and repression, but her encounters with Rocco (depicted, in the stereotype of the times, as a swarthy and predatory Sicilian immigrant) only create revulsion about her adult experience with men. Repeating the pattern of lies and secrets she learned at home, Barby hides the situation from the other girls, feeling that she is " *ruined anyway. Ruined at thirteen. Like an apple that looks nice and shiny, but is rotten at the core, black and moldy*" (83). At this point in the novel, she cannot envision her future, because she cannot envision herself falling in love or getting married.

Primed by her negative experiences with men, Barby is a character who would typically be a good potential "victim" of an experienced, older lesbian. In fact, the figure of the older lesbian as sexually predatory, jealous, and selfish is a stock character in lesbian pulp. For example, Taylor's earlier lesbian novel, *Whisper Their Love*, provides a classic depiction of the school mistress as preying on young, naïve students at an all-girls college. In *The Girls in 3-B*, however, Taylor treats the experienced lesbian with dignity. For Barby, Miss Gordon is a figure of identification as well as desire. She first admires Ilene's figure because she is, unlike Barby, *"slim and tailored, and not so damned sexy"*; she looks "all of a piece," "neat and integrated and without problems" (98). Ilene is, in fact, recovering from the breakup of a six-year relationship with a woman who has just left her to marry a man. However, her philosophy about moving on from the past allows her to have one without it haunting the new relationship with Barby, for whom lesbianism as an erasure of past is a profoundly cleansing experience. Miss Gordon, like her namesake, Stephen Gordon of Radclyffe Hall's *The Well of Loneliness*, is a chivalrous and protective lover. She cautiously questions Barby about men and marriage before she proceeds to court the younger woman, and introduces her gently to the subject of lesbianism. As it is depicted in the book she gives to Barby, lesbianism is "the passionate unselfish love of another woman . . . a relationship . . . without force or fear. . . . a love between two individuals who understood and cherished each other because they shared the same nature" (116–117). An idealized representation of love between women that emphasizes mirroring and sameness, it works to provide contrast with the negative experiences of heterosexuality from which Barby is fleeing. Ilene not only offers Barby a chance to escape from Rocco's unwanted sexual attentions, but a chance to do so without having to return to her father's home. When a visit from Barby's father threatens to intrude on the sanctuary of their new life together, Ilene deftly outmaneuvers him in his efforts to gain control over his daughter's actions, and he leaves Chicago reassured that his daughter is under the guidance of a sensible career woman. Ilene also offers Barby a chance to share in Ilene's upwardly mobile lifestyle, and to move up the ladder at the department store, making a career for herself.

One might expect Barby to find the closeted nature of the lesbian relationship to repeat the pattern of small-town repression that drove her away from home to begin with. She and Ilene lunch in secret; Ilene hides the lesbian novel that she gives to Barby under a box of clothing tags at her worktable; they develop the habit of taking separate routes to and from work; they rumple the spare bed on the cleaning woman's day, and they don't seem to have any community of lesbian friends. But the closet is represented as a matter of fact in the lives of middle-class women who had jobs to lose if they were open about their relationship. Thus, the secrecy surrounding Barby's relationship is not the kind of secrecy that Barby associates with the lives of married men whom she has been studying for five years, "wondering what fearful secret lives were hidden by their everyday faces" (117). In fact, lesbianism is strikingly free of the guilt that might be associated with the closet and precipitates a break in the isolation Barby has felt from other people. She finds the little restaurant that Ilene takes her to, obviously a gay establishment, "a different world from any she had ever seen," "more personal" than either the anonymity of the big city or the suffocation of the small town (114). Barby moves from cherishing the anonymity of the city and of "the Store," a city within a city, to discovering identification with the people around her. She sees that "the faces of clerks and customers held a depth of feeling that she hadn't noticed before," and empathizes with young mothers and older saleswomen. Startled to find that she feels less alone than she ever has before, she is convinced that, for the first time in her life, "everything would work out all right" (118).

In spite of its generally positive depiction of lesbianism, *The Girls in 3-B* is not unmarked by the constraints of the genre or by popularized Freudian understandings of homosexuality. Perhaps what contemporary readers will notice most about Taylor's representation of lesbianism in *The Girls in 3-B* is that the sexual relationship is muted almost to the point of invisibility. When Ilene asks Barby to stay the night, we anticipate a sex scene. Instead, Taylor cuts immediately to the post–love scene, when the two women are watching snow fall outside the bedroom windows. Barby alludes to the physical satisfaction of the encounter, affirming that "it's what I've wanted, all my life. How can anybody want a man, when there's this?" (137). But she emphasizes the emotional security and fulfillment that she feels, especially her sense that her experience with Ilene has "washed away all the hurt and terror" of her encounters with Rocco, and of her traumatic experience of being raped as a child (137). With Annice, the other character who loses her virginity, Taylor is much more graphic in her depiction of the physical aspect of female sexual desire and satisfaction. She allows the reader to witness the sex between Annice and Alan, to watch Annice undress self-consciously as she evaluates her body through Alan's eyes as well as her own, and to hear descriptions of Annice's "mounting tides of desire," the moment of penetration, and her sexual satisfaction.

The mutedness of the lesbian sex scenes might be seen today as a capitulation to the 1950s taboo around representing lesbians, and a reinforcement of the cultural invisibility of lesbianism. However, considering the invitation, or perhaps more accurately, the expectation that lesbian-themed pulp would offer male readers lesbian sex scenes, a more probable explanation for Taylor's discretion in depicting lesbian sex is the wish to avoid the voyeuristic imperative of pulp. As Yvonne Keller explains, voyeurism in lesbian pulp "worked as a form of pleasure and reassurance over anxieties about social hierarchies; it reinstated the power of the man over [lesbians as] the objects of their gaze" (3). In fact, Keller refers to Taylor as the paradigmatic example of a writer who reacts to "the conventional voyeurism of the genre" by refusing to acknowledge its existence in her writing (6). Taylor, she argues, "successfully avoided sensationalism and extraneous sex scenes and worked to normalize, humanize, and desensationalize the lesbian characters while keeping them central to each story" (6). According to this argument, then, Taylor takes advantage of pulp's ability to provide lesbians with images of themselves while resisting its demand that those images take particular form; she modulates the depiction of lesbian sex, in particular, to avoid the most exploitative patterns of representation in lesbian pulp.

The ideological construction of homosexuality in this novel is as complicated as its visual representation. It includes a psychological narrative of the origins of Barby's sexuality, reflecting the psychoanalytic establishment's postwar interest in homosexuality. In Barby's case, her history of rape and her unconscious sense of her father's incestuous feelings toward her constitute a typical narrative of origin for her lesbianism at a time when any deviations from normative heterosexuality required explanation. The necessity of providing an origin for homosexuality is especially strong for the feminine lesbian, because there are no outward markers of masculine identification, and nothing about her looks (especially for Barby, who epitomizes the feminine ideal of the 1950s—slender with womanly curves, and a graceful, hip-swaying walk) prevents her from "getting a man." The history of rape in the lives of lesbian characters is characteristic of Taylor's novels, including *Whisper Their Love*, *A World Without Men*, and *Journey to Fulfillment*. Although it is difficult to detach the frequent equation of rape and lesbianism from the historical imperative to explain homosexuality, it is notable that Taylor refuses psychoanalytic models of lesbianism as a disease, a neurosis that needed to be "cured," that predominated the 1950s discourse on homosexuality (Faderman 130–138). Taylor's reliance on the rape narrative as a point of origin for lesbianism could be read as a suggestion that the real sickness might lie in a culture where women are so often the victims of sexual violence.

It is this tendency of Taylor's to include social commentary on issues such as sexism, violence against women, gender and economics, and conventional sexual morality in a genre not noted for its radicalism that makes her such a remarkable writer. In order to fully understand her achievements, it is helpful to have an understanding of what it meant to be a lesbian writer of pulp fiction in the 1950s. Barbara Grier, a librarian and collector of lesbian fiction from a young age, dates "the golden age of the lesbian paperback" from 1950, which saw the publication of one of the very first lesbian pulps, *Women's Barracks* by Tereska Torres ("the frank autobiography of a French girl soldier"), to 1966, after which a new type of lesbian literature influenced by the politics of the emerging gay rights and women's movements made pulp fiction less relevant to lesbian readers ("The Lesbian Paperback" 4). Often set in all-female environments such as schools, hospitals, and department stores, as well as emerging "gay meccas" such as Greenwich Village, these pulps were sold as sensationalized stories of sexual taboo.

Blurbs for titles such as *Women in the Shadows*, *Stranger on Lesbos*, and *The Other Side of Desire* announced stories of strange lust, unnatural love, and perverse relationships in worlds of women without men.

It may seem paradoxical that lesbian paperbacks became so widely available during a historical time of intense homophobia, but lesbian pulp was a successful branch of the exploding paperback industry begun in 1939 by Pocket Books. For example, *Women's Barracks*, published by Fawcett, had sold 3 million copies by 1968 (Keller 2). Fawcett published lesbian paperbacks under three imprints: Gold Medal, Crest, and Premier. Cut out of the market for reprints of classic literature because of its contract with another company, Signet Books, Fawcett developed the Gold Medal insignia to sell paperback originals, or PBOs, and, at the same time, solicited books from unknown authors to write new, if formulaic, books for the paperback trade (Stryker 54). Other presses quick to exploit the trade in lesbian pulp novels were Midwood-Tower, Lancer Books, and Universal Publishing. The primary market for these paperbacks was not necessarily lesbian; most of these books were directed at heterosexual men who, the publishers thought, would be titillated by the subject. In fact, much lesbian pulp was male-authored and written as part of a larger market for erotic paperbacks. Valerie Taylor herself resented being thought of as a pulp novelist, characterizing pulp as trashy fiction with thin plots and flat characters that only served as devices for staging gratuitous sex scenes (Taylor qtd. in Brandt 51). Her goal, she contended, was to provide readers with stories about lesbians who "acted human, who had problems, and families, and allergies, and jobs, and so on" (Taylor qtd. in Brandt 52). Susan Stryker, author of *Queer Pulp,* estimates that "at least fifteen lesbian authors during the golden age produced over a hundred paperbacks in which lesbianism was presented in as favorable a light as publishers would allow" (61). Among these writers were Ann Bannon, Paula Christian, and Vin Packer. But marketing practices made these "pro-lesbian" pulps indistinguishable from others that were homophobic and exploitative in the extreme.[1]

Taylor's discussion of her first lesbian novel attests to the formulaic marketing practices and editorial demands on authors. The publisher changed the book's working title, "The Heart Takes Many Paths," which Taylor explained was based on an "old Arabic proverb" of her own invention, to *Whisper Their Love*. While Taylor felt that this was "a disgusting title" (Taylor qtd. in Brandt 52), it fit with publishing conventions that emphasized the secrecy, loneliness, and otherness of lesbian life. *Whisper Their Love* is also the only one of Taylor's novels to include a front-page introduction by a "Dr. Richard H. Hoffmann," an expert in adolescent psychology whom Taylor guesses was the publisher's office boy. In the tradition of Radclyffe Hall's *The Well of Loneliness,* the front page was intended to lend respectability to the supposedly salacious theme of the book, and to guide readers toward the lessons it provided. Thus, *Whisper Their Love* was presented with a warning to parents that they should attend to the moral education of their children or risk abandoning their teens to "the painful consequences arising from sexual and adolescent rebellion" (n.pag.). It tells the story of a young woman who, deprived of her mother's love, gives in to the temptation of an affair with the headmistress of an all-girls college, but is restored to heterosexuality through the attentions of an understanding local boy who convinces her that marriage will make her happy. Although the ending disappointed later readers of Taylor's fiction, publication standards in the 1950s practically guaranteed that lesbianism would end in the separation of lovers through heterosexual normalization, self-destructive alcoholism, or the death of a main character.

Looking at the chronology of Taylor's work, we can see the easing of such standards, perhaps in response to the awareness of a new audience of lesbian readers who wanted happy endings. As we have seen, *The Girls in 3-B* (1959), published only two years after *Whisper Their Love* (1957), is remarkable in providing a happy ending for the lesbian character, especially because it is juxtaposed to the trials and tribulations of the heterosexual characters. *Stranger on Lesbos* (1960) is much more typical in its plotline. It tells the story of a married woman who falls in love with an alcoholic and unfaithful lesbian and ends with the woman's return to her forgiving husband. The Erika Frohman series, which follows the same character through three novels, begins with *A World Without Men* (1963), in which Erika, the series' protagonist, meets the troubled and alcoholic Kate, who is healed by Erika's love. Although Kate is run over by a car toward the end of the novel, she does not die, but is comforted by Erika in her hospital bed, setting the stage for their continuing relationship. Oddly, the next novel in the series, *Return to Lesbos,* also published in 1963, begins with Erika grieving Kate's death in the automobile accident that Kate survives in the first novel. Taylor, who explained that she was "finished" with Kate's character and so killed her off, goes on to introduce Erika to Francine, the unhappy wife of *Stranger on Lesbos,* who finally leaves her husband and finds happiness with Erika. The last novel of the series, *Journey to Fulfillment* (1964), actually tells the story of Erika's childhood and adolescence—her survival of Nazi concentration camps, her adoption by an American couple, and her involvement with their sadistic, bisexual daughter.

In a sense, *Journey to Fulfillment* circles back to *Whisper Their Love,* for it ends with Erika being fostered by a lesbian school teacher, and suggests a happy future for the two that the 1957 novel could not provide.

During the 1950s and early 1960s, such novels offered the only readily available images of lesbians. Aside from reprints of *The Well of Loneliness* (1928), there were few other overtly lesbian novels being published and distributed. The Hays Code banned even the implication of "sex perversion" from motion pictures, and the self-censoring practices of the television industry also suppressed any obvious references to homosexuality. Joan Nestle, a self-identified "fifties fem" and cofounder of the Lesbian Herstory Archives, recalls that even purchasing and reading lesbian pulp was an act of courage for women with little other access to public representation of lesbian lives. The best pulp fictions were cherished and passed from woman to woman. The exchange of these paperbacks in itself was a significant act, as we see in *The Girls in 3-B,* where it signifies coming out for the woman giving the book, and self-discovery for the woman receiving the book.

Even if, by the mid 1960s, "having a sense of humor about lesbian paperbacks was the most charitable stance one could take" (Stryker 66), pulp fiction was recognized as an important element of lesbian literary history at least as early as 1957, when Barbara Grier, writing under the pseudonym Gene Damon, began yearly surveys of lesbian literature that appeared in *The Ladder.* These surveys expanded into Grier's later publication of *The Lesbian in Literature: A Bibliography.* The bibliographies use a rating system combining letters and asterisks to indicate both the quantity and the quality of lesbian material. The changing content of Grier's bibliographies reveals shifts in judgments about pulp's literary and cultural value, especially as other kinds of lesbian fiction became available. The first edition of *The Lesbian in Literature*, published in 1967, contains over three thousand titles marked "T" for "trash" that compilers of the third edition (1981) subsequently eliminated. Most of these entries were pulp novels of the 1950s, 1960s, and 1970s, although the works of lesbian writers, such as Taylor, who made significant contributions to the field of midcentury lesbian literature stayed; some (including *The Girls in 3-B*) are even given three asterisks to designate that they are among "the few titles that stand out above all the rest and must properly belong to any collection of Lesbian literature" (Grier, *The Lesbian in Literature*, 3rd ed., xx). As Grier explains in the introduction to the third edition, the "Trash" entries, indicating books of extremely poor literary quality, were deleted not only to make room for new, presumably better, titles, but also to "acknowledge the changing consciousness of the world" about what counted for quality lesbian reading material (xix). For the most part, these pulp novels are now hard to find, except through used and rare book dealers, in lesbian and gay archives, and at libraries that hold collections of lesbian pulp.

In the late 1990s, the appearance of books, essays, and archive-sponsored shows on lesbian pulp signaled the first emergence of scholarly interest in the genre after Grier's bibliographies, and the first resurgence of popular interest in the genre. Several academic papers were written on the work of Ann Bannon, whose novels became the most accessible of the vintage pulp titles when Naiad Press reprinted the Beebo Brinker series in the 1980s. Focusing on how the novels navigate sexual ideology in the conservative social climate of the 1950s, these essays recuperate pulp fiction by arguing that, in spite of the genre's limitations, lesbian writers such as Bannon are able to complicate stereotyped representations of lesbianism.[2] This is true of many of the pro-lesbian pulps, which not only bear witness to a lesbian and gay subculture that was becoming increasingly visible, but also explore sexual identity in ways that both reflect and resist the 1950s moral and medical understanding of homosexuality as a dangerous perversion or a disease of biological and psychological origins.

Taylor's social and political identities clearly informed her writing, and provide insight into how she worked within the constraints of the genre of lesbian pulp while also subverting the dominant discourse on lesbianism in the 1950s and 1960s. Over the course of her life, Velma Young authored hundreds of poems and articles and over a dozen books, published under the pen names Nacella Young, Francine Davenport, Velma Tate, and Valerie Taylor, the name she adopted as her permanent one. As Valerie Taylor, she is best remembered as one a few authors of pro-lesbian pulp fiction from the 1950s and 1960s. Living through a time that spanned the years before gay and lesbian liberation and after Stonewall, Taylor combined her career as a writer of mass-market paper-backs with an ongoing involvement in social activism, leading one of the most public lives of her contemporaries.

Taylor traced her interest in both politics and writing to her family heritage. Born on September 7, 1913, in Aurora, Illinois, Taylor came from a family of Midwestern farmers and workers. In a brief autobiography written in the third person that appears in *Love Image*, Taylor explains that she grew up in a household "short on money but full of books" ("About the Author" n.pag.). Her paternal great-grand-mothers were both feminists: one marched in the first suf-frage parade in Elgin, Illinois, in 1889; the other was a committed advocate of literacy and dress reform who demonstrated independence in a way that "infuriated vil-lage housewives" ("Autobiography" n.pag.). Her paternal grandfather was a follower of Bob Ingersoll, a famous nineteenth-century agnostic. Several of the women in her family, including her mother, were trained to be teachers and were avid readers. The family's literary traditions proved to be important in Taylor's upbringing. Her father worked as a building contractor, moving from job site to job site for much of her childhood. Consequently, Taylor did not complete a full year of school until the seventh grade. She and her sister were taught at home by their mother, who kept the house supplied with books and magazines. Due to her mother's diligence, Taylor had learned to read by age four and write by age eight.

Somewhere between the ages of seven and ten, Taylor developed a slight curvature of the spine, which was probably the result of a light, undiagnosed case of polio. She referred to this "handicap" frequently in interviews and autobiographies, often without comment. However, in *Love Image* Taylor wrote that the spinal curvature "never made much difference and is mentioned only to demonstrate that being handicapped (who isn't?), like being ugly, is relatively unimportant. Non-beautiful women may not have as many lovers as pretty ones, but they get the best lovers. Friends, too" ("About the Author"). This wry comment, typical of Taylor, suggests that her physical self-image was, in fact, an important part of her life, perhaps influencing her decision to marry in 1939. But it also expresses the strong sense of self-worth that carried her through many difficult situations, including living and writing as a lesbian during one of the periods in U.S. history most hostile to homosexuality. This sense of self-worth clearly influenced Taylor's political activism, which began in her twenties when the country was in the grips of the Depression.

Taylor's family fell on hard times during the Depression,

but in 1935, she was able to get a two-year scholarship to Blackburn College in Carlinville, Illinois, where she studied education. In her second year at Blackburn, she met lifelong friends Ada and Hank Mayer, who were committed socialists and labor organizers. They introduced her to grassroots activism, and she became a member of the American Socialist Party at age twenty-two (Taylor qtd. in Terkel 310). Her political activity in support of farmers and small unions paved the way for her later involvement in the civil rights movement, the feminist movement, the gay and lesbian rights movement, and the international peace movement.

After her graduation from Blackburn College, Taylor taught at various country schools in Illinois from 1937 to 1940. In the spring of 1939, she married William Jerry Tate and took the name Velma Tate. She described herself as "a victim of conventional sexual morality" ("About the Author"), who married out of fear that she would not attract a husband in an era when marriage was an important part of women's lives. She was quickly disillusioned about her husband and sex, and found that the only redeeming part of marriage to an alcoholic and financially unreliable man was her relationship with her three sons, Marshall, who was born in 1940, and twins Jerry and Jim, born in 1942.

During her marriage, she began writing to support her family, publishing poetry, short articles, and confession stories in various regional, religious, and women's magazines. Taylor published her first book, *Hired Girl* (Beacon Books), in 1953. More lurid than her lesbian novels, *Hired Girl* uses the characters of an impoverished drifter and an eighteen-year-old orphanage survivor, both "hired hands" on a run-down farm, to reveal a seamy side of Midwestern farm life and to explore social taboos such as adultery, abortion, blackmail, and drug dealing. The sympathetic representation of the main characters' grinding poverty and the brief appearance of an itinerant couple with socialist values mark the novel as Taylor's work. With the $500 that she was paid for *Hired Girl,* Taylor bought a pair of shoes, two dresses, and applied for divorce to end a fourteen-year marriage that had been marked by poverty and frequent illness ("About the Author"). She went to work in an office and supported the children on her own. She was forty when she received her divorce papers, and over the next three years had a variety of lovers, both male and female. Taylor identified herself as both bisexual and lesbian, where one does not seem to exclude the other. In an interview with Studs Terkel, she explains her sexuality as follows:

> I've always said I was bisexual. I was about thirty-six when I realized what a woman could mean to me. That was about eight years into my marriage. The failure [of the marriage] was not because of that.
>
> I never hid my lesbianism, but I didn't make a thing out of it either. In those days, you'd lose your job if you ever came out of the closet. I'm talking about the '50s and '60s in Chicago. (310)

Tee Corrine suggests that Taylor's involvement with women may have begun earlier (Tee Corrine, "Valerie Taylor: Chronology" n.pag.), and Taylor herself claimed that she first became aware of lesbianism in high school, when she had a crush on her French teacher ("Autobiography"). In any case, it appears that after her marriage, Taylor's primary emotional and physical attachments were to women. While she had good relationships with men, she "found that women are better—they may or may not be better sexually but the emotional depth of a relationship with a woman is better even in a short, casual affair" ("Autobiography").

After the publication of *Hired Girl,* her novels followed

a clearly lesbian trajectory. In 1956 she began aiming her writing toward the newly popular market for lesbian and gay-themed fiction, and sold her first lesbian novel, *Whisper Their Love*, to Fawcett. She continued to use the pen name Valerie Taylor, by which she became widely known as a writer of pulp fiction classics that followed, including *The Girls in 3-B* (1959), *Stranger on Lesbos* (1960), *Return to Lesbos* (1963), *Unlike Others* (1963), *A World Without Men* (1963), and *Journey to Fulfillment* (1964). At the same time that Taylor published what were to become some of the classic novels of pro-lesbian pulp, she was heavily involved in the early lesbian and gay rights movement. She was a member of the Daughters of Bilitis, a group organized to provide a sense of community and political unity for lesbians, and she was a regular contributor to its publication, *The Ladder*, the first national publication for lesbians. Sometime in the early 1960s, she met Pearl Hart, a civil rights lawyer twenty years her senior, whom she described as the love of her life. Along with others, the two women helped organize the Mattachine Midwest, an early homophile organization that united gays and lesbians against discrimination.

Taylor continued to work as a writer and an activist from the 1970s to the 1990s. In 1974, Taylor cofounded the country's first Lesbian Writers Conference in Chicago. She also continued to write, releasing the novels *Love Image* (1977), *Prism* (1981), and *Rice and Beans* (1989) through Naiad Press, a publisher of books for lesbians founded in 1974. Naiad also reprinted three of her earlier novels, and Womanpress published *Two Women* (1976), a reprint of her poetry, which was collected with that of her close friend Jeannette H. Foster, author of the classic *Sex Variant Women in Literature*.

As Taylor's health began to take a toll on her in the late

1970s, she moved to Tucson, and became the resident "lesbian grandmother" of the community. Always the activist, she became involved with the Gray Panthers, an intergenerational advocacy group fighting for health care, affordable housing, and disability rights, among other social issues, and she joined an active Quaker meeting. In 1992, she was inducted into the City of Chicago's Gay and Lesbian Hall of Fame. Taylor was eighty-four when she died on October 22, 1997, in Tucson, Arizona. Her lifelong concern with issues of social justice—especially for sexual minorities, for the poor, and for the aging—is reflected in her novels.

Lisa Walker
University of Southern Maine
Portland
June 2003

Notes

I would like to thank Professor Willard Rusch and Rebecca Redman for their interest in this project and for their helpful comments on drafts.

1. Yvonne Keller uses the term "pro-lesbian" to describe "a subset of lesbian pulps, often written by lesbians, with generally more positive lesbian representation" than male-authored pulps that she terms "virile adventures" (Keller 2). For other discussions of the history of lesbian pulp, see Kate Adams's "Making the World Safe for the Missionary Position: Images of the Lesbian in Post–World War II America" in *Lesbian Texts and Contexts: Radical Revisions*, ed. Karla Jay and Joanne Glasgow (New York: New York University Press, 1990), 255–74; and two short surveys, Susanna Benn's "Sappho in Soft Cover: Notes on Lesbian Pulp" in *Fireworks: The Best of Fireweed*, ed. Makeda Silvera (Toronto: Women's Press, 1986), 66–68, and Rebecca Yusba's "Odd Girls and Strange Sisters: Lesbian Pulp Novels of the 50s," *Out/Look* 12 (Spring 1991): 34–37.

2. Three essays of this period that develop extended readings of Bannon's work are Michele Aina Barale's "When Jack Blinks:

Si(gh)ting Gay Desire in Ann Bannon's Beebo Brinker," *Feminist Studies* 18.3 (Fall 1992): 533–549; Diane Hamer's "'I Am a Woman': Ann Bannon and the Writing of Lesbian Identity in the 1950s" in *Lesbian and Gay Writing: An Anthology of Critical Essays*, ed. Mark Lily (Philadelphia: Temple University Press, 1990), 47–75; and Suzanne Danuta Walters's "'As Her Hand Crept Slowly Up Her Thigh': Ann Bannon and the Politics of Pulp Fiction," *Social Text* 23 (1989): 83–101.

Works Cited

Breines, Wini. "The 'Other' Fifties: Beats and Bad Girls." *Not June Cleaver: Women and Gender in Postwar America, 1945–1960.*" Ed. Joanne Meyerowitz. Philadelphia: Temple University Press, 1994. 382–408.

Corinne, Tee A. "Valerie Taylor: Chronology by Tee A. Corinne." Unpublished ms.

Eisenmann, Linda. "Educating the Female Citizen in a Post-War World: Competing Ideologies for American Women, 1945–1965." *Educational Review* 54, (2 Nov. 2002): 133–141.

Faderman, Lillian. *Odd Girls and Twilight Lovers: A History of Lesbian Life in Twentieth-Century America.* New York: Columbia University Press, 1991.

Friedan, Betty. *The Feminine Mystique.* 1963. New York: W.W. Norton, 2001.

Grier, Barbara. *The Lesbian in Literature.* 3rd ed. Tallahassee: Naiad Press, 1981.

——. [Gene Damon, pseud.] and Lee Stuart. *The Lesbian in Literature: A Bibliography.* San Francisco, California: The Daughters of Bilitis, Inc., 1967.

——. "The Lesbian Paperback." *Tangents* (1966): 4-7.

Hall, Radclyffe. *The Well of Loneliness.* 1928. New York: Doubleday, 1990.

Keller, Yvonne. "Pulp Politics: Strategies of Vision in Pro-Lesbian Pulp Novels, 1955–1965." *The Queer Sixties.* Ed. Patricia Juliana Smith. New York: Routledge, 1999. 1–25.

Meyerowitz, Joanne, ed. *Not June Cleaver: Women and Gender in Postwar America, 1945–1960.* Philadelphia: Temple University Press, 1994.

Stryker, Susan. *Queer Pulp: Perverted Passions from the Golden*

Age of the Paperback. San Francisco: Chronicle Books, 2001.

Taylor, Valerie. "About the Author." *Love Image.* Bates City: Naiad Press, 1977. N.pag.

———. "Autobiography." Unpublished ms. Copyright Valerie Taylor, 1991.

———. Interview with Kate Brandt. *Happy Endings: Lesbian Writers Talk About Their Lives and Work.* By Kate Brandt. Tallahassee: Naiad Press, 1993. 51–60.

———. Interview with Studs Terkel. *Coming of Age: The Story of Our Century by Those Who've Lived It.* By Studs Terkel. New York: The New Press, 1995. 309–14.

———. *The Girls in 3-B.* 1959. New York : Feminist Press at the City University of New York, 2003.

———. *Hired Girl.* New York: Beacon Books, 1953.

———. *Journey to Fulfillment.* New York: Midwood-Tower, 1964.

———. *Return to Lesbos.* New York: Midwood-Tower, 1963.

———. *Stranger on Lesbos.* New York: Fawcett Publications, 1960.

———. *Whisper Their Love.* New York: Fawcett Publications, 1957.

———. A *World Without Men.* New York: Midwood-Tower, 1963.

———. *Unlike Others.* New York: Midwood-Tower, 1963.

———. *Prism.* Naiad Press, 1981.

———. *Rice and Beans.* Naiad Press, 1989.

———. *Two Women: The Poetry of Jeannette Foster and Valerie Taylor. Womanpress: 1976.*

**A daring new series uncovers the forgotten queens of pulp—
and subversive new viewpoints on American culture**

Femmes Fatales: Women Write Pulp celebrates women's writing in all the classic pulp fiction genres—from hard-boiled noirs and fiery romances to edgy science fiction and taboo lesbian pulps.

Beneath the surface of pulp's juicy plots were many subversive elements that helped to provide American popular culture with a whole new set of markers. Much more than bad girls or hacks, women authors of pulp fiction were bold, talented writers, charting the cultural netherworlds of America in the 1930s, 1940s, 1950s, and 1960s, where the dominant idiom was still largely male, white, and heterosexual.

The pulp fiction revival of the last decade has almost entirely ignored women writers. Yet these women were sometimes far ahead of their male counterparts in pushing the boundaries of acceptability, confronting conventional ideas about gender, race, and class—exploring forbidden territories that were hidden from view off the typed page. The novels in the Femmes Fatales series offer the page-turning plots and sensational story lines typical of pulp fiction. But embedded in these stories are explorations of such vital themes as urbanization and class mobility, women in the workplace, misogyny and the crisis of postwar masculinity, racial tensions and civil rights, drug use and Beat culture, and shakeups in the strict codes of sexual conduct.

The Feminist Press at the City University of New York is proud to restore to print these forgotten queens of pulp, whose books offer subversive new perspectives on the heart of the American century.

For more information, call 212-817-7920.

Career—marriage—or intrigues with a dashing stranger?
What's a girl to do?

SKYSCRAPER
FAITH BALDWIN
Afterword by Laura Hapke

"**A captivating and quietly subversive novel**. . . . *Skyscraper* declares that despite all challenges—cultural, political, historical— women should insist on their right to have it all."
—**ALICIA DALY**, *Ms.*

"With its sexual bargains and betrayals, insider trades and financial maneuvers, *Skyscraper* **is pulp fiction at its best.**"
—**MARIA DIBATTISTA**, author of *Fast-Talking Dames*

First published as a serial in *Cosmopolitan* in 1931, the year the Empire State Building opened its doors, *Skyscraper* marks the advent of the working-girl romance. Ambitious and bright, Lynn lives for her job in the gleaming new skyscraper—until she meets Tom, the archetypal boy-next-door. If they don't get married soon, something improper is bound to happen. But if they do, Lynn will be fired—it's the Depression, and jobs are reserved for men and single women. Complicating matters is David Dwight—rich, charismatic, and a well-known seducer. Rather than just choose between suitors, Lynn and young women like her must decide whether to abandon their careers—or abandon their men. They can't have both—or can they?

Even as she turned out fast-paced love stories for popular consumption, best-selling romance writer Faith Baldwin had a finger on the pulse of the economic and social changes facing women in her time. Among Baldwin's best works, *Skyscraper* both exemplifies and transcends the trappings of the romance genre as it explores choices and challenges that still affect women today.

288 pages, $14.95 paperback, ISBN 1-55861-457-5
Available at bookstores, or call 212-817-7920.

A hard-boiled tale of American machismo gone mad—basis for the classic 1950 film noir starring Humphrey Bogart

IN A LONELY PLACE
DOROTHY B. HUGHES
Afterword by Lisa Maria Hogeland

"**A tour de force**, laying open the mind and motives of a killer with extraordinary empathy. The structure is flawless, and the scenes of postwar L. A. have an immediacy that puts Chandler to shame. No wonder Hughes is the master we keep turning to."
—SARA PARETSKY, author of the V. I. Warshawski series

"**A superb novel by one of crime fiction's finest writers of psychological suspense.** . . . What a pleasure it is to see this tale in print once again!"
—MARCIA MULLER, author of the Sharon McCone series

"**This lady is the Queen of Noir**, and *In a Lonely Place* her crown."
—LAURIE R. KING, author of the Mary Russell series

"If you wake up in the night screaming with terror, **don't say we didn't warn you**."

—*NEW YORK TIMES BOOK REVIEW*

The setting of this classic 1947 noir is post–World War II Los Angeles. Here, the American Dream is showing its seamy underside, and there's a strangler on the loose, preying upon the city's young women. At the center of the suspense is the suggestively named Dix Steele, a cynical vet with a secret life and a chip on his shoulder about women. Brilliantly narrating the novel from the inside of Dix's tortured mind, Dorothy B. Hughes dissects the anatomy of American misogyny, and invites us to watch as the killer is unmasked by a couple of femmes fatales with brains—a stunning undoing of the conventional noir plot.

272 pages, $14.95 paperback, ISBN 1-55861-455-9
Available in bookstores, or call 212-817-7920.